Summer at the Chateau

Annabel French is a bestselling author of several contemporary romantic fiction stories for HarperCollins. Based in southeast England with her family, when she's not busy locked in her study writing, or daydreaming, she can be seen in the great outdoors, running after her two dogs, Wotsit and Skips. This is the first novel in the chateau series.

ANNABEL FRENCH

Summer at the Chateau

avon.

Published by AVON
A division of HarperCollins*Publishers*
1 London Bridge Street
London SE1 9GF

www.harpercollins.co.uk

HarperCollins*Publishers*
Macken House, 39/40 Mayor Street Upper
Dublin 1
D01 C9W8

A Paperback Original 2023

1

First published in Great Britain by HarperCollins*Publishers* 2023

A catalogue copy of this book is available from the British Library.

ISBN: 978-0-00-855821-5

Typeset in Birka by Palimpsest Book Production Limited, Falkirk, Stirlingshire

Printed and bound in the UK using 100% Renewable Electricity by
CPI Group (UK) Ltd

This book is produced from independently certified FSC™ paper to ensure responsible forest management.

For more information visit: www.harpercollins.co.uk/green

To my family.
Thank you for your constant support.

Chapter One

'It must be so upsetting! How do you even get over something like that?'

Lizzie Summers narrowed her eyes at the computer screen, ignoring the whispers coming from behind her. She knew exactly what her colleagues were talking about. The two women might have been holding a handful of papers and pointing at various sections with a pen, but they weren't fooling anyone, least of all her. The sly glances and muttered comments told Lizzie that her being jilted at the altar three months before wasn't old news yet.

She supposed it was a natural reaction when someone had undergone a life-shattering experience and lived like a virtual hermit since. Even her friend had intervened, banning her from watching *Dirty Dancing* after she'd started reciting it in her sleep. Apparently, watching it several times a day was a 'bad sign' and called for some kind of 'action'. Lizzie couldn't even think about the drunk-dialling episode where her phone had been wrestled off her after she'd started listing her ex's faults in great, very specific, penis-shaped detail. (It wasn't actually that small, but she'd been upset. What else was she going to say?)

Lizzie continued to type up the article due on her editor's desk by 5 p.m. She wouldn't normally leave her work to the last minute – Lizzie prided herself on her organisation and focus – but the famous designer who rarely gave interviews had only been able to fit her in today and Lizzie needed this piece. No one else on the team at *Lifestyle!* magazine had managed to speak to him, and this could be the winning ticket to the pay rise and additional column inches she desperately needed.

After narrowing her eyes at the two women who dropped their gaze and returned to their desks, Lizzie retied her long blonde ponytail, squared her shoulders and typed furiously, aware of the ticking clock above her editor's door. Just as she'd regained her focus, her phone rang.

'What now?' She pulled her mobile towards her and saw it was her mum. Why was she calling? Of course, Great-Aunt Sarah's will reading was today. According to the solicitor, will readings didn't really happen nowadays, but Sarah had always had a flair for the dramatic and despite living in France for sixty years, her will was still lodged with the solicitors in her old hometown. Sadness and guilt washed through Lizzie. Their relationship had been complicated to say the least. Two different personalities conflicting whenever they were together. The mixed emotions that had swamped her on hearing news of Sarah's death had only added to the maelstrom already ringing inside ever since she'd stood outside the church, patiently waiting for her husband-to-be to arrive. Of course, he hadn't, and she'd been slowly – very slowly – coming to terms with that fact for the last few months. Hence the *Dirty Dancing* marathon and eating her bodyweight in chocolate.

Regardless, she couldn't answer the phone right now. Her mum knew she might not be available, and Lizzie had to get this article finished. It was already 4.30: the clock was ticking . . . loudly. She'd call back as soon as she'd submitted it. Refusing the call, Lizzie re-read the last line she'd written and continued typing.

Her phone immediately rang again and for a second, she wondered if this time it was Will, her ex. Whenever her phone buzzed into life there was always a fleeting moment where she imagined him calling to apologise. To say it was all a mistake and could they start again, but it never was. Maybe that was a good thing. Her heart felt like a deflated balloon, all floppy and empty, and she wasn't sure it would cope with having to work again. She wasn't one hundred per cent sure it would resemble anything like an actual proper heart ever again.

Seeing her mum's name, Lizzie answered with a quick, 'Hi Mum, sorry can't talk now. On a deadline. Call you back after 5.' She hastily ended the call. Perhaps something had gone wrong at the will reading even though they'd all assumed it would be a straightforward affair, or perhaps it had been too much for Mum. Although Lizzie hadn't really got along with Great-Aunt Sarah, her mum had been shaken by the news of her death.

Lizzie wrested her attention back to her interview and typed.

After a final read-through and a flourish, she pinged the finished article over to her editor with a minute to spare and immediately hunkered down behind her screen for some privacy. She tapped the screen to call her mum, and the dial tone started ringing.

'Hey, Mum, everything okay?'

The sound of a tissue being pressed to her nose crackled down the line followed by snuffling. 'Sort of, I suppose. No. I mean yes. I'm okay, I think.' Lizzie frowned, trying to figure out which of the options was likely the right answer. 'I've got something to tell you and it's important. I know you said you had that interview today. The one with that designer who makes massive pillows out of second-hand jumpers—'

Lizzie rolled her eyes. 'Eye-wateringly expensive luxury oversized scatter cushions woven from the finest cashmere.'

'That's the one. I've put the one you gave me for Christmas on the spare bed. I'm too afraid to use it in case your dad spills something on it. You know what he's like when he eats from a sofa tray. I found a piece of spaghetti stuck to the arm of the chair yesterday. When I asked him how it got there, he tried to blame me, but I never sit there. Don't try to—'

'Mum,' Lizzie said gently. 'What's happened?' Her mum always babbled when she was nervous or upset.

'It's – it's – I don't really know how to say this.'

'Just say it, Mum. It's fine,' Lizzie replied, calmly. 'We already knew Sarah wouldn't have wanted me to have anything. We never really got on and—'

'She's left you the chateau!'

Aware that her mouth had fallen slightly open, Lizzie's heart beat erratically, the once steady rhythm growing faster. 'I'm sorry, what? What did you say?'

'The chateau, Lizzie. You know, her place in France. You used to go there every summer.'

'I – huh?'

'Oh, darling. Didn't you hear me? I can't believe it myself.' Her voice was shaky with sadness as well as shock.

'No. I mean yes, but . . .' Lizzie's brain had stopped working altogether and was currently shouting 'Whaaaaaaaaaat?' with a large neon sign flashing above it. This couldn't be right. 'There must be some mistake, Mum. We all thought she'd sell it or leave it to the locals. Let's face it, as I got older, my trips there became so much more difficult and—'

'She loved you,' her mum replied indignantly.

'Please Mum, she used to see me arriving and say the same thing every year, "Still not got a boyfriend then?" Or "Cheer up, it can't be as bad as all that".'

'In her defence, you were a bit of a sulky teenager.'

'That's what teenagers do!' Aware of a sly glance from the desk opposite, Lizzie lowered her voice. 'And I wasn't always sulky. Sometimes I'd be asleep.' She could hear her mum smile on the other end of the line. 'I just wanted to be at home with my friends, not off to France with no one my own age to hang out with.' Saying it out loud, she suddenly realised how spoilt it sounded and moved the conversation on. 'I don't understand this at all, Mum. Are you sure there's not been some sort of mistake? What did the solicitor say?'

'It's all there in the will in black and white. You should have heard what your father said. He actually swore in the solicitor's office, which Mr Devlin did not like at all, I can tell you. But he was very clear about it, and he said I'm the executor and it's apparently my job to tell all, the beneficiaries what they've got, and you've got the chateau. Sarah didn't have much money, but she's left you and me a bit, and some of her jewellery too, which is sweet of her. I always remember her wearing those enormous kaftans and reams of beads. She wasn't everyone's cup of tea but once you got to know her . . .' Her mum's words were replaced with more snuffling.

'Oh, Mum. Are you okay? I wish I could give you a hug.' She was beginning to regret not moving the interview.

'Thanks, darling, but your dad's here and the worst is done now. Sarah has some bits and bobs she wants me to have so I'll send you a copy of the list. When do you think you can go down there?'

'Go down there?'

'Yes. What else are you going to do? Surely you want to see it.'

Lizzie's mind started running at a million miles an hour and memories of the chateau filled her brain. It had been a beautiful and enchanting place when she was younger. Before she'd grown out of the idea, she'd dressed as a princess and run up and down the grand staircase, Cinderella arriving for the ball. She'd stood at the top window of one of the pepper-pot turrets and flung out a bed sheet, the other end secured to her head with a headband, Rapunzel in her tower. Then she'd fought dragons in the nearby wood, climbed trees with dirty knees and picked mushrooms. But as she'd grown, turning from a child to a teenager, the summers had dragged with envious thoughts of all the fun her friends were having back home without her. These memories hadn't surfaced in years and as they came to that last, disastrous summer, an unsettled feeling inched up her spine. She began to fiddle with a paperclip.

'I can't go down straight away, Mum. I used a lot of my time off after . . . you know what.' Remembering her colleagues from moments earlier, she didn't want to say the words out loud. 'I'll have to speak to Hilary.'

'As soon as you can, poppet. Get everything sorted out as quickly as possible, you know? You're probably going to want to sell it so the sooner it's on the market the better. Though I do hate to think of it not being Sarah's anymore.' She sniffed again and the ruffling of the tissue filled Lizzie's ear.

'Yeah, I guess you're right.'

Really, there was no question that she'd sell it. She had no wish to move to France. Her life might not be quite how she hoped at the moment, but it wouldn't be forever, and she loved her job. It was the only thing she had left. Hilary had hinted at possibilities to come and once she secured a promotion she'd have enough for a place of her own. With the sale of the chateau as well, she might even be able to buy her own place in London, somewhere that wasn't the size of an ant's shoebox.

'Well, let us know when we can call and talk more. You need to get the keys from the solicitors, they won't give them to me. I told Mr Devlin I'm your mother and would pass them on, but he still refused. I mean, what did he think I was going to do with them? But apparently, there are rules about this sort of thing. I'm glad it's all over though.'

'I'm sure you are, Mum. You've been really brave about it all. I know how close you were.'

'You're a good girl.' She snuffled again. 'Anyway, toodle-oo poppet. I'll let you get on. Love you.'

'Love you too, Mum.'

As she placed her phone back on her desk, Lizzie heard scoffing from behind the screen opposite where her annoying acne-ridden colleague Matthew worked. 'You love your mum! How old are you?'

'Oh, grow up, Matthew. This is why you're only allowed to write the zodiac column.'

What had he come up with for Libra? Whatever it was, it wasn't going to predict the unbelievable turn of events that had just befallen her.

Glancing at the glass office to her left, she stood and went to Hilary's door, tapping gently.

'Come in, Lizzie.'

Hilary's chin-length bob swished around her face as she lifted her head. A few grey hairs scattered the roots of her light brown hair, but they suited her, and Lizzie admired how she accepted them with pride. Will had always joked about dying his hair when he found his first grey. Had he found any yet?

'The interview went well – it's in your emails.' Lizzie flopped into the chair Hilary motioned towards, banishing thoughts of Will from her mind.

'You did well to secure him. I'm not sure how you managed it.'

'Stubbornness and a talent for stalking, I think. I was a bit worried my daily phone calls to his assistant were going to land me in prison, but thankfully not.'

Hilary laughed. 'So what's up?'

Lizzie shook her head slightly, still unable to believe the news she'd just received. 'So—' She opened her mouth to speak, then closed it again, unsure where to begin.

'I've inherited a chateau.' Hilary stared as if she'd just admitted to stealing the office Post-its or photocopying her behind at the Christmas party (Matthew had, but Lizzie had politely declined). 'It's crazy and a bit mad but . . .' She gulped down a laugh at the absurdity of it all. 'I hate to ask but I need some time off to go and see the place and get it on the market. And I need to bring some bits back that my great-aunt wanted the family to have.'

'Wow, Lizzie. I mean . . . I don't know what to say. Firstly, I'm so sorry for your loss.'

'Thank you. We weren't close.'

'Sounds like you were closer than you think.'

Lizzie's stomach knotted and she let her eyes drift to the view of the London skyline behind Hilary's head. The summer sun shone through the window and the sky, a bright cloudless blue, reminded her of lying on the grass in front of the chateau, bored to tears and wishing she was at home. She didn't want to go back there. She'd left the place behind years ago, physically and mentally. Especially after . . . No, she wouldn't allow herself to think about that now. Her life was here, and besides, she'd only just picked herself up from her breakup with Will. One day she'd have an office like Hilary's with a view just like this. One day, she assured herself, feeling the fire of ambition that had grown since the split. 'I know I haven't got much time off left, if any.'

'I think you've only got a few days,' Hilary replied, wincing. 'I could give you a couple more as compassionate leave, even though that's normally only for close relatives. How long do you need?'

'I don't really know.'

How long would it take to get it on the market? After all, she could sell it with all the possessions in it. Lizzie remembered the beautiful Louis XV chairs they'd sat in around the large mahogany table in the formal dining room, though most of the time they ate at the simple wooden table in the kitchen. But the house would still be full of Sarah's possessions, her documents. Her life was in that place and given that she'd lived there for over sixty years, there'd be quite a lot of stuff to sort before people came to view it.

'More than a few days,' she said sadly, noting the way Hilary's eyebrows pulled together. 'But believe me, I want to make this trip as short as possible.'

After how supportive Hilary had been when she'd been jilted, letting her work from home (or at least the apartment she was bunking in while her friend's flatmate was in Australia) Lizzie knew she was asking a lot.

A kernel of an idea made its way to the forefront of Lizzie's mind, pushing aside all the confusing emotions, and she looked to Hilary, a smile forming on her lips.

'What if we made an article of it? We could call it "Living the French Dream" or something like that and I could talk about how to sell or buy property in France, how to negotiate with French estate agents, that sort of thing? I think our readers would love it. It's a beautiful property and you know how many people have a dream of packing up and moving to France. The wine, the cheese, the culture . . .'

If she had a purpose, something to focus on, returning might not be too bad and this could be the piece that really showed Hilary what she was made of. Coming straight off the back of her star designer interview, it would definitely impress an interview panel. Hilary leaned forwards and tapped the pen she'd been holding on her notepad. It was a good sign, but she wasn't convinced yet.

'It has turrets,' Lizzie added.

A sparkle came to Hilary's eyes, and she sat back in her chair. 'You can have 5,000 words and as much time as you need but—'

Why was there always a but?

'I'm not paying your travel as you needed to go anyway, and don't stay longer than you have to.' As she said this last part, her mouth pulled up in a grin.

'No worries there,' Lizzie replied firmly, remembering again the welcome she'd received whenever she arrived for the summer. 'My plan is to get in, get it on the market, and get out again as quickly as possible. I definitely won't be staying long.'

Chapter Two

Standing in front of the large wrought-iron gates to Chateau Lavande, Lizzie steadied her breathing. Her heart fluttered and the air in her lungs vibrated with anxiety. The last time she'd been here – over fifteen years ago – words had been exchanged that were less than pleasant.

After she'd spoken to Hilary, Lizzie had hightailed it to the solicitor's office to collect the keys. She'd stood on the doorstep, opposite the solicitor's shiny gold plaque, the clock ticking down to closing time, building up the courage to go inside. She'd given herself courage by thinking of the article she'd write. The future she was building for herself. It had been the only thing to get her over the threshold and into Mr Devlin's office with mere seconds to spare.

An image of Sarah's disapproving expression formed in her mind and Lizzie gazed at the view to distract herself. She'd known coming back here would bring up certain difficult memories she'd spent the last fifteen years trying not to think about. Was she ready to now?

It was mid-afternoon and a lazy sun beat heat onto her legs. How could she have forgotten how much warmer summers in Provence were? Her jeans and T-shirt were sticky with sweat.

After a short flight, the drive hadn't been arduous and as she'd passed purple lavender fields, the heady scent lingering in the air, long-forgotten memories had attempted to surface. She'd focussed on the road, on the radio, on her plans for the feature, anything to draw her mind away from the past. But as she'd driven deeper into France – a country she'd always loved – an unexpected feeling of escape had accompanied her. Every passing mile, every lush green field, every tiny village full of cobbled streets, medieval buildings and of course, picturesque cafés, helped her leave Will behind and the wedding they'd been planning for two years.

They'd only spoken a handful of times since the wedding day. Will had called, apologising profusely, saying he'd had no choice. He just couldn't go through with it after realising he didn't really love her after all. Ouch. That had really hurt. But was that all? Had he cheated too? She'd wondered for a while if he had. There'd been work do's he didn't talk much about, a pretty female colleague he was a little shifty over, but she had no proof and he'd never said anything. After that one single call, there'd been nothing. Nada. Zilch. It was like he'd swipe lefted her from his life. Gone. Erased. Forgotten. He hadn't been there when she'd moved out and had soon stopped answering her drunk-dialled calls or responding to her less than polite messages. She hadn't called him in quite a while, though, and raising her head a little, she was rather proud of that achievement.

Lizzie narrowed her eyes as she surveyed the entrance to Chateau Lavande again, still unable to believe that any of this was actually real. The chateau gates were rusted in places, a dark reddish brown pushing through the black paint. Render fell from the wall that spread out encompassing the grounds and the grass was higher than Lizzie ever remembered it being except in the wild areas kept for the deer and the bees. They were normally located in the furthest acres, far, far away from the house itself. The chateau had never been in tip-top state. Sarah wasn't really one for decorating when there were more exciting things to do: trips to go on, places to explore either near or far, fun to be had. But the rust was noticeable now and Lizzie made a mental note to add painting the gate and walls to the list of jobs she had to complete.

The keys she'd been given by the solicitor hung loosely in her fingertips. They were a strange assortment of ancient, monstrously large gaoler keys and regular everyday ones. She stepped forward and unlocked the padlock strung through the bars. After driving through, she re-locked them behind her.

The long gravel drive curled its way through high-grassed grounds and mature, leafy plane trees provided shade from the bright Provençal sun that dappled the windscreen. Lizzie nudged her sunglasses further up the bridge of her nose and opened the window, hearing the buzz of insects and feeling the air on her face.

The pepper-pot turret of the east wing came into view, followed swiftly by the rest of the chateau. Lizzie's hands tightened on the wheel, and she sat forward, her breath catching in her throat just as it had when she was a child. She slowed to a stop in front of the stone steps leading to the front door, pulled her sunglasses down and gazed up. The perfect symmetry of the arched windows was breathtakingly beautiful, as was the sweeping arc of the stone balustrade that led to the front door. Two urns at the base of the steps were full of something more weed than plant and the compact, rectangular main building of the house nestled between the two towering turrets. Yet all were drawn together by the matching dark grey tiles of the roof.

The chateau was even more fairy-tale perfect than she remembered and Lizzie let out a breath that had been trapped somewhere in her ribcage. The cream walls shone in the sun, and she remembered just how thick and sturdy they were. The house had existed for hundreds of years. It had a life and soul of its own and it was crazy to think it was now hers.

Inside, she'd find high ceilings and large fireplaces where Sarah had taught her how to build a proper fire. Lizzie had never fully realised how grand the place was, but children took these things for granted. They assumed everyone had the same as them and it was only when the teasing began in her teenage years that she'd realised most people went to a caravan in France for a week, not a large turreted chateau where they'd stay for the entire summer. Back then their envy had confused her because they didn't know Sarah – didn't know how her enthusiasm could be intimidating, too much – but today Lizzie was seeing the chateau with fresh eyes.

Reminding herself she was here to sell the place, Lizzie climbed out of the car and studied the exterior, taking in every detail. Moss crept from the gravel path onto the steps (that would need removing) and the light blue paint flaked from the double front door, revealing the dark wood underneath (she'd have to repaint that too). Sage green shutters hung slightly off kilter, obscuring some of the windows, their hinges bent or missing altogether. Lizzie pursed her lips. Had this decay happened in the short weeks since Sarah's death or had she been living like this for some time? Guilt and shame prickled the back of Lizzie's neck harsher than the sun's rays ever could.

She found the right key on her first attempt. The lock on the front door hadn't been changed since she'd last visited and muscle memory had sent her fingers to it without hesitation. She ran her hand over the peeling paint before opening it, sending tiny flakes fluttering to the ground.

It was dim inside, the only illumination coming from a large broken window at the top of the grand central staircase. Dust motes floated in the beams of sunlight, falling onto the chessboard-pattern floor. The black and white tiles looked more brown and grey as they were covered in muddy footprints. The air in the small hallway was heavy with damp and decay. As she edged inside, her eyes were drawn to Sarah's study at the back of the hall, and she quickly turned away.

Cobwebs hung from the corners of the ceiling and in the darkest recesses mildew climbed the walls. The feeling of escape that had grown on the journey vanished, pushed out by a rising anger. Was this a punishment for not doing what she'd asked all those years ago? For not appreciating the place as Sarah had? Lizzie brushed her blonde hair back from her face, tucking it behind her ear, and moved further into the house.

Strange noises emanated from one of the doors off the hallway and fear squeezed her chest. Sarah had once tried to convince her of ghosts that roamed the house at night. The chateau had been built in the eighteenth century and Sarah was certain some must exist: a desperate lady in white, wringing her hands; a headless aristocrat fresh from the guillotine; but Lizzie had never seen one. The house had always creaked and moaned but it was the floorboards, or the breeze edging around the tiny gaps in the old windowpanes. This noise was different and despite the heat, Lizzie shuddered.

Her steps left footprints in the covering of grime that coated everything like a dusting of snow, and she made her way to the living room. The strange noise grew louder. A scratching and shuffling sounded from the other side. Lizzie steadied her nerves, ready to fling the door open and surprise whoever was daring to poke around the house uninvited. After counting to three she twisted the handle and shouldered the door in one quick movement, stumbling forward, almost tripping over her feet as her eyes fell on the unwanted guest.

A goat stared at her disapprovingly from the other side of the sofa as if she had rudely interrupted its dinner. Its chewing slowed for a second, then keeping beady eyes on her, it craned its neck forward and took a bite out of the arm of the sofa. It was taunting her. A goat was taunting her! And it had clearly been munching away for a while as stuffing puffed out like cotton candy.

'What the heck? Shoo! Get out of here.' Lizzie waved her arms, and it took a step back. It was then she realised she was blocking the door. The goat dipped its head, and she could have sworn it sneered before charging as fast as it could towards her. 'No, no, no, no, no, no, no!'

Lizzie ran from the room, the goat suddenly very close behind. She jumped onto the staircase and ran to the top, taking them two at a time. Surely it wouldn't follow her. Considering she'd misjudged its fear of humans, and its ability to understand English, she crossed her fingers she hadn't got this one wrong as well. Were goats good at climbing stairs? There were mountain goats, of course, but this goat didn't look particularly athletic. When she turned around, its tail was disappearing through the still-open front door. Thank goodness. She really didn't fancy playing hide-and-seek with an angry goat all afternoon. They weren't the cute, docile creatures she remembered from childhood visits to the petting zoo.

Allowing her heart rate to calm down from the unexpected burst of exercise, not to mention the fear of being mauled, she sat on the large windowsill only to feel cobwebs cling to the hairs on her arms. And where there were cobwebs, there were spiders. Big, hairy, terrifying spiders. With a screech, Lizzie bolted back to standing, rubbing her hands over her body to disperse any creepy crawlies that might have taken up residence in her clothing.

'I hate this place,' she said out loud, feeling exactly as she had at fifteen. 'I really hate this place. Why am I here, Sarah, hey? Why?'

But Lizzie's words only echoed around the empty chateau. Sarah's ghost wasn't resident any more than other so-called spirits were, and Lizzie pressed a hand to her forehead, pinching her temples. Did she really own this place now? And how long would she be here?

It was clear a lick of paint and a quick scrub round wasn't going to do much, and rocklike dread hardened in her chest. She tried to shake it off. Perhaps she was just tired and grumpy from the journey. A new sofa wouldn't cost too much. Neither would fixing the window. Regaining some courage, Lizzie headed back downstairs and into the living room.

The intricate cornicing around the wonky and dangerously loose chandelier barely clung to the ceiling and lumps of plaster littered the floor. The giant rugs that covered the black and white tiles were threadbare and had been nibbled at too. This room had been an all-you-can-eat buffet to her goat guest.

Lizzie's heart sank. The state of the place was so much worse than anything she'd pictured. There was only one thing for it. Tea. She needed a good strong cup of tea before exploring the rest of the house. Maybe the living room was the worst she was going to find and everything else would be better, requiring nothing more than a coat of paint. Leaving the dirt and mire behind, Lizzie went across the hall to the kitchen.

The sun spilled in through the large windows that lined

one wall, but the cheerful light did nothing to hide the carnage. More windows had been broken, cupboard doors were hanging off and the floor was even dirtier than in the hall. It was like one of those home makeover games, except this wasn't a game, it was real life. Her life. Broken crockery lined the open shelves and a large, ancient, grease-ridden stove sat in the alcove, a black pipe, thick and tacky with dirt, climbing from its back. Even Sarah's souvenirs, gathered from her frequent and varied escapades, were coated in grime. The large dining table Lizzie remembered dominated the space, its surface scattered with newspapers, magazines, and months of correspondence. They too were thick with dust and when she pushed aside the detritus, mug rings, scars and dents were clearly visible on the table's surface.

Lizzie flung her hands into the air. This was not what she'd been expecting at all. The place had never been perfect, but it had always been clean. This? This was something else. What had caused Sarah to live like this? Age? Illness? What would her mum say when she told her? On their semi-regular phone calls, Sarah had always assured Lizzie's mum that everything was fine. Clearly, she'd been lying.

Looking around, Lizzie found a normal electric kettle on the counter and went to the sink to fill it. It took both hands to turn the stiff tap and when she managed it, dirty water spurted out, bouncing off the butler sink and soaking her T-shirt. A sound halfway between a growl and a groan escaped her mouth but she bit back the swearwords desperate to escape. She let the water run clear, though it intermittently sputtered and trickled away to nothing, and filled the kettle. A frightening fizzle made Lizzie jump as she switched it on, then it hummed before exploding in a loud crack. The noise disturbed something behind her, and tiny feet scurried across the floor. Lizzie spun, still gripping the worktop, but whatever it was had vanished.

'I'm not sure I can take much more of this,' she said to the empty room, hoping it wasn't a rat. When she flicked the kettle again, nothing happened. Lizzie tried the light switch. Nothing.

'Brilliant, no electricity whatsoever.' Tears stung her eyes.

She had intended on staying at the chateau and getting started on Sarah's possessions straight away, but there was no way she could sleep here tonight. If this was what the downstairs was like, how bad would the upstairs be?

The answer was 'even worse', as Lizzie explored more rooms, including the old bedroom she'd slept in years ago. The sky darkened outside, and the bright sun vanished behind thick, black clouds. The heat of the day grew close and oppressive as a summer storm rolled in, and the breeze grew fiercer, gusting through the trees. Lizzie had always enjoyed summer storms. She loved the way the air cleared as the rain washed it clean and the world seemed fresher and brighter once it was done. A crack of thunder echoed around the empty chateau and rain tumbled from the sky. Lizzie watched as the drops bounced off the ground like tiny silver balls thrown from the heavens, then something cold and hard hit the top of her head. She looked up. Water dripped from the ceiling and a splodge hit her in the eye.

'Oh, for the love of—' Taking a step to the side she

wiped it away. 'Wonderful. A knackered roof too. Just what I need.'

There was no way she could afford to fix all this before putting it on the market. The list of jobs was just too big. The dark clouds outside the window rumbled and bumped into each other. All she could do was hope someone wanted a doer-upper. Maybe if she included the property details in the article she was writing, a reader would be so tempted they'd make an offer. Fat chance, but anything was worth a shot. She ran downstairs to the now dark kitchen to find something to catch the water, but it seemed fruitless. Rain dripped through the ceilings of all but one of the eight bedrooms and the overpowering smell of mildew made her gag.

In a final insult, as she descended the stairs a bird flew above her and something wet landed on her head. She let out a groan.

'This is not happening.' She pressed her fingers to her hair. Bird poo. 'Urgh. That's it. I'm out of here.'

She'd find an estate agent and come back tomorrow when hopefully it wouldn't be raining inside as well as outside the house, goats wouldn't be eating the furniture, and birds wouldn't be pooping in her pricey cut and colour.

Locking the front door behind her, Lizzie ran to the hire car and jumped in. She was soaked, her body shivering in stark contrast to the earlier heat of the afternoon. At least she hadn't unpacked the car. The nearest town must have a *chambre d'hôte* or *gîte* she could stay in until she'd arranged everything. She turned the car on, blasting the windscreen where it had clouded from the steam radiating off her. As soon as she had enough visibility, she eased the car back down the drive, concentrating intently through the torrential downpour bouncing off the window. If she remembered right, there was a village a few miles away. She'd head for there.

With the windscreen wipers frantically swishing, she drove back through the gates, pausing to re-lock them once she'd passed through. Not that there was any point. No one was going to steal anything. If they tried, the demon goat would probably get them. By the time she got back in the car she looked as if she'd jumped in a swimming pool fully clothed. Mascara ran into her eyes and down her cheeks but at least the rain had washed the bird poo from her hair.

Slowly, Lizzie chugged along. Water pooled at the sides of the narrow roads and at one point, when she'd finally made it a couple of miles from the chateau, the lights on the dashboard flickered as she drove through a deep puddle covering the entire surface of the road.

'Don't you dare,' Lizzie murmured to the steering wheel. Obediently, the engine continued to run.

By now the rain had intensified further, even though that hadn't seemed possible. Visibility was non-existent and she could barely see beyond the waterfall on the windscreen. It was like being in a car wash and just as disorientating. Lizzie's neck ached and a headache pounded behind her eyes. Thunder cracked the air around her and a bolt of bright white lightning rippled down through the sky. It seemed to land next to her, and she counted to see how far away it had fallen.

Today was, without doubt, one of the worst days of her entire life. She'd been charged by a hungry goat, narrowly avoided electrocution, and been soaked to the skin. It made being jilted at the altar a mild inconvenience by comparison.

The tiny lane was obscured by another puddle and Lizzie slowed, pressing the brakes. The back of the car suddenly swerved out from behind, aquaplaning out of control. Lizzie gasped and tightened her grip. Were you supposed to brake or not? Fear slammed her foot down on the brake and the car began to spin. Wrong choice, wrong choice! Lizzie shrieked. Another bolt of lightning crashed down from the sky, followed by a deep, rumbling clap of thunder. It was too hard to focus. The world was obscured by the spinning car and the rain hammering down. She only knew one thing for certain.

She was going to crash.

Chapter Three

Instinctively, Lizzie straightened the wheel. The car swerved until it was almost sideways on the road. Her throat burned and then, with an almighty shunt, the car stopped dead. Lizzie's whole body was rocked by the crash, ricocheting in her seat. Now she could add whiplash to the list of things that made today the worst day in history.

'Please be okay, car. I don't want to pay for you too,' she muttered as she climbed out.

Lizzie stared at the bonnet. The front bumper hung off, and part of it was rammed into the grass verge. She'd expected a crumpled mess, the bonnet crunched up like a piece of used paper, but maybe sheer terror had made it all seem worse than it was. She climbed back in and turned the ignition key. The car didn't respond. She tried again, pleading for it to start, but it refused.

'Oh Lord.' Lizzie raised her eyes to the roof of the car. 'Please tell me what I've done to deserve this? I always help older people carry their shopping. I recycle. Maybe I don't always rinse out cans and jars, but I do recycle. I give my seat up on the Tube. Was I a murderer in a past life?'

She tried once more but the car was dead.

Though her hands were still shaking from the cold and now the crash, she pulled out her phone to call the emergency breakdown cover. As she stared at her phone, the bars showed her signal strength had disappeared. She waved it around the car, but it refused to flick into life. Lizzie leaned over the seat, almost breaking a rib on the headrest in her attempt at contortion, but the short distance between the front and back of the car hadn't brought even the tiniest of signals. She was well and truly stuck.

With no signal to call for help and no Google Maps to check, wherever she went next, she'd be walking, which wasn't normally a problem in warm Provençal weather. The only thing Lizzie had been looking forward to was a few strolls around the area, roaming the chateau grounds in the sun and enjoying the local food.

If she went back to the chateau she'd have to stay there overnight with no electrics and no decent water. Not to mention whatever wildlife decided to join her. Would the demon goat have found its way back in? A hot bath would be out of the question, and she shuddered at the thought of the musty bedding she'd climb into. Her only option was to go forward towards the village.

Lizzie removed some essentials from her suitcase in the boot of the car, ramming them into her handbag. Trudging onwards she followed the path of the road, certain that if she stuck to it, it would lead her to the village. Despite her hopes, the rain didn't ease off, though the storm itself moved further away, which was a relief because the way her luck was going, she'd probably be struck by lightning and die alone in a field.

After walking for another twenty minutes, Lizzie stopped. Had she totally lost her bearings or did she remember the village being closer than it actually was? There was still no signal on her phone and her feet were blistering where the wet fabric of her socks rubbed her heels. Her legs ached and she shivered from the cold seeping into her bones. Lizzie hopped onto the verge to avoid a particularly deep puddle.

'Just nip down,' Mum had said. 'The sooner the better.' Lizzie tutted. It was all supposed to be a lot easier than this. Maybe not easier exactly, but simpler. Lizzie's steps slowed as she tugged each mud-caked foot out of the mire. 'Did I murder kittens or something, God? Did I harass nuns or scam people?'

As more thick clouds amassed in the sky and Lizzie's hopes of finding the village faded, a ray of light pierced through dark clouds reflecting off something on the horizon. A small house stood on the brow of a hill, and she made her way towards it. Surely someone there would be able to drive her to the village, or at least let her shelter from the rain for a while. She left the road behind and crossed a field, keeping her eyes on the lights in the windows. A small wall blocked her path and she hopped over it into a vineyard.

Rows of grapevines stood like soldiers on parade. Thin stumps of trunk erupted into a mass of wide green leaves, and stalks of blackening grapes peeked through the foliage. Raindrops dripped from the leaves and though she was soaked to the skin, Lizzie remembered the heady scent of the grapes she'd eaten in her childhood. The fresh produce from the local market made eating here a pleasure and Sarah had always liked simple meals cooked with the best ingredients. Looking back on it now, Lizzie had taken that for granted too. She thought back to the state of the kitchen and sadness swept over her so strongly that tears appeared in her eyes, though she forced them back, unwilling to let them fall.

'Hey!' came a deep male voice from behind her. '*Qu'est-ce que tu fais ici?*'

Lizzie spun round, trying to remember some basic words of French. 'Whoa!'

Well, that wasn't very French, but whoever was dishing out forgiveness would have to forgive her because the man marching towards her was hot. Hotter than the sun in a heatwave. Hotter than Captain America mixed with Jamie Dornan – and just thinking of *Fifty Shades of Grey* in the presence of this Gallic god made her body tingle all over. She couldn't tell what colour his hair was as the rain had plastered it to his head, but he had a well-trimmed dark brown beard that couldn't hide his strong jaw. Rain soaked his shirt where his jacket hung open, and muscly legs ended in thick boots. Rugged. Handsome. He was the sexiest man Lizzie had ever seen and she momentarily lost the ability to form sentences. He repeated the question, scowling at her, though all it did was make him more attractive.

'Right,' she answered. 'Yes, umm . . . hello. *Bonjour*!' She gave an awkward wave. What had he said to her? She attempted to decipher as much of it as she could. She hadn't understood all the words, but his angry expression made it clear he was asking something along the lines of, 'What the hell are you doing on my land?' Before she could answer he spoke again.

'*C'est une propriété privée*.'

She wasn't sure what he had said exactly, but it seemed he was telling her she shouldn't be there. Realising her broken French would only lead to more confusion, she replied in English. 'I'm so sorry to intrude. I had an accident in my car.' She pointed behind her, towards the road and his eyes followed then flicked back to her face. 'I was wondering if you can point me towards the *chambre d'hôte* in the village.'

'You are trespassing.'

Excellent, he spoke English. Not very friendly English but English all the same.

'Did you hear me? You are trespassing on my vineyard.'

He had a point.

'Yes, I know and I'm very sorry, but you see—'

'Where have you come from?' She was sure he wanted to add, 'You crazy English lady', but was gallant enough not to.

'Just over there. Well, I guess my car is somewhere over . . .' She turned on the spot, trying to figure out where the road was and where her car had been abandoned. Taking a reasonable guess but not wholly sure, she pointed over her right shoulder. 'There.'

'*Merde*.'

Now *that* she understood, and it wasn't very gallant at all. A blush crept over her cheeks, warming her body. There was no need to be quite so rude. It wasn't exactly her fault she'd ended up on his property. What she needed right now was help rather than this, admittedly gorgeous, French man swearing at her.

'Listen, I'm sorry to disturb you but—'

He looked her up and down one last time, sighed, and turned on his heel, marching back towards his house. 'Come with me.'

Lizzie followed, the sting of scoured skin rippling through her feet. 'I don't suppose you have any plasters, do you?'

'Plasters?'

'For my feet. I think I've got blisters.' She wracked her brain and dragged something up from the depths. '*Le pamplemousse*?'

He stopped. '*Pamplemousse*? You want a grapefruit for your feet?'

'What? No!' She thought some more, replaying a memory of Sarah taking her into the village to buy supplies. '*Le pansement*! That's it. *Le pansement*?'

'*Oui*,' he replied, without looking at her. 'I have some of those.'

'Thank you.'

'*Touristes*,' he muttered under his breath, but Lizzie ignored him. No matter how unfriendly he chose to be, she'd just be grateful for a sit-down.

Within minutes they had left the vineyard and reached

an open garden in front of his house. It was much bigger than she'd thought from the road; a large farmhouse rather than the small hut she'd imagined. While it lacked the symmetry of the chateau, it was beautiful, nonetheless. The small, square windows were framed by shutters painted a bright and vibrant blue, and the oddly shaped stones of the walls gave it a mosaic-like appearance of muted earthy browns. A gnarled tree stood sentry a few metres from the rustic wooden door the man was walking swiftly towards.

He opened it and stood aside to let her through into the kitchen. Lizzie took a moment to admire her surroundings while the man lit the fire already prepared in the grate. Exposed beams lined the roof, and the walls were painted a rich cream. If she wrote about here, she'd definitely be capturing the French dream her readers so fiercely coveted. Once the fire was burning, he motioned her towards it. Lizzie didn't linger and though her shoes squelched with each step, she held her hands out to the growing flames.

Feeling her body warm, Lizzie relaxed for the first time that day. She gave a sly glance over her shoulder to see what the Gallic god was doing. He shook off his jacket and grabbed a small towel from the back of a chair, drying his hair with it. When he finished, she was struck once more by how sexy he was, with dark brown curls most women would love to run their fingers through, and eyes of shining emerald blue. Lizzie turned back to the fire, not wanting to be caught staring, however much she would have liked to.

She hadn't had this sort of reaction to a man in years. In fact, the last man to make her body tingle had been Will. Knowing she needed to drag her thoughts away from the loser who'd broken her heart before the familiar sting of betrayal came flooding back, she said, 'I'm Lizzie, by the way. Thank you for helping me.'

He filled and placed a kettle on the hot plate of the large range cooker nestling in the alcove. It wasn't anywhere near as dirty as Sarah's. 'Luc,' he replied, banging around, gathering whatever he needed.

Lizzie turned back to the fire, concentrating on the thawing in her fingers and the warmth on her cheeks. She was starting to feel human again, though she must look anything but. She ran a hand over her hair where the bird had pooed and checked it had all disappeared. Forcing herself not to glance at Luc, she watched the flames wriggle and dance, mesmerised until something heavy hit her shoulders, bouncing off the back of her head. Luc had given her a blanket, or at least thrown one at her. She pulled it tighter, surprised at its delivery but grateful for the extra layer. 'Thank you.'

The rain was easing now, tapping lightly against the windows rather than pounding incessantly, and a pale watery sun appeared in the breaks in the clouds. While the kettle boiled, Luc took two tumblers and a bottle of brandy down from a shelf, splashing some into each of the glasses.

'Drink this. It will warm you up.'

His chair scraped along the stone tiles as he pulled it out and sat at the dark wooden table. Lizzie joined him, taking the glass and sipping the brandy. He was right. The amber liquid pleasantly burned her throat, warming her from the inside. It was strong stuff, and she repressed the urge to cough. With how grumpy he was, he'd probably take it as an insult, and she didn't want to make things worse.

The kettle whistled and Luc made a pot of tea. Without speaking he poured her a cup and pushed it towards her. Lizzie swallowed the last of her brandy, coughing loudly this time, and the corner of Luc's mouth lifted in amusement. She wondered what he would look like if his entire face lit up with a grin. She could imagine the blue eyes bright against the darkness of his beard. Her heart flipped and she stared at the tabletop.

'Where have you come from?' Luc asked.

'Chateau Lavande.'

Lines formed on his forehead. From those and the gentle crow's feet around his eyes, Lizzie put him in his late thirties. 'The chateau?' His beautiful accent made her tingle again. 'I thought it was unoccupied since Sarah passed away?'

'You knew my great-aunt?' The idea shouldn't have surprised her – they were neighbours after all – but given the state of the place, Lizzie had presumed Sarah had cut herself off from others or lied to them as she had her family, insisting everything was okay, which today had shown wasn't the case.

Luc nodded. 'Sarah was well known in the village. She was a very nice lady.'

Nice? Sarah had been many things, but Lizzie hadn't

imagined anyone from the village would describe her as nice, after what had happened. An uncomfortable silence settled on the room, broken by Luc clearing his throat.

'We will have this,' he said, gesturing to the tea, 'then we will find your car and I will tow it back to the chateau.'

'Oh no,' Lizzie said, shaking her head. 'No, no, no. No way – I mean . . .' thank you, but I can't stay there. It's full of . . . wildlife. Animals that should live outside are currently living inside and I'm sure that earlier today I saw a rat. I'm not normally prissy, but there's no way I can stay there overnight. In the dark. Something will try to eat me in my sleep.'

'Prissy?'

'Snobby or umm, squeamish.'

Luc shook his head. 'There are no rats. It will not have been a rat.'

'How do you know?'

'Because we do not have rats in French houses. It was probably my cat.'

Lizzie raised an eyebrow. '*Your* cat?'

'Yes. Albert likes to wander. Especially to Sarah's. She used to feed him fresh meat from the market.'

Sarah hadn't liked cats. Had she? Then again, if Luc had described her as nice it seemed Lizzie hadn't known her very well at all, or she'd changed. Maybe calmed down in her later years?

'Is there no way you can take me to the village, and I'll stay at the *chambre d'hôte*? I'd really rather not go back to the chateau.'

'The *chambre d'hôte* is full.'

'How do you know?' She didn't mean to sound

accusatory, but they had to have a room. If she was forced to sleep at the chateau tonight it wouldn't be at all surprising if a ghost appeared for a one-off haunting just to top things off nicely.

Luc studied her for a second. 'I went into the village this morning and Chloé, the owner, told me.'

'Oh.' Lizzie's heart sank, hitting her empty stomach. It rumbled loudly in answer. She'd been so busy dealing with each problem, she hadn't had a chance to eat today. 'Isn't there a *gîte* or a hostel or something I can stay in? Someone somewhere must have a room?'

Luc stood up again and went to the fridge, taking out some cheese, a few ripe, juicy tomatoes and butter. Then from the worktop he grabbed a long, crusty baguette and tore off a sizeable piece. After placing each item onto a wooden board and picking up a knife, he handed them to her. 'Eat.'

Shocked, but too hungry to argue, Lizzie obeyed without question. She spread the soft goat's cheese covered in herbs onto the crusty bread, her mouth watering with anticipation. She closed her eyes, letting the flavours fill her senses. The cheese was creamy and rich, and the deliciously crunchy bread was as soft as a cloud inside. After a bite, she took one of the tiny tomatoes, popping it in her mouth and letting the sweet, tangy juice hit her tastebuds. When she opened her eyes, it was to see Luc glancing away from her. Self-conscious again, she kept her eyes open for the remainder of the meal and as soon as she'd finished, Luc stood.

'There is nowhere else to stay, and you cannot stay here.'

'I didn't ask to.' Mildly affronted he thought that was what she was hinting at, Lizzie pushed herself up to standing. She had absolutely no wish to stay in the house of a man she'd known for less than half an hour.

'I have a friend who can look at your car, but it will not be until Monday.'

The thought of being stuck in the chateau for another day made her nose sting with unshed tears, but Lizzie refused to cry in front of Luc. So, she was here for the weekend, at least. She'd make the most of the time. Find the items Sarah wanted her mum to have, research her article. What else could she do? 'It's kind of you to help me.'

Luc went to another cupboard, taking out a small medical tin and opening it. Lizzie caught the plasters he tossed to her as he instructed, 'Time to go.'

Chapter Four

Stiff and sore, on Sunday morning Lizzie opened her tired and gritty eyes, blinking at the bright sunlight blasting through the threadbare curtains.

Then she screamed.

Despite checking the doors were locked before finding a bedroom to sleep in, the goat had somehow got back in the house and was now straddling her, staring into her eyes. And it was not staring lovingly.

The scream had done nothing to move it. Paralysed, Lizzie couldn't decide if she should sit up or wait until the goat got bored and wandered off. The one thing she did know for certain was that he or she had the worst morning breath she'd ever smelled.

'Christ, Goat, what have you been eating? You really need to floss, or at least start brushing. Either will do.' The goat cocked its head and after a second backed down the bed. Was it sad that this was the most bedroom-based excitement she'd seen in months? Even before the breakup, hers and Will's night-time antics had become more a cup of tea and a good book than candles and *Magic Mike* moves. They'd blamed work and stress but maybe it was a sign she'd missed. One that screamed, 'Hello! Your relationship is dying. Time to start CPR'.

Slowly, she drew her legs up and the goat wriggled backwards and sat down. Was it settling down for a nap?

'So you're just going to sit there, huh?'

Unsurprisingly, it didn't reply.

'I'm going to get dressed now, okay? Don't go charging at me, or getting upset, all right? I'm just going to slip some clothes on and then casually leave the room and brush my teeth. Nothing for you to worry about.'

Lizzie climbed out of bed and began to dress. She'd brought her suitcase inside with her last night and pulled on shorts and a vest top. Judging from the strong sun shining through the window, it was going to be a bright, hot day and to be honest, she needed something to lift her spirits.

By the time Luc had driven her to the chateau last night, unspeaking and stern, all traces of the storm had vanished. The ground was still wet, and puddles eclipsed the lane, but the clouds had rolled away and the sun had filled the sky with golden light. Warmth had suffused the evening air, perfuming it once more with lavender and the smell of fresh, rain-soaked grass. Luc had then left with a brusque *au revoir* and not so much as a backward glance.

With no electricity, Lizzie had found and lit some candles ready for the night to descend. She'd boiled water in a pan on the gas hob and after a cup of tea had found the only bedroom that didn't have a hole in its ceiling. The bedding had been damp and fusty but she'd discovered a clean set in an old cupboard that, while not exactly fresh, was at least a lot more pleasant.

Sleep had been fitful, as Lizzie had expected it to be. In fact, she'd anticipated dreams of Sarah or the recurring nightmares she'd had since the day she should have got married. Dreams where her teeth fell out, or she couldn't find her clothes, or she was desperately trying to call someone, but her fingers constantly hit the wrong numbers. All anxiety dreams, according to Google. Her subconscious dealing with the humiliation and heartbreak her 'wedding' day had brought her. How could Will have done that to her without any hint that something was wrong with their relationship? Leaving it until their wedding day, until the very day she was standing in her gorgeous wedding dress, holding a bouquet of cream-coloured roses had been cruel. No matter how many times she went over it, she was sure he'd simply made a last-minute decision that she wasn't what he wanted and that hurt.

The goat bleated and Lizzie studied it. It looked a lot smaller than yesterday's one. Was it a different goat (that there might be more than one was a terrifying thought) or had she misjudged its height from when it charged at her? It was actually quite cute now she came to look at it. Its creamy hair was soft and strokable, and its little ears tipped forward as if the tops were too heavy to hold up. Darker hair crowned its head and its black, shiny nose reminded her of a puppy's.

Grabbing her toothbrush and toothpaste, she went to the bathroom across the hall and the goat stood up and followed her.

'Coming with me?' Lizzie said, as it trotted behind. She felt a bit silly for being so scared of it yesterday. 'I'm going to have to think of a name for you, aren't I?' She brushed her teeth while running through a list of possibilities. 'What about Henry?' she asked when she'd finished. She was assuming it was a boy and had no inclination to check if that assumption was correct. 'Or Tony?' The goat looked distinctly unimpressed. 'Okay, what about Gary. Gary Baaarlow?' A tiny bleat escaped the goat's mouth and for the first time in months, a burst of unadulterated laughter rang from Lizzie's. 'Excellent. Gary it is.'

On her way to the kitchen, Lizzie noted again the desolate state of the place. Though she'd hoped it wouldn't look as bad after some sleep, tiredness gave way to frustration and anger. What was she going to do now? Not only was she sharing the chateau with Gary the goat, but there was so much to do. She needed someone to fix the electrics, the taps, the roof, decorate . . . it was going to cost a fortune. A fortune she didn't have. Her only option was to sell it in its current state, which would mean a lot less money but at least then it would be someone else's problem.

Lizzie made a cup of tea as she had the previous night, boiling the water that spurted from the tap in fits in a saucepan on the hob. She grabbed the stale croissants she'd purchased from a service station on the drive down and shared one with Gary. Better he eat that than the sofa or a chair. Where had he snuck in from last night? It wasn't the kitchen or living room. She'd have to check the other rooms later.

As she was going to be here for another day, supplies were called for. Something for lunch and dinner, and maybe even a bottle or six of the local rosé. She'd need a drink by the time she started going through Sarah's things. Last night, Luc had pointed out a shortcut to the village that cut across the fields at the back of the chateau. It was a much more direct route and one she would have undoubtedly taken in her youth. Funny that she hadn't thought of it yesterday.

Before all of that, the first thing to do was to email a local estate agent. The tiny village nearby was unlikely to have one; it hadn't when she'd been here last. She'd have to search for one. Lizzie grabbed her phone, thankful that today the chateau had a tiny bar of signal. As soon as she found one, she emailed, giving the address of the chateau and asking them to come and give a valuation. It felt good to have achieved something after the disaster that was yesterday, but something niggled at the back of her mind as though she was doing something wrong. She shook the thought away and was just gathering her wallet and bag when her phone buzzed.

'That was quick, Gary. I didn't think they'd get back to me so fast.'

Once she'd shown them around and they had everything they needed, she could be out of here. Lizzie checked the screen and her heart dropped as she saw a text message from Hilary.

How's the chateau? You must be so excited! Can't wait to

read the feature. Our readers are going to love it. Make sure you get pictures of the turrets!

'Oh god.' She groaned.

Lizzie slumped back down on the hard wooden chair and laid her phone on the table. How was she going to admit to Hilary that the feature was a non-starter? That any pictures would terrify their readers and that she was going to sell the place as quickly as possible? It was too big a job. Too big an ask. She didn't have the time, the money, or the resources and she was leaving tomorrow as soon as her car was fixed. The chateau wasn't someone's dream, it was a nightmare, and any article she tried to write would turn their readers off the idea of ever moving to France. The icy chill of failure crept over her skin. This was supposed to be her big break and instead she was letting down a person who had been incredibly supportive to her. Racked with guilt, Lizzie stared at Gary.

'What am I going to do, hey?'

It turned out that goats weren't the chattiest of companions as Gary continued to munch on his piece of croissant. Deciding she'd think about it on the walk, Lizzie grabbed a wicker basket from the pantry that must, at one time, have been stacked full of food, and used the last of the croissant to lure Gary outside.

The grass in the fields had dried in the intense heat of the day and the long blades tickled her legs as she walked. Lizzie tuned in to the prickle of warm sun on her skin. Even the hottest of British summers couldn't compete with this, and for a second, her fears melted in the freedom of the wide, open countryside. She loved London and all the distraction it provided, but it had been a long time since she'd been alone in nature. She expected it to feel isolating, as it had when she was younger, but it was calming. Peaceful.

As she came to the end of the chateau's grounds, purple lavender fields filled the scene before her. A mountain rose in the distance, peppered with bushes. The view was mesmerising. Small, squat rows of amethyst rolled away, and to her right, in the distance, was the small wall she'd climbed over into Luc's vineyard. He'd told her to follow its line and she'd come to a path that would lead her into town. She couldn't have been that far away from it yesterday, but the storm and the crash had turned her around. Tucking the basket further into the crook of her arm, Lizzie walked on.

Doing as Luc instructed, she followed the wall until the scrubby dust track running alongside a lavender crop came into view. The scent was almost too overpowering when combined with the fierceness of the heat. Almost. Lizzie took deep breaths of one of her favourite scents. It smelled of summer, of playing in the turret dressed up in one of Sarah's bright coloured shawls, and excitement built inside her as she thought of the food and drink she was about to buy. Her appetite had died somewhat since the breakup, but it was coming back now.

Anger at the state of the chateau still fizzled below the surface, as did guilt about what she'd say to Hilary, but since *Dirty Dancing* had been banned and she'd had to go back to work, Lizzie had learned to compartmentalise her feelings, ignoring the things that hurt or worried her and focussing on something else. Back home, that had been her career and for now, it would be visiting the little town ahead of her.

The dust track, dotted with tufts of brown-green plants, soon led onto cobbled streets and winding alleyways. Some of the tall buildings were made of the same mosaic-like stones as Luc's farmhouse while others were painted in a palette ranging from rich ochre to pale peach. It was like walking inside a painting. Surely this was one of the prettiest towns in the whole of France, if not the world. Bougainvillea climbed over garden walls, tickling her shoulders as she ducked underneath, and following the noise and chatter growing louder with every step, she found her way to the town square and the local *marché*.

The medieval square bustled with people of all ages perusing the market stalls and buying fresh produce, joking and haggling, or smelling the fruit and vegetables. Lizzie watched and took some photos with her phone.

Stalls with vibrant awnings in red and white stripes, or dazzling blocks of green and blue, were crammed into the square, the tables underneath bursting with colour. Crates of fresh onions and garlic sat alongside piles of vivid yellow and red peppers while the purple skins of aubergines shone beside plump, red tomatoes. Lizzie wanted to buy a little of everything, to spend the day walking around each of the stalls, photographing their beauty for use in future articles. Perhaps she could write a piece about French markets, linking it to French culture? No, that didn't seem quite hooky enough for a feature. Though it would be great for a freelance article. She'd have to think of something else to placate Hilary and keep her dreams of a promotion alive.

Lizzie entered the throng, glancing around for anyone who may remember her, relieved that there was no one she recognised. What welcome would she get? She didn't want questions. Would Sarah have told them why she no longer visited? Unlikely.

Pausing at the cheese stall and admiring the giant wheels with their thick, rough rinds, she spied some of the cheese Luc had given her yesterday. In embarrassingly rough French, she asked for some, and the handsome man smiled as he served her. Were all French men gorgeous? Here as a teenage girl, she surely would have remembered that. Next up was charcuterie.

When she eventually left the stall, she'd bought more than she'd ever be able to eat in a day, but the different flavours had been too hard to resist. Perhaps she could give some to Luc to replenish the food he'd given her yesterday and thank him for finding a mechanic. It wasn't that she wanted to see his handsome face again, or to see if her body tingled in his presence. This was just a courtesy, as she would have done for anyone who'd helped her. Anyone at all.

After gathering some vegetables and salad items, Lizzie paused at a stall selling locally made wines. She wondered if Luc's wines were stocked here but didn't know the name of his vineyard. The man was offering a taste to those who wanted it and tourists flocked towards him. It was strange how she didn't quite consider herself a tourist, though she really was given that it had been fifteen years since she'd last visited. When the man held out a small plastic cup, she declined, but she did purchase a bottle for later. Cold, crisp, rosé was one of her favourites and would be delicious sat in the garden of the chateau in the afternoon sun while munching on a baguette.

'Élisabeth? Is that you?'

Lizzie turned from admiring a flower stall overflowing with huge, happy sunflowers. An old woman, slightly weathered and stooped, smiled in front of her.

'It is you! I knew it as soon as I saw you from across the square. How wonderful to see you again. We were so very sorry about Sarah. Such a loss.'

It took a moment to place her, and worry flew into her stomach that this might be someone who hadn't been fond of Sarah. Someone who hadn't forgiven her. But Lizzie smiled as recognition dawned. It was Sylvie, a friend of her great-aunt's whom Lizzie had met on summer vacations. Sylvie had grandchildren around the same age and Lizzie used to play with them when they met in town. Two boys and a girl, if she remembered correctly. She shielded her eyes from the strong sun as she bid her good morning.

'It's lovely to see you again, Sylvie. How are you? And how did you recognise me? I must look very different now.'

'Ah, it is the smile.' Sylvie gestured with her hands, brushing them up either side of her face. 'I would know it anywhere. It has been too long. Far too long. Why have you not come back before? You enjoyed it here, did you not?'

Lizzie had, at one time, but more than just teenage sullenness had taken that from her. When princesses and dragons failed to exist, the towers had lost their appeal and soon the rest of the chateau had followed. But that wasn't what had ultimately stopped her coming. Her mind flew to that sunny afternoon when her and Sarah's relationship had imploded. After that, life had moved swiftly on and she'd never reached out to Sarah, but then, Sarah had never reached out to her. Lizzie had done enough interviews to learn how to avoid a difficult question and asked her own instead. 'How are your grandchildren, Sylvie? What are they doing now?'

Sylvie puffed with pride, growing taller. 'Pierre is a surgeon; Jacques is a teacher; and Brigitte is a florist. She also has a family of her own. I am still waiting for Pierre and Jacques to settle down.' She gestured again with her hand, rolling it over, showing how she wanted time to move on and more grandchildren to arrive. 'They are taking their time about it.'

'I'm sure you're a wonderful grandmother.' Remembering the name of her husband, Lizzie added, 'And how is Henri?'

Sylvie grinned and pointed to a bench away from the hubbub of the market, shaded by mature plane trees. An old man with a cane resting between his legs spoke to another aged man. From the way they threw their arms into the air as they talked, it was clear they were putting the world to rights.

'He is the same as always. He talks more than I do when he sees his friends. But it is good to see you, Élisabeth. Are you here for just a holiday?'

Lizzie didn't want to say she'd only come here because she had to and even then, with her career in mind. Sylvie loved her town and had never ventured further than its borders. 'I was here to see the chateau, but unfortunately I go back to England tomorrow.'

'Oh, that is a shame.' Sylvie seemed genuinely disappointed. 'I hope I will see you again soon. Well, it's been lovely to see you back. Excuse me, I must just go and speak to Claude about some patisserie.'

Lizzie relaxed, grateful not to face more questions about the chateau. She wasn't sure how to answer any of them. But yet again, her memory had played tricks on her. She'd forgotten how friendly the village was. How kind everyone had always been. No one had cared that her French had been dreadful, except for Sarah. They'd done their best to teach her, to decipher what she wanted and had smiled and waved each summer when she'd returned. How had she forgotten those things? She knew full well how the good memories had been wrapped in the dark clouds of her and Sarah's parting. It had obscured everything that had gone before it.

As Lizzie glanced at her basket, scanning the contents to see if there was anything else she needed, her eyes rested on the bottle of wine and an idea occurred to her. What if she featured Luc's vineyard in her article rather than the chateau? She needed a topic strong enough to make Hilary change her mind. Maybe she could switch it from focussing on buying and selling property in France to running a vineyard? Surely, their readers had that dream as well. Maybe a day-in-the-life-of article would work?

In the corner of the square was a sign reading La Maison Café. The small tables were already filling up with tourists seeking a late breakfast and locals taking a break from shopping. Lights had been strung from the sign to a large tree nearby and Lizzie almost wished she had the time to come back and see the place lit up in the dusky sunset. A corner table, in the shade of a flowering, bushy climber looked perfect. Lizzie made her way over to it, deciding a strong espresso was just the thing she needed to top up her energy levels before she headed back. Then she'd be ready to convince Luc about the article. As she was leaving tomorrow, she'd need to interview him today and if her time with him yesterday was anything to go by, convincing the grumpy gallic god to do her another favour wasn't going to be easy.

Chapter Five

A gift shop sat opposite the café and Lizzie called in before she went back to the chateau.

The huge shop was more like a medieval fortress set in an old stone building. Large archways led into the store and through each one, Lizzie spied shelves lined with bottles of wine and olive oil. She edged around the spinner full of the obligatory fridge magnets and postcards and immediately the scent of lavender filled the air, mixed with a heady aroma emanating from the thick bags of *herbes de Provence*. Lizzie picked one up and studied the flecks and dots of the different herbs. Her mum loved to cook and would adore something like this. She wanted something more for her though: a special something to remind her of the chateau before it left the family for good. Lizzie strolled on past tiny cloth bags of lavender soaps and an assortment of perfumed goodies, picking up something for herself – though she might have to wait to use it until she got home. The water system at the chateau wasn't robust enough to attempt a bath.

'*Bonjour!*' the cheerful woman called from behind the counter. 'Can I help you with anything?'

'I'm just looking for a gift for my mum,' Lizzie replied.

'We have plenty to choose from.' The shopkeeper picked up a box from the floor and re-filled some of the shelves. A tall, slim, elegant woman, the epitome of French style, paused next to Lizzie. She took a bag of *herbes de Provence* and smiled.

'I know just the thing you need.' She leaned in to speak conspiratorially. 'Everyone buys *herbes de Provence*, but if you want something special . . .' She pointed to the top shelf and a row of exquisitely made white ceramic jugs, all decorated with blue fleur-de-lis.

Lizzie hadn't noticed them at all, overpowered by the beauty of everything else around her. 'They're lovely.'

'They are. And all made locally by someone who does it for the love, not because they want to make pots and pots of money.' Her laugh was warm and friendly even though she appeared to have stepped out of one Lizzie's magazine shoots. Her long, blonde hair curled around her shoulders in elegant waves, flawless make-up made her skin luminescent, and her brown eyes were like saucers. 'Are you here for long?'

Her English was perfect, and Lizzie wished her French was as good. She'd really wasted her time here as a child. Her mum and Sarah had given her an amazing opportunity and she'd squandered it.

'No, I go back to England tomorrow. I—' She hesitated,

unsure why she wanted to tell this woman more, but her approachability encouraged her to continue and the burden she carried made her lonely. When Lizzie had confided in the friend she was living with about the chateau, she'd acted like Lizzie had won the lottery, encouraging her to move there immediately. Lizzie wondered if she'd be glad to be rid of her, if the *Dirty Dancing* marathons had proved too much. 'I've inherited the Chateau Lavande,' Lizzie began. 'I came back to sort through things but . . .' The sentence trailed away and again a feeling of failure consumed her as she prepared to admit she was running away from it all.

The woman's face softened. 'I heard of Sarah's death. I'm so sorry. She was quite a favourite in the town.'

Lizzie couldn't hide her surprise, but perhaps it was easier for the townsfolk to forget. Sarah had always been fun, able to win people over. The only trouble was, sometimes being fun meant being impulsive and that led to hot-headedness and mistakes. For Lizzie, though, some mistakes were more easily forgiven than others.

'Everyone liked Sarah,' the woman continued. 'She was always so cheerful. So chatty and full of life. And she spoke very good French considering she was an English woman. Sometimes you'd never have known. Except when she swore. She couldn't help but do that in English.'

A young girl stood by the woman's side, her eyes pinned to the mobile phone in her hand. She was about twelve and shuffled from foot to foot self-consciously. Lizzie had been just as awkward at her age. Perhaps that was partly why she hadn't enjoyed her holidays here with only Sarah for company.

‘Hello,’ Lizzie said, including her in the conversation. ‘I’m Lizzie.’

The young girl raised her head but didn’t answer.

The woman tried to catch the child’s eye, then tutted and turned back to Lizzie. ‘This is my daughter Amélie, and I’m Margot. It’s a pleasure to meet you. It must be very painful for you being at the chateau. If there’s anything I can do, please do ask.’

‘Thank you. It’s not painful, exactly.’ Margot’s brow furrowed and Lizzie worried she sounded unfeeling. She wasn’t, she was a mess of mixed emotions when it came to Sarah. ‘It’s just that the chateau’s in such a terrible state. I wasn’t really expecting it. I seem to have inherited a goat as well as a house. The electrics have blown, and I don’t think there’s any running water.’

‘It is probably an airlock.’

Lizzie’s eyebrows shot up and Margot laughed again. It was a dirty laugh that made you want to join in.

‘I know. I do not look like I should know this, but I used to live here. I grew up in the town and it can happen with old pipes. I cannot help you with the goat though. That is beyond my skillset.’

‘Thank you for the tip.’ Lizzie had worried all the pipes would need ripping out and replacing. An airlock sounded more easily resolved for whoever bought the house and shouldn’t affect the value too much. She didn’t have hopes of a windfall from the sale, but anything would help her get her own place back in London. ‘And don’t worry about Gary.’

‘Gary?’ Margot asked.

'The goat. I've named him Gary. I couldn't keep calling him Goat, especially after he woke up on my bed this morning.'

Amélie finally lifted her head from the phone screen. She wasn't exactly smiling but the idea of Gary the goat had lifted the corner of her mouth.

'Then at least you have made a friend. Three if you count me and Amélie too.' Lizzie warmed at the idea and mentally added lovely old Sylvie to the list too. It was more friends than she had back home since the split. 'And it's not all bad. You are in France at least. The best country in the world with the best food and the best wine. And in Provence! There is no better place to be, except for maybe Paris.'

Now Lizzie came to think about it, she was happy to be away from England, and though her heart still hurt, the distance from Will and the breakup, from the humiliation of being the most talked about subject in the office (even when *The Masked Singer* was on), and from sleeping in her friend's room amongst another person's belongings, gave her space to breathe. Waking up to see Gary the goat wasn't anywhere near as bad as waking up to walls covered in framed rugby shirts and a bed she'd have to give up in a couple of months' time. At least here she could ignore all those problems. But there was one problem she had to face immediately, and that was what she'd write about instead of the chateau, and the vineyard was still looking like the best option.

'It's been lovely to meet you both,' Lizzie said, sad that this would be their one and only meeting. She had a feeling that she and Margot could have become good friends if they had the time.

'And you, Lizzie. I hope we will see you again.'

Lizzie made her purchases and left, ready to face Luc, hoping that this time her body wouldn't simmer at the sight of him. She wasn't emotionally ready for simmering or tingling.

The journey back was as peaceful as her walk into town had been. She flattened her palm, allowing the wild grass and tallest lavender buds to skim her hand. Ambling slowly, time stood still. When the vineyard came into view, she approached it cautiously, not wanting to be accused of trespassing again. There was no reply after she'd knocked on the farmhouse door and so she made her way back through the rows of vines, hoping to stumble across him.

Certain this topic was the only one Hilary might be interested in, Lizzie needed to speak to him immediately and had already thought of some questions to ask. Hunting the grounds, she entered the track he'd led her up the night before and heard loud voices that even with her limited French sounded like an argument. As Lizzie weaved between the vines, she caught sight of a white skirt similar to the one Margot had been wearing as it disappeared from view. It hadn't sounded like Margot, though, and there was no sign of her daughter. Whatever the disagreement had been, she hoped it wasn't going to affect her chances with Luc. Venturing on, she found him alone, inspecting the grapes.

'Luc! *Bonjour*.'

He glanced up, scowling, then turned his attention back to the fruit. 'Have you broken another car, or have you come to stomp all over my vineyard again?'

Her stomach knotted. Whoever he'd argued with had put him in an even worse mood than yesterday. She hadn't expected a hug and a warm welcome, but he wasn't even meeting her eye. Despite the sour expression that this time did mar his attractiveness a little, Lizzie carried on.

'I bought you some bits to replenish what I ate yesterday and to say thank you for helping me.' She pointed to one side of the wicker basket where her gifts for Luc were stacked. 'Don't worry, I haven't tried to poison you.' His head shot up and she felt the blue eyes pin on her. He didn't smile at her joke and Lizzie's cheeks began to burn. It hadn't been particularly funny, but at least she was trying to be neighbourly.

'Gifts?' he said, finally meeting her eye.

Lizzie tried not to focus on the way his curls sprung out in all directions and how she wanted to touch them. His blue shirt, which almost exactly matched the colour of his eyes, was open at the collar and rolled up at the sleeves, revealing tanned skin. Lizzie forced her eyes back to his face. The piercing gaze focussed directly on her like a laser beam, and the tingling started in her spine, seeping out through her nervous system until her entire body was buzzing.

Damn you, body! When she got back to England, she'd have to get her big girl pants on and try one of the dating apps her friends were always moaning about. It was a terrifying thought but clearly her body was trying to tell her something, and it wasn't that she should join a convent and become a nun.

'You want to give me a gift, so you buy wine from my rival?' Luc angrily jabbed a finger towards the bottle in her basket.

'Your rival? I – No, I didn't know. I just fancied a drink.' He checked his watch. 'Not right now,' she added quickly. Great. It was eleven o'clock in the morning and she sounded like a lush. 'Later,' she clarified. 'This afternoon – I mean evening. I thought you might want a drink *later this evening*.' He wasn't convinced. 'I just bought some from the guy in the market. Don't you sell at the market? It was very busy. I bet you'd make a killing if you did.'

Obviously this too was the wrong thing to say, as Luc huffed and stomped away. He might be the sexiest Frenchman she'd ever met but he really was insufferably moody. For the sake of the article, Lizzie hurried after him.

'Look, I'm sorry—'

'I couldn't make the market today, okay? Are you happy now?'

Yet again the words 'crazy English lady' hung in the air, but he didn't say them. He had, however, said 'appy instead of pronouncing the 'h' and a single butterfly fluttered so violently in her stomach, Lizzie placed a hand there to calm it. She really needed to get a hold of herself. 'Okay.'

Luc paused to inspect another bunch of fat, black grapes poking out from beneath the green leaves. He took a pair of shears from his back pocket and trimmed some leaves from around it.

Seeing a way to bring up the article, she said, 'What are you doing there?'

'What does it look like? I'm checking the grapes.'

'For what?

'For disease and bugs. Why do you want to know?'

It wasn't the gentle way in she'd been hoping for, but it seemed now was her chance. 'Listen, I know this may not be the best time to ask, but I was wondering if I could interview you about your vineyard? I work for a British magazine called *Lifestyle!* and I thought it would make an amazing feature. Everyone dreams of giving up their office jobs and moving to France and this place looks pretty ideal to me. I was hoping to ask you some questions and take some pictures of the place.'

Luc watched her in silence. He narrowed his eyes, the crow's feet becoming slightly more pronounced, and his mouth had gone from full and kissable – *kissable?* – to a thin line. *Lizzie. Get. A. Grip. Rein it in.*

'*Non.*' He began to march off again.

She scurried after him like a tourist after a particularly militant tour guide. '*Non*?'

'*Non*,' he barked. 'It means no in French.'

'I know that, but why?'

Panic rose inside. How could he be saying no? If he said no, she'd have nothing to write about and rather than securing a promotion she'd probably lose her job. They might even give her feature to annoying Matthew, the ultimate humiliation. Lizzie told herself to calm down. This was not the time for ridiculous catastrophising, a habit she'd fallen into since the wedding that never was. It was tiredness talking, not the normal her. 'We have a great readership,' she rallied. 'It's one of the top lifestyle magazines in Britain.'

By now they were nearing the farmhouse. 'Still no.'

'Can I ask why not?' She tried to control the shake in her voice.

'Because I don't want to.'

'But it could be great for your business. It'd be excellent publicity.'

'I do not need the publicity.'

'Every business needs publicity.' She sounded a bit desperate now.

He stopped and scowled at her. 'Mine does not.' Each and every word was emphasised, fired at her like bullets from a gun. Why was he so impossible? 'Besides, I know you have not really come here to talk about wine but for your chateau. Isn't that so?' He pointed his finger accusingly.

The weight of the basket pulled her arms down. He was right. Luc had every right to be affronted. She'd told him last night she'd inherited the chateau and now she was making out the sole reason for her visit was to write a feature on him. She felt ashamed of herself. Maybe honesty was the best policy.

'You're right,' she admitted. 'And I'm sorry. I was supposed to write a feature on Chateau Lavande, on buying and selling French property and the dream of living here, but I can't now. The place is a mess. To be honest, the broken-down car is the least of my problems. If I write about the chateau, I'll be turning readers off the idea, not selling it to them. I'm leaving tomorrow and if I've got nothing to show my editor, I'll be in more trouble than I can imagine. I thought, maybe, if I could switch the topic to your vineyard, I might still be able to write something she'd accept. She's been so kind to me since—' Lizzie stopped herself just in time. He wouldn't be interested in the drama her life had become and she didn't particularly feel like sharing all the humiliating details with the grumpiest man to have ever walked the planet. Lizzie forced herself to be cheerful and tried again. If she kept going, maybe something would convince him. 'Packing up the nine to five and running a vineyard in Provence is still a dream for a lot of people and this place is gorgeous. You're incredibly lucky.' She gazed at the beauty around her, taking it all in. 'And the food I brought was a genuine thank you for last night. I really do appreciate your help.'

A flicker of something passed over his face and a softness eased the wrinkles from his brow. Then the curtain came down again. 'My answer is still no.'

Okay, maybe honesty hadn't been the best policy.

'But—'

'*Non*. Crazy English lady.'

And there it was.

Luc lowered his head and marched back towards the house. This time, Lizzie didn't follow. She had nothing more to say, could think of no other argument to make, and it was clear he wasn't going to listen to anything else.

What could she do now? She was fast running out of ideas. Hilary's scowling face formed in her mind. She'd be so disappointed, and Lizzie was disappointed in herself. She'd made a mess of everything since she set foot on

French soil – and things hadn't been much better on English soil, either.

With the gifts for Luc still in her basket, she trudged back to the chateau, and even the sun couldn't dry the tears falling down her cheeks.

Chapter Six

Black tea was disgusting but without electricity for the fridge, the milk had gone off in the heat. Lizzie sat on the front steps of the chateau, rubbing her tired, achy eyes. It was now Monday morning and after a long, sleepless night in which the shadow of Will had lurked, the possible loss of her career had circulated, and that last, difficult goodbye with Sarah had replayed over and over again, she perched on the cold stone steps and stared expectantly down the drive, waiting for Luc's mechanic friend to arrive.

After her trip into the village and the unhelpful meeting with Luc, Lizzie had sat alone in the garden drinking rosé and nibbling on bread and cheese. The wine tasted gorgeous even though it was made by Luc's rival, and she wondered how his would measure up. He was such a serious man she could only assume he was just as serious about his job. Yesterday afternoon, she'd contemplated returning to the vineyard and begging for the interview, but although she didn't have much pride left after being jilted, what little she did have wouldn't let her.

At least her mobile phone signal was inexplicably stronger today. She had two tiny bars instead of one and as she swiped at the screen, a notification she'd missed caught her attention. The estate agent had emailed back saying he could come today. A tiny spark of hope flickered inside and for a moment a weight lifted from Lizzie's shoulders. If she could get the place valued and on the market, and the car fixed today, she could be out of here by this afternoon. With no time to lose, she called the estate agent, whose English was, thankfully, perfect, and arranged for them to come immediately. He said he'd be there in half an hour. She hoped he'd bring his camera; she didn't want to have to arrange follow-up visits to take photographs. If he thought she could reach a decent price – or even a semi-decent price – she'd get it on the market as soon as possible. Sign the paperwork today. Now she needed to tidy and clean. She wasn't sure it would make any difference, but she had to at least try.

She was just taking a moment to listen to the birds singing when the sound of her ringtone startled her and she accepted the call. '*Bonjour Maman.*'

'Oh, so some of it's coming back to you then?'

'A little,' Lizzie laughed. She might not remember much French, but her accent was still pretty good when she tried. 'Everything okay?'

'Well, I don't really know how to say this, dear.'

Whatever it was, it couldn't be as mad as inheriting a chateau. 'Out with it, mother of mine. Is it to do with Sarah?'

'No.' Her mum hesitated. 'It's to do with Will. Have you seen on Instagram he's now with some woman called Melody?'

'I . . . My signal's a bit dodgy so . . . No, I didn't see that.'

'Oh love, I'm so sorry. I can't believe it. Only three months after doing what he did and he's moving on like nothing happened. My poor girl. I should have seen what a wrong 'un he was. I just can't believe it. Your dad's furious. Absolutely raging. I've had to stop him going round there. Are you still there, Lizzie?'

'Yeah. Yeah, I'm still here, Mum. I just didn't know. I unfollowed him after we split.'

'I know. And I didn't want to upset you, but I thought you were better off hearing it from me than finding out from someone else. I don't follow him anymore but I do like to stalk him now and again, just to see what he's up to. I was hoping to see him miserable and lonely, but there you go. It probably won't last, darling. There's always that.'

Whether it did or didn't was beside the point. The point was he'd moved on already. Had she been the girl Lizzie thought he'd cheated with? She didn't have any proof, only vague suspicions that could easily have been the result of her heartbreak. 'I *am* glad I heard it from you. But listen, I have to go. I'll call you back later, okay?'

'All right, love. Take care of yourself. Have a nice big glass of wine tonight. You deserve it after all you've been through. But you'll be fine, do you hear me? You're better off without him.'

'Mm-hmm.' Tears clouded her eyes, blurring the lines of the chateau.

'Say it for me so I believe you.'

'I'll be fine,' she replied, hiding her quivering voice with a strained laugh. Lizzie bid her goodbye and hung up.

She immediately searched for him and found the post. Her heart shrank in her chest. Will grinned wildly at the camera, his arm around a pretty, dark-haired woman. Lizzie swiped to see the next photo. He was kissing her. Several had been uploaded, all with the same theme: kisses, laughter and love. He couldn't be happier, he said in the text underneath. She was the love of his life.

Her throat tightened. 'The love of your life? Are you joking?'

It had only been three months since he'd jilted her. Three tiny months. Each word cut deeply, slicing through her skin down to her still-bruised heart. It had felt a little stronger since being in France but now it was back to a deflated balloon. A wave of heat rose from her toes to the crown of her head.

It was unbelievable.

Now she'd be faced with even more sympathetic glances, more office whispers, and the pitying consolation of their friend group. Not that she saw many of them anymore. She'd tried not to put them in the middle and the easiest way to do that had been to stay away from them altogether. Since then, they'd drifted away, hardly contacting her. Not only had Will stolen the best day of her life, but he'd also stolen her friends. He was oblivious. Totally oblivious. Just as he had been when he'd posted this. He would never have thought what it would do to her. Never considered what his actions would mean for her. He had no clue the social anxiety it would cause, the personal pain. In all their years together, since they'd first started going out after university, ending up in London in their first proper jobs, Will had never been that aware of what his actions did to others. It was the first thing her mum had pointed out after she'd been stopped outside the church by her dad and told Will wasn't coming to their wedding.

Needing to move, to do something, Lizzie stood and drank the last of her tea, grimacing at its bitterness, and an aged tatty Land Rover appeared around the bend in the drive. Through the windscreen Lizzie made out Luc's unsmiling expression. He really would look better if he smiled. It was a shame he was so determined not to. Just behind the van came her own small car, driven by the mechanic. It was fixed! She was a giant step closer to going home. Though that wasn't quite as appealing after the news she'd just received.

Lizzie placed her cup next to one of the stone urns and ran her hands down her summer dress. Luc jumped out of his Land Rover and the mechanic exited her car. She swallowed down the sadness that engulfed her and stuck on a smile.

'*Merci!*' Lizzie cried. '*Merci* . . . so much!' *How do you say so much in French again?* Walking to the mechanic, she pressed her hands together in prayer. She really was grateful he'd fixed her car so quickly. 'I really can't thank you enough. How much do I owe you?'

'I'm sorry but it is nine hundred and fifty euros.'

'What? Oh my god.' Luc shot her an evil glance. It wasn't that she thought he might be ripping her off, she hadn't suspected that for a second. It was that she hadn't anticipated it costing so much. She simply didn't have that much money. There might be just about enough room on her credit card if she never bought anything else again, ever. 'What was wrong with it exactly? Apart from me crashing into the verge that is.' She laughed to ease some of the tension she'd inadvertently created. The mechanic gave a small smile, but Luc's gaze remained hard and angry.

'The bumper needed replacing, along with some of the fuses. The water got to them. That's why it wouldn't start.'

'Right, I see,' she nodded. 'I'm afraid I don't have that in cash. I'll need to pay on my credit card. Is that okay?'

He nodded. 'Stop by the garage. It is on the way into town. Luc can show you.'

Luc glowered at being volunteered for the job and Lizzie shifted uncomfortably. Blimey, he really didn't like her at all, and though she'd been a pain in the butt since she arrived, she didn't think she'd been that bad.

'I'm sure I'll be able to find it. Thank you again. I really appreciate you helping me out. I promise I'll stop by this afternoon.' She could easily call in on her way home once the estate agent had been and the chateau was on the market. Speaking of which, she really needed to get on with the tidying. It was going to be hard enough to make a good impression with the holes in the ceilings and the sofa half eaten by Gary. Maybe she'd be able to find a throw she could chuck over it?

The mechanic left and Luc was just walking to his car

when Lizzie called out to him. 'I just wanted to say thank you to you too, Luc. It was really nice of you to help me get the car fixed. And you must have shown him where it was, so, umm . . . thanks. *Merci*.'

He didn't answer straight away; instead he took a few steps towards her, studying her with a slightly quizzical expression, and in his silence, pain washed over her again at thoughts of Will. It was like a dark, heavy cloud wrapping around her, devouring her. But she couldn't sink down into that spiral of self-loathing and depression again. She didn't want to go back to the feelings that had held her hostage in the days after their relationship ended, forcing her onto the sofa to hide and weep. Still, how could Will have done this? How could he have moved on so quickly? Didn't he remember all the good times they'd had? The special moments between them.

'Are you okay?' Luc asked, the question and the softness of his tone shaking her.

His expression had changed, so much so that she could hardly believe it was the same man. His dazzling blue eyes were dimmed with disquiet and rather than a scowl, the lines on his forehead spoke to a genuine concern for her welfare. But the tingling she'd felt before didn't materialise, unable to compete with the pain pulsing through her.

She swallowed down the lump in her throat and stared at her mobile. The screen was blank now but she could still see Will's smiling face. The love in his eyes. 'Just a personal thing. Bit of a surprise, that's all.' A tear fell from the corner of her eye, and she swiped it away, plastering on a smile again. 'Thanks, Luc.'

'Are you sure you're all right? You seem—'

'I'm fine. Really.' She hid her quivering voice with a strained laugh. 'Thanks again. You've been really kind to me. Sorry to have put you out.' She jogged to the stone steps, eager to hide in the house. Closing the door behind her she pressed her forehead against the cool, bare wood.

Gravel crunched as he drove away, and after several deep breaths she lifted her head from the door.

Why did this have to happen now? The day she was heading home. The pain left a bitter taste in her mouth as the shadowy hand of despair threatened to grab her again. As she had done before, Lizzie focussed on her refuge: her work. What questions would she ask the estate agent? Not just for her own purposes but for the article as well. The estate agent was going to give her everything she needed to know on selling property in France, whether he wanted to or not. Right now, she was quite prepared to hold him hostage if necessary. She opened the note-taking app on her phone and began typing while moving through each room and tidying what she could. Just as she'd done before, the pain would be buried deep down under her ambition.

About an hour later, as the stunning Provençal sun shone through the windows, the rev of an engine indicated the arrival of the estate agent and Lizzie stopped mopping the black and white tiles of the hallway floor. They were looking better but the water had become so grimy, and the mop was so old and mouse-eaten, it would need another once-over, probably two. As the estate agent made his way towards the chateau steps, Lizzie edged the bucket into the corner with her foot and rested the mop against the wall. She gave her best smile as she opened the door, happy to see his impressed expression as he surveyed the front of the chateau from the bottom of the steps.

'*Bonjour*, and welcome to Chateau Lavande.'

The estate agent's smile didn't last long as he spotted the mossy stone steps, the weedy urns, peeling front door and broken windows. If he was frowning like that now there was no way he was going to like what he found inside.

Lizzie faltered but felt some background might help explain the state of the place. 'I apologise that it isn't quite as tip-top as I'd like. I've just inherited the chateau and there are a couple of little jobs that need doing. It's beautiful though, isn't it?' He climbed the steps, placing each foot carefully and when he reached the top, he picked a flake of paint from the front door. 'I'd love to stay, but that's not possible. So I'm hoping to sell quite quickly. Maybe to someone who wants to refurbish and do it up themselves.' A look of confusion settled on his pudgy features but then she had been talking at a million miles an hour. Perhaps she should slow down and let the poor man step inside out of the heat. He must be sweltering in his dark suit. 'I'm Lizzie, by the way.' She held out her hand. 'Lizzie Summers.'

'Charles-Claude Baudin. Pleased to meet you.' He shook her hand but held his large leather folder close to his chest like a shield. Definitely time to calm down. Less crazy English lady and more professional journalist.

'Please, come in. Or did you want to look around the outside first?'

He gazed at the impressive lines of the house, the magnificent pepper-pot turrets. It was still spectacular as long as you didn't look too closely. 'I think we should start inside.'

'Of course.' She was just about to offer him a cup of coffee then remembered she didn't have any electricity. Perhaps if she popped him in the living room, she'd be okay to nip to the kitchen and boil some water in a pan. She supposed she was going to have to tell him everything about the state of the place for him to list it and give a valuation. She couldn't lie and pretend the electrics worked like a charm. Maybe if she said it cheerfully it wouldn't seem so bad. 'Would you like a cup of coffee? I'm afraid the electrics have gone so it might not be the nicest and it'll have to be black because the milk went off without a working fridge, but . . .'

Mr Baudin's eyebrows met in the middle, forming a rather long, ruffled-looking caterpillar. 'I'm fine, thank you.'

He was probably worried he'd get legionnaires' disease or something. Lizzie carried on regardless. 'Shall we begin in the living room?'

He nodded and followed her into the house, making notes in his leather pad with a traditional fountain pen.

'As you can see it needs some work but there's so much potential here. The fireplace for example is original and really quite stunning.'

It actually was. She hadn't really looked at it properly before, probably because of the rampaging goat and assorted wildlife living rent free, but now she looked at the pale white stone, at the intricate carving, she could imagine a fire roaring, and people gathered around it. She told him as much.

'*Bon*,' was his response, with an indulgent smile.

They toured the house, his face either unreadable or frowning. She'd made the most of the size of the rooms – they really were on the large side – and of the beautiful hallway floor which would look even better when she'd washed it again and had the window fixed so the sun could shine down on it. Dread now weighed down Lizzie's chest. Her attempts at small talk had been curtailed by Mr Baudin's miserable expression and her inability to decide whether she should attempt French or stick to English. In the end, she'd simply followed him around, answering his questions whenever he raised one. Some she knew the answer to, some she didn't.

'May I see the exterior?' he asked solemnly when they arrived back in the hall.

'Yes, of course.'

She led him back out to the front of the chateau. He made more notes, and even scratched his temple once or twice with the end of his pen. The sun beat down stronger and hotter under the pressure of the situation and Lizzie wished she'd applied sunscreen to her shoulders. She was sure they were burning already.

'Isn't it beautiful? I know some of the shutters need fixing but that's not a huge job. I used to love the turrets when I was a little girl. I used to play in them all the time.'

He gave her another smile and after walking around the entirety of the house, and asking about acreage, they moved back to the coolness inside. Lizzie opened the front door and let Mr Baudin walk through first. He paused just inside the doorway and Lizzie wondered what had halted him. Perhaps he was seeing the place through fresh eyes and admiring the grand staircase now the light was bouncing off the chessboard floor of the hall.

'Is that a goat?' he asked in slightly panicked tones.

'A goat?' Lizzie peered over his shoulder. Not again. How had Gary got back in? Now really wasn't the time for him to be trotting in for lunch. She rushed in and gently shoed Gary towards the door. Mr Baudin jumped out of the way in as comical a fashion as Lizzie had when Gary had charged at her. It really had been a stupid reaction to such a small, cute creature. Gary trotted past, eyeing Mr Baudin like a guard dog eyes a burglar's ankles. Then he disappeared around the side of the house. 'He's a – a pet!'

'A pet?'

'Yes. My aunt was quite eccentric. Loved goats. Hated dogs.' Crikey, what rubbish was she spouting now? 'Shall we go through?' She motioned to the living-room door.

Once seated on the old, worn sofa, Lizzie clasped her hands together in her lap. Nerves tingled her stomach. She didn't have butterflies; that could be a pleasant sensation. This was worse. Like someone was tying her internal organs in a giant knot – one of those ones it's impossible to undo. She took a deep breath.

'So, Mr Baudin, how much do you think the chateau's worth?'

'Well.' He cleared his throat. Then spoke in slow, controlled English. 'Miss Summers, I'm afraid that with the extensive work required on the property we're unlikely to find a buyer.'

The knot in her stomach quickly unwound as it dropped to the floor. Queasiness settled in the base of her throat. 'Until I get it fixed up, you mean?'

Mr Baudin sighed heavily. 'There will be a lot of work to do, I'm afraid. The best option would be to sell to someone who will knock it down. It does come with a lot of land.'

'Knock it down?'

The idea was simply horrible. Though she and Sarah had fallen out, this had been Sarah's home and there had been some good times here. No matter where Sarah travelled in the world, and she had travelled a lot, she always came back to the chateau. To France. There was no way Lizzie could sell it merely for someone to knock it down. It felt like a betrayal, not just to Sarah but to her mother too. Selling it to a family to love and enjoy, like Sarah had, was very different to selling it to someone who'd demolish it and do what? Build flats? Build some ghastly new architecturally designed modern monstrosity?

'I'm afraid those are your options.' He stood, fiddling until he'd placed the fountain pen back in the leather notepad. 'I'd be happy to come back once you have made some improvements, but until then, I really cannot list the property with any expectation of a sale. It would be a waste of your time and mine.'

And time was running out. In a state of shock, Lizzie simply nodded and gave a perfunctory goodbye.

Her thoughts ran from Will and his new girlfriend, to

Sarah and their problematic relationship, to her mum and what she'd think if she let someone knock the chateau down. She pushed the image of her mother's tear-stained face away. What the hell was she going to do now? She couldn't stay but she couldn't go home either. Just when she'd thought things couldn't get any worse, they had. Swallowing the lump in her throat, she wondered if she would ever catch a break.

Chapter Seven

Lizzie trudged to the kitchen, taking the mop and bucket with her. Was there any point in giving the floor another clean? The water was cold now with a grimy scum sitting on the surface. She'd need to replace it and boil another huge pan on the hob. It was all too much effort. What was the point if the place was only good for knocking down? She tipped the water away and turned to survey the kitchen once again.

A high shelf held mementoes of Sarah's trips. She'd travelled extensively and had carried those experiences within her soul. She'd worn bright kaftans and strings of beads had jangled from her neck and wrists. Her clothes were as colourful as her character. She was full of life. She'd been exactly the type of person Lizzie would have loved now: exciting and voracious. But as a teenager Lizzie had been unable to cope with her enthusiasm for everything. Amongst these memories, her mind tried to wander into the realms of arguments and endings, but it didn't feel right. Whatever had happened between them, this was Sarah's home. Her greatest love.

There was a carved wooden mask from somewhere or other (Sarah hadn't labelled it), and a silly stuffed camel, mangy and unwell from the dust and grime on its plush. Beautiful shells collected from exotic beaches were next to a giant stone pestle and mortar. Though her summers here hadn't always been the happiest, could Lizzie really just wipe out all that Sarah had held dear in the blink of an eye? In the time it took to sign a contract selling it all? Her character, her life, was in these walls, in the very fabric of the building.

Lizzie's skin prickled. The chateau had so much life left in it. All it needed was some love and care. She wasn't the one to give it all but surely someone could love this place as much as Sarah had.

Looking with fresh eyes, there was gorgeous stonework around the door frames; dark green tiles that once polished would shine in the sun sat behind the sink. There were so many features in this room alone that it would be a shame to lose them, and she couldn't bear the thought of the house being dismantled piece by piece as elements were stripped out that people deemed worth saving.

Was there any solution? The only one Lizzie could think of was staying and doing it up herself, but that could never work. Could it? She had to go back to London. To her job. Okay, there wasn't much more than that to go back to. She had no significant other, no flat to give notice on. She loved her family, but they'd understand. Her mum would probably be pleased, given the chateau's alternative. Lizzie's heart quickened as a nebulous idea began to solidify. Was there any way it could work? A pinching in her gut told her it might. It wouldn't be easy, but if she finally had some luck . . .

Lizzie checked her phone. As usual, there wasn't much signal, so she raced through the house, out into the sunshine of the front steps. The tiny bar had flickered in and out of life as she'd moved through the house but now she was outside it stayed miniscule but intact. With unsteady fingers she dialled Hilary's number.

'Lizzie! Hello! How are things?'

'Ah, *comme ci*, *comme ça*,' she replied.

'Make sure you put touches of that lingo in your article. I love it. What can I do for you?'

The pinching tightened into a knotty bundle. *Here goes*.

'I thought I'd ring and give you an update because it's not been exactly plain sailing.'

'Okay.' A clear note of concern rang in Hilary's voice and Lizzie continued quickly.

'So, I know we agreed that I'd write a piece on selling the chateau and living the French dream but . . .' She took a deep breath, knowing that right now her career prospects could be irreparably damaged if Hilary didn't go for the new idea. 'The chateau's in a state. Far worse than I ever expected. I've had it valued today and the estate agent said it's really only good for knocking down.'

'Lizzie, I'm so sorry. That must be awful for your family.'

It was typical of Hilary to be more concerned with her and her family than the article. She really was an amazing boss. Lizzie's thoughts ran to her mum and how upset she'd be when she heard the news. She and Sarah had been the closest out of everyone. All those summers Lizzie stayed, her mum had hoped they'd grow close too, but it wasn't to be. All her life Lizzie had assumed that it was Sarah's fault the relationship wasn't there, but hearing people in the village speak of her, knowing how she herself had been ungrateful during the summer holidays, she wondered now if it had been partly hers, too.

Hilary's voice was tinged with disappointment. 'So I guess writing about living the French dream is out of the question?'

'That's what I thought at first,' Lizzie replied, excitement bubbling up at her new idea.

'At first?'

'Well, when I saw the state of the place, I thought I'd need to switch topics and I considered writing about the vineyard next door but—'

'Wait, wait, wait. There's a vineyard next door?' The slight chuckle helped Lizzie relax a little. 'This place sounds perfect.'

'It would be if it wasn't run by a handsome but very grumpy Frenchman. Anyway, Luc wasn't in favour at all.' Saying his name brought his face to mind. The wet hair of the night they met, the concern of earlier that day. If it was concern, that is – it could have been annoyance. 'To be honest, I thought it was all pointless until the estate agent came.'

'And told you the place was only good for knocking down? I'm confused.'

'I promise it'll all become clear. I considered selling for

a second, but I just can't bring myself to do it. Not for it to be destroyed. You should see this place, Hilary. It's in a bit of a state now but underneath it really is gorgeous. It's like Cinderella in her servant's clothes. All it needs is a fairy godmother to wave her magic wand and sprinkle some fairy dust. I couldn't picture it before, but walking around with the estate agent today, I could really see its potential.'

'So what's your plan?'

Lizzie paused, organising her thoughts and ensuring the words buzzing around her head were exactly the ones she wanted. She'd only have one shot at convincing Hilary this was a good idea and she needed to make the most of it. 'I warn you this is probably the cheekiest thing I've ever said, but here goes. How do you feel about giving me a regular column? I know it's a lot to ask but this is a long-term project. I can't fix everything in a week or two, there's just too much to do, and I don't have the money. I'm going to have to do things as and when I can afford to until I reach the point that I can sell it to someone who'll cherish it, and that means staying here and doing as much of the work as I can by myself. Then, once I'm offered a decent price, that's when I'll sell. It's just not the two-minute job I was hoping for. I still think an article like that would appeal to our readers and it's basically what we agreed in the first place but over a longer period of time. I promise it'll be informative and entertaining, It'll just be more real because it'll be about my experience doing this.'

There was no response and Lizzie didn't know whether to carry on speaking or give Hilary space to take everything in. The connection wasn't the strongest and she worried half of what she'd said had been missed altogether. But finally, Hilary spoke.

'So, it would be a regular column documenting you doing up the chateau? All the ins and outs, the nitty-gritty, the successes and failures. Everything from finding local tradesmen to fixing broken taps yourself.'

'Exactly.' Lizzie feigned a confidence she didn't feel. She'd never been that great at DIY but what other option did she have? 'There are windows to fix, ceilings to mend, furniture to restore, plus I need to find out where Gary comes from.'

'Gary?'

'He's the goat that's taken up residence. He's actually quite sweet.'

Hilary laughed and it was a reassuring sound. 'I like this idea, Lizzie. I like it a lot.'

'You do?'

'Yes I do.' The sound of Hilary's fingers tapping on her keyboard tinkled in the background. 'This really is living the dream for a lot of people. How many of our readers are actually in with a chance of inheriting a chateau or buying one that can be lived in straight away? The reality is, that if someone does want to disappear to the south of France, they're going to buy a fixer-upper and do a lot of the work themselves. I really like this idea. This is much more accessible for our readers. And a regular column, Lizzie, it's a big step up for you. I've been pitched lots of ideas for regular columns but none of them have made me as excited as this one. I might even be able to give you a sort of advance to kickstart your efforts. One that you don't have to pay back, but I'll need clearance from above so I can't promise anything.'

Lizzie nearly dropped the phone in shock. 'Really? Hilary, that's . . . that's more than I hoped for. Are you sure?'

Hilary chuckled and Lizzie's tense shoulders dropped. She hadn't realised how hunched she'd been. A cool breeze tickled her neck, and the sound of birdsong came back into her ears.

'I'm positive. I can't guarantee it'll be much—'

'Every little helps, and I should be getting some money from Sarah's will as well.'

It seemed only right that she should use the money to restore the place Sarah had loved most in the world.

'Right, well, I've got another meeting, so I have to go. I'll email you about deadlines and I want lots of pictures of everything. I want our readers to see it before you've done anything to it and every step of the way too. We might even put the ones we can't get in the magazine on the website. What's your first job today?'

'Find someone to fix the windows, I think. If it rains any more the water will come straight in again.'

'Again?'

'I'll let you read that in my draft. It'll give you a laugh. Let's just say my first night here was an adventure.'

'Then I look forward to receiving it. Take care, Lizzie, and stay in touch.'

Lizzie signed off with copious thanks and closed her eyes, savouring the sun on her bare skin. She sank down in relief. Tension released from her muscles and as she listened to the crickets in the long grass, she appreciated the peace and calm around her. She hadn't felt this alive in a long time.

Now she didn't have to go back and hear everyone talking about Will and his new girlfriend, or worry about finding somewhere to live because her friend was kicking her out in a matter of weeks. There was a lot to do, and it was going to cost a ton of money, but it was an investment. This whole thing was an investment in her future both professionally and financially. She laughed to herself at the absurdity of it all. What had seemed such a disaster had ended up with her getting a regular column and somewhere to live. The chateau wasn't exactly The Ritz, but it was better than being homeless or living in a tiny bedsit. And a regular column could make her career. This could be it. The key to a promotion at the magazine. She'd shown she had a nose for a good story, for what their readers wanted. It certainly wasn't going to do her CV any harm.

For the first time since she'd arrived, Lizzie pulled her phone from her pocket and gave a full dazzling smile. She snapped a selfie with the chateau in the background, ready for the magazine's blog and her own social media channels.

Things were finally looking up.

Chapter Eight

Gary came gambolling past as she tucked her phone in her pocket.

'Oh, come back have you, now you've scared my estate agent away?' He tilted his head and his silly crooked ears flopped forwards. 'Well, you can't come in now. I've got to go into town. I need to find someone to help me fix this place up, and I'm going to need way more food if I'm staying for a bit.'

After gathering her keys and wallet to buy more supplies – which reminded her that she really should get the electricity and water sorted first so she could have a bath and put her food in the fridge – Lizzie made her way into the village using the shortcut she'd followed yesterday.

As before, lavender filled the air and long grass tickled the backs of her legs. What was the weather like in rainy old England? The world seemed so much better when it was bathed in sunshine.

The village was quieter today without the local *marché*

and the crowds. Tourists were still snapping pictures on phones and bulky cameras, and shop owners chatted with each other. The café she'd stopped at was full and the smells emanating from the tables woke her stomach. She was always hungry here in France. Back home, food had become a necessity but not something she took enjoyment in. Here the food was fresh and appetising, and she found herself thinking about the next meal as soon as she'd finished the last one.

Lizzie made her way through the arches of the gift shop – she had decided to call there first as the owner had seemed kind. The smell from the bags of herbs hit her first. She'd buy one for herself as soon as the kitchen became operational. The owner was bustling around behind the counter again as Lizzie approached wishing her good morning in French.

She received a warm welcome, but with such rapidly spoken words, Lizzie panicked.

'I'm so sorry, my French is still very rusty.'

'No problem. Are you well? Is there anything you need?'

'I'm very well, thank you. And there is something I need but it's advice, really. I don't know if you know but I've inherited—'

'Chateau Lavande from Sarah. Yes, I heard. I am sorry for your loss. So sad. We all miss her.'

It still dumbfounded Lizzie to hear people say things like this. She pulled her mind back to the matter in hand. 'That's kind of you to say. I'm Lizzie, by the way.'

'Violette.'

'Nice to meet you, Violette. The umm . . . the chateau

needs some work doing to it. Quite a lot, really, and I need some help. Do you know—'

'Luc.' She gave a curt, confident nod. 'You will want Luc.'

'Luc?' Surely she couldn't mean *Luc* Luc?

'Yes. Luc. Luc Allard. He runs the vineyard next to you.'

'Yes, I know Luc.'

Why did it have to be him? The town was small but there must be someone else who could help. Luc didn't like her and wouldn't take kindly to any request for help. He wouldn't even do an interview, so the chances of him fixing her shutters almost made her laugh. 'Are you sure Luc's the best person? I haven't told you what I need help with yet.' Lizzie added a laugh to ensure Violette didn't take offence.

She waved her hand dismissively. 'It doesn't matter. He will be the best.'

'But I need someone to fix the windows—'

'Luc can do that. He replaced a window for me once.'

Lizzie frowned. 'And I'm pretty sure the electrics need completely re-wiring.'

'Who do you think wired the farmhouse?'

This couldn't be happening. Surely there was a glazier nearby and an actual electrician. 'And I think there's an airlock in the water system.'

The owner tutted. 'Luc can do all these things for you. He is very good. And he will not charge you a fortune like some people can.'

'Right.'

Lizzie thanked her and made her way back outside. So

Luc was one option, but she had only asked one person. Perhaps Violette simply didn't know of anyone else or had always relied on Luc. She'd have to try someone else.

Lizzie crossed the square and joined the queue for the boulangerie. So many people were waiting that she had to stand on the pavement and as she did, she listened to the conversations in front of her, remembering odd words and their meaning. It would be a long time till her French was good enough to hold a conversation. The people in front said various helloes and good mornings that Lizzie returned, feeling welcomed. It was such a change to the head down, speedy commutes she'd become used to in London where eye contact would either mean people thought you were mad, or you risked being accosted by someone who actually was.

The queue grew smaller, and Lizzie was soon at the counter ordering two baguettes and fresh croissants for the next morning. The smell of fresh-baked bread was heavenly. That warm yeastiness tinged with sweetness and a hint of salt from the butter tempting her to buy more and more. There was so much she could have ordered from the delicious display but in the name of moderation she held back. The baker was large and slightly intimidating despite his friendly demeanour but as she handed over the money, she said, 'And can I ask you for some advice, please?'

The baker's meaty brow crinkled in concern, the folds of skin forming a series of mountain peaks. 'I will try.'

'Is there an electrician around here? And a plumber?'

He shook his head. 'Luc. Luc Allard, from the vineyard. He will help you.'

'Luc,' she replied with a dim voice. 'Got it.' She really didn't want Luc. Why, out of all the Frenchmen in Provence, did he have to be the only one they recommended? 'Do you know of anyone else I can ask?'

'No, there is no one. Luc is very good at this sort of thing.'

Lizzie nodded and retrieved her goods from the counter. 'Thank you.'

After a quick visit to a small bookshop that sold the most beautiful second-hand books, and asking the same questions, it seemed everyone was giving the same answer. She needed Luc. The nearest plumber lived in a small village much further away and was very, very busy. The same for an electrician. Everyone praised Luc, who had a reputation as a jack-of-all-trades as well as running the vineyard, and had done various jobs for them all over the years. The lady behind the counter of the patisserie where Lizzie had gone for a chocolatey pick-me-up had seemed rather offended when Lizzie had asked if Luc had any actual qualifications. He didn't, as it turned out, but no one had ever complained about his work. Slightly afraid of her scary stare, Lizzie scarpered, wishing she'd bought a few more cakes so she didn't have to go back in for the next few days. She might not be forgiven.

She should have known after her first two attempts that everyone would recommend the same person. It was that sort of town. The sort of place where everyone knows everyone else's life story. Who'd dated who, who left, who came back, who was so-and-so's great-great-grandfather. And Luc seemed a particularly favourite resident.

So, it was Luc again whom she had to speak to and ask a favour of. He really wouldn't be pleased at all. It was going to be a difficult conversation. She thought back to the difficult conversations she'd had to have with the wedding DJ and the caterers. Will had left her and her family to deal with all of that. Surely it couldn't be as difficult as those.

On her way to the shortcut, Lizzie noticed a sign sticking out between the houses, advertising the garage. She still needed to pay the mechanic and had promised to do so this afternoon. She'd imagined calling in on her drive home, leaving the chateau with a promotion-making feature under her belt and the promise of financial security from the sale . . . How her plans had changed so quickly! But with Hilary now on her side, she couldn't be despondent and she headed into the garage with a spring in her step.

The garage was little more than a small stone arch with barely enough room for the car he was working under. His feet stuck out and Lizzie called a gentle hello, not wanting him to hit his head in surprise. He slid out and smiled at her.

'I've come to pay my bill,' she said, cheerily, fetching her card from her wallet.

'Ah, yes. You said you would come and here you are. That is very English of you.'

She thought back to her wedding day when Will had promised he'd be there and then decided he'd rather not. She didn't bother correcting this unknowing mechanic that some people were untrustworthy no matter what their nationality.

'This way.' He motioned towards a small office no larger than a broom cupboard rammed with files and an old computer.

Lizzie stayed in the doorway as there wasn't enough room for two. After finding her bill and entering something on the computer, he reached out and took her card, running it through the grubby card machine on the desk. Lizzie gave a silent prayer that it would go through. She was almost sure there was just enough room, but she'd been sailing pretty close to the wind.

As an uncomfortable silence enveloped them, and partly to relieve her nerves as the card machine buzzed, Lizzie said, 'So you're a friend of Luc's? Have you known him long?'

'All my life,' the mechanic answered. 'He's a good man.'

Grumpy though, she wanted to add. 'Everyone keeps telling me he's the one to help me fix up the chateau. He seems to be the go-to man for all sorts of problems.'

The mechanic nodded. 'When he started at the vineyard, the farmhouse was barely liveable. He did everything and now it is beautiful.'

'It is.'

'Everyone knows Luc. He's always lived here, apart from a little stay in Paris. Sorry,' he said, taking her card and trying the machine again. 'The connection has broken. I must try again.'

'Oh, okay. No problem.'

Another silence enveloped them, broken by the mechanic giving her a strange look up and down, then saying, 'Luc is a nice man underneath the exterior. He has had a tough time with love. It has made him like . . . like cheese.'

'Cheese?' If he hadn't been speaking English, Lizzie was sure she'd have misinterpreted him.

'Yes. A cheese with a hard rind that underneath has a soft and gentle flavour. That is like Luc. He is a bit difficult when you first meet him but that is because he has put up his defences. Once you get to know him, he is good and kind.'

Lizzie had to stifle a laugh at his lyrical description; if she was going to compare Luc to anything, it certainly wouldn't be cheese. A tiger maybe, or something prickly like a porcupine. Maybe a hedgehog. She'd always found them cute, too. Why the mechanic was mentioning this, though, Lizzie had no idea and decided it best not to ask.

After the card machine gave a final wheeze, the payment went through, and Lizzie breathed a sigh of relief. She took her card, bidding the mechanic goodbye.

A gentle breeze blew as she ambled back along the path towards the chateau. She was just deciding whether to call in at the vineyard or leave it until tomorrow when Luc appeared on the horizon. He was wearing a shirt that had come half untucked from the waistband. With his curly hair ruffled by the breeze, Lizzie's heart beat a little faster, but she put it down to nerves at having to ask him to help her with the chateau. A question she was sure would receive a resounding no, no matter what anyone in the village said. He drew closer and Lizzie put her hands in her pockets, hoping to appear casual and not the least bit unnerved by his presence.

'Hello.'

'*Bonjour*,' he replied with a slight sneer that Lizzie took as disapproval at her using English. He moved around her, eager to continue on his journey.

'Luc, do you have a moment?' Unable to launch straight into it under his piercing blue eyes, she pushed away the strands of hair that had blown into her face. As he stared at her, waiting, the fizzing started again in the pit of her belly. It made her feel vulnerable, and she switched to professional mode to conceal it. 'I'm actually going to be staying at the chateau and, clearly, it needs doing up. I've been told you're the person to help me mend the windows and fix the electrics and . . .' He was still staring at her, his face totally unreadable. She had no idea if he was amused or annoyed. 'And such like. I was wondering if—'

Luc focussed on the panoramic views around them, then turned back. 'Me?'

'I asked everyone, and apparently you're the one.' Both his eyebrows shot up and Lizzie blushed at the phrase. 'For DIY, I mean. I know you've already helped me with the car, and I know you're very busy, but is there any way you can help me do a few things, or at least, point me in the right direction? I'll pay you of course.'

Under his intent gaze her insides were throwing themselves around, but she ignored it. He was just a handsome Frenchman with a killer accent. He wasn't likeable at all. What's more, he seemed even more offended at her last comment, but if she hadn't offered to pay him, he'd have thought she was taking advantage. *Chance would be a fine thing*, a voice in her head offered and Lizzie bit her lip, hushing that part of her brain. This time, it was she who turned her head and surveyed the beautiful landscape around her.

'Fine, I will help you with what I can. But I will teach you so you can do it yourself. I do not have time to do everything for you and run the vineyard.'

'Of course. I don't expect you to be there all the time. If you could just help me with—'

'I will be there tomorrow at nine and we will get started. I must go now.'

He strode away, leaving her frustrated. Why did he always have to be so blunt? She was making such an effort to be polite despite his rudeness, couldn't he do the same? She didn't expect him to just come and work at the chateau full time. Hadn't she made it clear she was looking for help, not someone to do it all for her? Sometimes it really did seem like he only heard what he wanted to hear. And why had the mechanic gone on about what a nice man Luc was? If he was, he was definitely doing his best to hide it.

Chapter Nine

The next morning, Lizzie eyed her old dungarees. They were paint-splattered from when she and Will had moved in together and decorated their small one-bedroom flat. Things were great then. Their relationship full of laughter and love. Sometimes she wished she couldn't remember those times and only recall the rows all couples had; the disagreements and not the nights snuggled on the sofa, cuddled up and kissing.

Unable to afford new clothes, she'd brought them with her to France, and at the time, she hadn't thought slipping them on over an old vest top would be so painful – but then she hadn't counted on Will finding someone else and plastering the news all over Instagram. It hurt more than it should. It was probably a good thing she hadn't brought *Dirty Dancing* with her. She might have regressed to watching it ten times a day, in which case nothing would get done.

Securing the buckles over her shoulders, Lizzie scraped her hair back into a ponytail and made her way downstairs.

She hadn't bothered with make-up. There didn't really seem much point as she had no idea how dirty she was going to get today.

Gary was nowhere to be seen but Lizzie had saved him some bread from her supper yesterday in case he turned up. She'd also snapped more pictures than she could ever use for her column and the *Lifestyle!* website. Somehow Lizzie knew that when she looked back on them after this journey was finished, she'd be proud. At least she hoped she would be.

It was a quarter to nine and Lizzie pottered about the kitchen making a pot of tea, eating her croissants and waiting for Luc to arrive. He always made her so nervous. It wasn't just that he was attractive and that when he was around, her heart decided to do things it hadn't done since Will, it was his manner as well. After the way they'd first met – her soaked to the skin, looking like a soggy ghost – she wanted to make a better impression this time.

Everyone spoke so highly of him. Had she just not seen that side to him yet? Perhaps he didn't like English people. But then, he'd liked Sarah. He'd told her so. So maybe he just didn't like her. A depressing thought given they were going to be working together for the foreseeable future. She'd just have to show him she wasn't the crazy English lady he thought she was. She stared down at her paint-smattered dungarees. That wasn't likely to happen.

At precisely 9 a.m. a knock sounded on the kitchen door, and Lizzie answered it.

'*Bonjour*,' she trilled happily, excited to get started. To take the first step on this grand adventure. 'How are you today, Luc? Would you like some tea? Or maybe coffee? How about a croissant? Have you had breakfast?'

Aware that she'd fired five questions at him in the space of a few seconds, she stopped talking. He stared at her like she was a gibbering idiot (which to be fair, at this second, she was) and walked in, taking a seat at the table. There was an ease to his movements that spoke of routine. Had he done this with Sarah?

'Coffee would be nice, thank you. Then we will get started.'

She began using a cafetiere she'd found in the back of a cupboard, and ground coffee from a pot on the counter. 'Help yourself to a croissant if you haven't eaten.'

'I have.'

All right then, she thought. Was this how the day was going to be? Her chatting away and him acting like the human version of a brick wall. Her hopes about the grand adventure she was embarking on began to fade.

'What is the first thing you need help with?'

Down to business straight away, but Lizzie refused to let her good cheer disappear.

'There are three main jobs that need doing first as far as I can see.' She counted them off on her fingers. 'Electrics, water and windows. There's the roof as well but I need a proper roofer for that. No offence.' She paused, worried that she had inadvertently insulted him again. He was so touchy it was difficult to tell what he'd take offence to and what he wouldn't.

'None taken.'

Phew. That was something at least.

'I'm going to need to get a few quotes and see who can give me the best price.'

'Yes, I cannot do the roof.' Luc relaxed back into his chair. 'I am afraid of heights.'

'You are?' Lizzie took the cafetiere to the table with two cups and the sugar. When she went for the milk, she checked over her shoulder to ensure he wasn't watching before sniffing it to make sure it was still fresh.

'That is why I run a vineyard rather than an orchard. The trees are too high in an orchard.'

Lizzie laughed. He'd cracked a joke! Who was this man sitting at her table and speaking to her like she was a human being?

'I'm afraid of heights too.' She returned to the table with the milk. 'And spiders and rats and snakes and fairground rides and . . . Actually I think that's about it.'

'Are you sure?' The corner of his mouth had lifted into a smile. It really did lighten his features when he allowed himself to cheer up.

'Oh, there is one more thing. You know when your foot gets stuck in mud, and you can't really pull it out? You have to kind of grab hold of your thigh and tug your own leg up? That terrifies me because I'm convinced I'm going to get sucked into the ground and die.'

'Wow. Does that happen to you often?'

'Not on a daily basis, no.'

She was just about to clarify that she wasn't insane when he laughed. As the kitchen grew silent, he peered at the mess around them. 'I'm sorry about Sarah. It must be hard being here with all her things.'

'I still need to sort through everything,' she admitted, picking up a random letter from the table and tossing it onto another pile of papers. 'These last few days have been so crazy I haven't even started yet. I'd forgotten how many strange things she'd gathered from her travels. Every room I go into has some random thing from somewhere exotic. I wish I'd got to know her more and talked to her about these things.' The thought had popped out of her subconscious unbidden, and it shook her. She sipped her coffee, aware Luc was still watching her. 'What job do you think we should tackle first?'

'We will measure the windows. The glass will have to be cut to size.'

'And you can do that?'

His brow furrowed. 'No. I will order it online, but when it comes, I can replace it.'

Online. Of course. Stupid. 'Okay. After that I need to get the electrics checked and the water sorted. Margot from the village said she thought there might be an airlock in the pipes.'

'Margot?' His voice had taken on a steely edge.

'Yes. I didn't get her last name, but she's very beautiful. Gorgeous long blonde hair. Do you know her?'

'Yes. We grew up together.'

'I met her in town yesterday and she mentioned it might be that. She said it can happen a lot with older houses.'

Luc stared into his coffee and took a sip. 'It can.'

Did he not like Margot? His reaction was hard to decipher as glum seemed to be his default setting. Lizzie carried on, deciding not to probe, hoping he might brighten again if they talked about the chateau.

'After that it's cosmetic things really. Re-plastering, painting, but like you said, I need to clear Sarah's things from each room before any of that can happen. Do you have a measuring tape?'

'A what?' Luc hadn't been listening to a word she'd said.

'A measuring tape. I'm afraid I don't know how to say that in French. Umm, *mesure*—'

'Don't worry. I know what a measuring tape is. Yes, I have one.' He pulled it out of his jeans pocket. As he'd moved to fish it out, his shirt, which had the top button undone, had opened slightly, revealing tanned skin just below his collar bone. A shot of desire ran through Lizzie and she cast her eyes back to the tabletop. Time to get started.

Lizzie took the pencil and notebook she'd found earlier from beside her. 'Shall we start outside?' Drawing her eyes from his chest where they'd treacherously wandered, she opened the kitchen door. With any luck, the breeze might cool her down.

It took far longer to measure the windows than she'd expected because so many more needed replacing than she'd first thought. When they'd finished, she and Luc ate a picnic lunch, similar to the one he'd served her, out on the rickety table in the kitchen garden. He leaned on his elbow while Lizzie sat opposite, unable to fully relax. Though he'd been kind and even cracked another couple of jokes as they were measuring the windows, she felt self-conscious around him and didn't know where to put her arms and legs. Every time she sat back how she normally would it felt unnatural, and she had to adjust her pose. The hard shell he'd wrapped himself in made it difficult to connect, even as neighbours.

'How long have you run the vineyard?' Lizzie asked, shuffling for the fourth time and re-crossing her legs.

'About six years.'

'Your friend the mechanic said you'd lived in Paris for a while. That must have been fun.'

'It was not.' He placed a tomato in his mouth and chewed, clearly not pleased his friend had mentioned it or that she had asked. 'I missed my home. The city was too busy and the relationship I was in, it didn't work out.' He sighed, but it seemed to contain a lot more emotion than most sighs did.

Lizzie wisely changed topic. 'This is a very beautiful place. I'd forgotten just how much. When I was younger and used to stay for the summers with Sarah I just wanted to be at home with my friends. It feels like such a waste of time now.'

'It is a quiet place for a teenager. Then and now,' he conceded. Had he felt that when he was younger? Perhaps it was something he'd missed when he moved to Paris and came to appreciate later, like she did now. Lizzie waited for him to say more, but he continued eating, tearing a piece from the baguette. After a moment, he said, 'You are very brave taking on the chateau. Sarah let a lot of things fall apart towards the end.'

'Was she sick?' His eyes widened that she didn't know. Lizzie toyed with the kitchen roll she'd been using as a napkin. 'We lost contact after the last time I visited. She kept in touch with my mother but didn't say anything about being unwell or the chateau going downhill.'

'She was old,' he said softly. 'And had become quite frail, but she was not unwell. I think she just didn't care about such minor things. When she knew she didn't have much time left she wanted to make the most of every minute. You know what she was like. It was how she lived her life. She visited friends and went out for lunch and dinner. She couldn't travel anymore, but she saw many people as often as she could. Her social calendar was always far busier than anyone else's. Even to the end.'

Tears stung Lizzie's eyes. She should have made more of an effort to get in touch, especially as so much time had passed. Her anger at their last meeting was now overshadowed by guilt. Sarah had been old, and Lizzie should have made more of an effort as the years had moved on, but her life had catapulted her from one event to another and she'd been caught up in it: moving to London, her romance with Will, getting into journalism. She'd confided everything in her mum on her return, and she'd understood why she didn't want to go back, but Lizzie hadn't wanted it to affect their relationship. Her mum hadn't approved of Sarah's actions, but she'd promised not to say anything unless Sarah did and as it turned out, Sarah hadn't mentioned a word. What had that meant? Anger? Guilt? Shame? She'd never know now.

Luc broke Lizzie from her thoughts of the past. 'I think she would have been happy with what you're doing to the chateau. Perhaps that is why she left it to you.'

Would he still think that if he knew the truth? Right now, it felt like a final punishment for not appreciating it all those years ago. 'Perhaps,' she replied with a faint smile.

'So, you're a journalist in England?'

'Yes. In London.'

'Ah. Another city.'

Why had he said it like that? So dismissively. 'Why don't you like cities? I love them. They all have a different feel. I mean, London's very different to Paris. That's what's wonderful about them.'

'One city is much like another,' he replied, standing up. 'Full of people who enjoy being busy. Scurrying around like ants.'

'I wouldn't quite say it's like that.'

Luc shook out the paper the baguette had been wrapped in, sending crumbs over the grass. Hungry birds flew down and began pecking at the ground and Lizzie watched them happily. If she'd done that in London a swarm of pigeons would have attacked her and had the remaining food out of her hand before she could hide it.

'Let us tackle the water,' Luc said with a slight nod. Whatever lightness had come to his face as they'd talked about Sarah had vanished, and they went back inside. Whatever he'd gone to Paris for and whatever he'd done there it clearly didn't bring back happy memories.

Chapter Ten

Sorting out the water system had been easy even though it had taken a length of hose (that Luc had begrudgingly gone back to his farmhouse to get), several taps, and some physics Lizzie simply didn't understand, but it had worked, and last night she'd sunk into the first hot bath since leaving England, scented with lavender bath oil from the gift shop. Her muscles had relaxed completely, and she'd climbed into bed, zombie-like, and slept soundly – her body and mind exhausted.

This morning, Luc was set to arrive a little earlier and Lizzie was up and dressed, ready to see him again. At times yesterday, there'd been glimpses of the Luc the village had talked about and she was keen to see more of him. With energy to spare and time to kill before he arrived, she'd been tidying, making more headway than she thought possible in such a short amount of time. There was now a neat pile of rubbish at the top of the stairs from three of the bedrooms she'd been in and cleared.

There still hadn't been any sign of Gary the goat and this afternoon, if time allowed, Lizzie was going to look for him. She almost laughed at the idea of searching for a goat like you would a missing dog or cat, but her life had become a sort of madcap comedy lately and there didn't seem much point in fighting against it.

Yesterday had also brought home the realisation that, at some point, she really did have to begin sorting through Sarah's possessions and for that she'd need boxes. Lots and lots of boxes. A trip to the gift shop was in order. Violette would have some, but for now, the first task of the day was the electrics.

The back door to the kitchen was open and heat seeped in from outside. Birdsong filled the air and before putting the pan of water on to boil, Lizzie stepped outside and took deep breaths. She'd never have done that in London. The air would have choked her, and she could see how Sarah had fallen in love with this place all those years ago. How could you not when nearly everyone in town was so relaxed and welcoming? Now she thought of it, she felt more at home here from the few short trips into town than she had in recent months living her life in London from her friend's spare room.

'*Bonjour*, Lizzie.' Luc appeared from around the side of the house, holding a paper bag. The smile was back, and Lizzie relaxed. 'I thought I should bring breakfast this time.'

'I should be supplying you with all the help you're giving me.' The heavenly smells of hazelnut and chocolate emanated from the bag. 'Still, I won't say no. What have you brought us?'

'Freshly baked pains au chocolat. They are sprinkled with hazelnuts which make them even more delicious. I always go to the bakery early. You get the freshest bread that way.'

'I'll have to remember that. Shall I make some coffee?' He nodded and they walked into the kitchen and sat at the table. Lizzie pushed some of the papers to one side, creating room for them both. 'Do you think we can look at the electrics today?'

'Of course.' Luc pulled out the two pains au chocolat and Lizzie handed him two plates. They were huge, the chocolate seeping out of the ends. It wasn't the healthiest of breakfasts, but it would give them the energy they needed to make headway with the house. Having got the glass measured for the windows and the water sorted yesterday they were already taking giant leaps forward. If the momentum continued, it really wouldn't take long to get the chateau up and running again. The only obstacle would be money, but she cast the thought aside as the cafetiere bubbled.

Luc wiped his mouth with his handkerchief as Lizzie filled two espresso cups. 'After, you will need to clear some rooms so we can see what more needs doing. I can teach you to plaster the walls and anyone can paint, but you cannot do any of that while the house is so . . .' He searched for a polite word.

'Messy?'

'Yes.'

'I was thinking about asking Violette from the gift shop for some boxes. She's bound to have some with all the stock she gets delivered.'

'Good idea.' He continued eating and Lizzie twisted her cup in the saucer, watching the black liquid swirl. 'There is a lot to do here, but I think it will be worth it. The house is beautiful. It has a lot of potential. I have always thought so.'

'Do you go into the village every day?'

'Most days, yes. I like to buy fresh food. Not things in cartons or cans.'

'Do you like to cook?'

'I used to.'

Her senses pricked up at this short but telling statement, but she couldn't pounce on him with her next question. If there was one thing she was learning about Luc it was that he had to do things at his own pace. There was no rushing or pressuring him. Like a snail, he'd curl tightly into his shell when he felt threatened. She smiled at the analogy.

'Why are you smiling?' he asked, a slight teasing note to his voice.

'No reason,' she replied, shaking the image from her brain and placing her cup back down. In the silence that followed, though she tried to stop it, her inquisitiveness got the better of her and she found herself saying, 'Sorry, but I have to ask. You don't like cooking now?'

'*Non*.'

'Why did you stop?'

'It does not matter.' Luc picked a piece from his pain au chocolat. His hands were large and rough from his job, but what would it feel like to slip her hand into his? Her fingers tingled at the idea. After a second he added, 'Cooking for one is a challenge.'

'I hate cooking for one, but it's much easier to eat here than it is in England. The rain and cold makes you want stodgy comfort food but that sort of thing takes ages to cook. Here it's just as nice to have some bread and cheese with a salad.'

'The best meals are simple, I find.'

'Me too.'

He met her eye, and his gaze stirred something in her chest. She wasn't sure why, or what had happened, and was unlikely to find out with how private he was, but there was a lightness to his features today.

'What is wrong with the electrics?'

'The first time I tried to put the electric kettle on there was a hum and a bang and then nothing worked.'

'Did you check the fuses?'

'Umm . . . no. I was a bit stressed out at the time and in my defence, I have no idea where they are.'

Thinking he was going to roll his eyes or march off annoyed, Lizzie prepared to defend herself, then Luc smiled. 'Come with me.'

He went to a door at the back of the kitchen that led down to the basement. Lizzie hadn't dared go down there alone in case something horrible lurked in the darkness. Luc used the torch on his phone, and she followed him down a wooden staircase into the depths of the house. In the small cellar was a fuse box attached to the wall. He studied it.

'The fuse has tripped, which I can fix for now, but from the troubles I remember Sarah having, the whole place will probably need re-wiring.'

'That sounds costly. Can you do it?'

'Me?' He seemed shocked at the idea. 'No. I can change fuses and plug sockets, re-wire a plug, fix a toaster, that sort of thing, but I cannot re-wire an entire house.'

'Oh. Violette was under the impression you'd re-wired the farmhouse.'

'The farmhouse is different. It's my house and if I do something wrong, it doesn't matter. I had a friend who helped me. He is an electrician. I can do lots of odd jobs, like I've done for Violette, but I am a vintner not an electrician. A whole house is beyond my skill.'

There was a hint of regret in his voice, but Lizzie left it; she didn't want him to think she wasn't happy for his help and if she was going to sell, she'd need a qualified electrician anyway. There would be certificates and things needed for the new homeowners. 'Do you think your friend could come give me a quote? I'm happy to contact him myself if you have a number.'

'I will write it down for you later.'

'Great.' She stepped away and went back upstairs. No one wanted someone watching over their shoulder while they worked. She had to admit to being a little disappointed. Not in Luc. He was right, he was a winemaker not a qualified electrician, but it meant spending more money. Hopefully the money Sarah had promised in her will would cover it. Mentally ringfencing it, Lizzie let the problem go.

Back in the kitchen, she started sorting through the rubbish scattered around while she waited for Luc to return. She found some bin bags under the sink and began clearing the papers from the table, stacking bills and anything personal in one pile and ditching everything else. Guilt once more overtook Lizzie as she remembered the meals she'd had there as a child. Each letter she picked up sent a wave of sadness over her and she was happy to stop and make another cup of coffee when Luc arrived back.

As she turned to the kettle, her bottom hit a stack of papers, sending them falling to the floor like confetti.

'Oh, for god's sake. Why is this place such a mess?'

It was an overreaction but the shame she'd been pushing down was bubbling to the surface. She bent down to pick them up, surprised to find Luc inches from her face as he helped to gather them. She could smell the peppery earthiness of his aftershave and see the soft curly hairs of his beard. How would they feel pressed against her skin? Heat rose up her back and when his fingertips brushed hers as they reached for the same piece of paper, her body answered his touch with a longing that took her by surprise. He gave a reassuring smile and, unnerved by her feelings, with the last sheet collected, Lizzie shot back to standing.

'I will help you sort through this,' Luc said gently, gesturing to the kitchen.

'No, you don't have to. If you want to get back to the vineyard I totally understand. You must be so busy with . . .' She couldn't think exactly what he might do on a day-to-day basis. 'Grapes and stuff.'

'Grapes and stuff?' His eyes shone with amusement.

'Yeah.'

'I will tell you one day what I do.'

'I'd like that.'

He watched her again, scanning her face. 'Sarah was my friend. I'm happy to help. What can I do?'

'I guess we just start in one corner and work our way around the room?'

They got started and a moment later he asked, 'Are you all right?'

This was the Luc the village spoke of and when she thought back to their first meeting, she saw the softness underneath his brisk demeanour. He'd fed her, made sure she was warm and dry and given her the plasters she needed. He'd organised someone to fix her car and was even helping her now. Lizzie glanced at him from the corner of her eye. Had he not felt the fire that seemed to ignite in her when they were near each other? It was probably all in her head, a silly crush. She felt too damaged for anyone to be interested in her. A part of her wanted to send him away if her body was going to react to him in this way, but she also wanted him to stay.

'I think so,' she replied. 'It's just strange to think Sarah's really gone. Being back here, I keep thinking she'll walk in the door and tell me to cheer up. That was one of her favourite things to say to me. I was a bit of a sullen teenager.'

Luc chuckled and it was the first time she'd heard anything near a laugh. 'She did have a habit of saying whatever was on her mind. She told me to smile many times when I came back from Paris.'

'Really?'

'Yes.' He ran a hand through his mop of curly hair, then down his beard. 'If you haven't noticed, I don't smile a lot.'

'Why is that?' she asked, knowing she was taking a big risk. Would he shut down again?

He shrugged. 'Life is complicated.'

Luc was a master at giving vague, closed answers but Lizzie let the matter drop. He wasn't wrong.

'I always thought it's only as complicated as we make it. I've always tried to keep my life simple but . . .' She contemplated the chateau kitchen. 'I suppose sometimes it gets complicated even when we don't want it to.'

They worked quietly together, clearing the table and tackling the rest of the kitchen. When it came to the shelf containing Sarah's souvenirs, Lizzie faltered. She reached a hand out to take down the wooden mask but couldn't quite bring herself to touch it. It felt like an invasion of Sarah's space, of admitting that she had lost the chance to find out about Sarah and her adventures, to see if they could have mended their fractured relationship now she was older and, she hoped, wiser.

As if sensing her unease, Luc reached over and took the mask down. 'Where was this from?'

'I don't know. I never asked her and if she said I don't remember. I wish she'd labelled them. Some of them look like they belong in a museum.'

'I don't think this does.' He placed the mask on the table and grabbed the mangy stuffed camel that had stood next to it.

'You're right. But he'll spruce up nicely after a wash. Now the water and electricity are working again I might pop him in the washing machine. Maybe there's someone in the village who'd like him.'

Her thoughts ran to Margot and her daughter Amélie. She'd been meaning to contact her, especially once she knew she'd been right about the water pipes. The first time they'd met, Lizzie had thought they could end up friends, but she'd been so busy she hadn't got around to asking her to meet yet. Lizzie made a note to find her and go out for coffee. Was Amélie too old for teddies? Lizzie hadn't been at that age, but life was different now with social media and all kinds of pressures that made children grow up far more quickly. Still, it was worth thinking about.

Without boxes to store anything in, Lizzie made neat piles on the long kitchen counter that ran along the back of the room. By the time they had finished, nearly all the mess had been cleared. She could see clearly the number of doors hanging off their hinges, the tiles that needed cleaning and the walls that needed painting but more than that, she could see the potential of the room.

'If you have a screwdriver,' Luc said, 'I will fix the doors.'

'Are you sure?' Lizzie checked her watch. It was well past lunch and edging towards dinner time. She hadn't realised how the time had flown, she was so comfortable in Luc's company as they'd discussed the objects Sarah had collected. They'd worked well together.

'I would not offer if I minded.'

'Well, thank you. I think there's one in that drawer, but I don't know if it's the right type.'

He crossed the kitchen, finding what he needed. 'This kitchen would look beautiful with the cupboard doors painted. Maybe cream or French blue. Perhaps a pale green as the tiles behind the stove are green.'

'I love that idea.' A pale green would really set the tiles off and with cream walls so it didn't clash, the kitchen would look beautiful. It looked like her colour scheme for this room was decided. 'Would you like a glass of wine?' Lizzie asked a little nervously. 'And I've got some bread and some of that lovely local cheese you introduced me to if you'd like to stay for dinner. The bread's from yesterday but it should still be okay.'

'What? Sacrilege! Eating yesterday's bread!' he joked. 'Actually, that would be nice. Thank you.'

As she prepared everything, he fixed the remaining doors. A few required her to help hold them in place while he adjusted the hinges. Another had to be taken off completely, but Lizzie preferred it that way with the shelves open. When he'd finished there was still a lot of work to do but the kitchen no longer looked like someone was squatting there.

With the table cleared, Lizzie spread out the food and placed the wine in the centre with two tall glasses.

'I think we deserve this,' she declared when he joined her at the table. 'We've made so much progress today. Cheers!'

She held her glass up for him to toast and he tapped his gently against hers.

'*Santé*.'

'*Santé*. That means health, doesn't it?'

'It does.' His dazzling smile returned. 'You are learning. Or remembering?'

'A bit of both, really. I never bothered learning before but must have picked up a few things without knowing it. I'd like to make up for it now.'

'Then I will try and teach you.'

'As long as you don't go too fast. I made the mistake of saying *bonjour* to Violette and she spoke so quickly I couldn't keep up.'

'Sometimes I cannot keep up with Violette.' He laughed and drank his wine. 'Why have you decided to stay in France? I thought you couldn't wait to get back to England.'

Should she tell him? It was a lot to admit to someone she didn't know but sometimes that could be easier. Maybe her honesty would encourage him to open up too.

'It's a bit of a sad story really. My fiancé left me at the altar about three months ago, so I've been staying at a friend's house. She needs to kick me out when her flatmate comes back from Australia, so when my editor said she was happy for me to stay and write about the transformation of the chateau, there didn't seem any point in going back. Especially as I've got no significant other to think about and I'll have to find somewhere else to live anyway.'

If he was surprised by her confession, he didn't seem it. His left eyebrow raised slightly when she admitted to being jilted but that was about it.

'I'm sorry. That must have been very hard for you.'

'It wasn't the most fun I've ever had.'

'Relationships can be . . . difficult,' he said quietly. 'Complicated.'

'Very. Just like life.'

He tapped his finger against the stem of his wine glass. 'You remind me of Sarah, you know.'

'I do?' She didn't think she could be anything less like her if she tried. She wasn't adventurous, and was only doing this because of circumstance, not her spontaneous spirit.

'Sarah used humour to deal with life's ups and downs too.'

'I suppose she did.'

Had she mistaken some of Sarah's comments in her stroppy teenage youth? Had her great-aunt simply had a sense of humour that was foreign to her? They had always been very different, but there had been times when they'd laughed together, like when Sarah had enjoyed Lizzie's tales of gossip from school. Lizzie worried her memories weren't as true as she'd always believed them to be and the thought sent an icy blast down her spine. Sarah had always grabbed at life, taking every opportunity and throttling the last drop of life from it. She'd wanted Lizzie to be the same, but back then, as an awkward, shy teenager, she hadn't been built like that. She wasn't sure she was now, even though for all intents and purposes she'd moved to France.

'Have you thought about colours for the chateau?' Luc asked. 'Some of the rooms are a little . . . can I say dated? I can show you some samples that would suit such a historic building.'

'How do you know about paint colours? I thought you were a . . . a vintner, was it?'

His eyes held a mischievous glint. 'I enjoy work like this. There is something wonderfully simple about painting, sanding, decorating, and they are skills that bring something to life. Of course, I cannot have you painting this beautiful house in bright greens or luminous yellows. Something garish you would find in a city hotel.'

'I wouldn't dream of it. Totally a pastel kind of girl. All about the heritage.'

'I am glad.'

Quiet settled on them but it wasn't uncomfortable. Lizzie's shoulders relaxed and she was sure Luc too felt more at ease.

Their conversation continued and they discussed the house until the wine was gone. Laughter rang through the kitchen as Lizzie teased him with outlandish decorating ideas she had no intention of carrying out, and Luc pretended to believe and then admonish her. It had been a pleasant evening but as she bid him goodnight the comments about Sarah disturbed her.

Would looking back over the past reveal she was as much to blame as Sarah for their difficult relationship?

Chapter Eleven

By the time Sunday rolled around, progress on the chateau had slowed. Lizzie kept her efforts to tidying small areas and in some of the rooms clear surfaces could finally be seen. She'd condensed the stuff in many of the bedrooms so now only a few were packed with Sarah's possessions and bags of rubbish. The others were clear. Or clearer. But still, in many of the rooms there was more work to be done, both decorative and structural. The re-wiring was still on the list, but the electrician Luc knew was so busy he hadn't been able to come and give a quote. Lizzie was reluctant to go with someone who hadn't been personally recommended so decided to wait, even though the fuse had tripped a few more times since Luc had fixed it.

She stared at the empty fridge then gazed over her shoulder at the just as empty cupboards. Time to re-stock. She and Luc had agreed to a day off today, leaving her free to write her column and wander into the village, while he went back to his vineyard for the magic of winemaking. She hadn't realised quite how low stocks were until, with an empty belly, she had made her supper last night. The slightly wilted salad and stale bread hadn't been anywhere near as appetising as the fresh food she'd grown used to.

A gentle bleat from behind made her jump.

'Gary! Where've you been?'

It was a stupid thing to admit but she'd been worried about him. Every day she'd expected him to pop by to nibble on the sofa or wander around the house like a nosy guest, but he hadn't arrived, and her thoughts had jumped to horrible conclusions: he'd been hit by a car or fallen down a ditch and was crying for help with no one to rescue him.

Without thinking, she went to his side and stroked him. He bleated again and began chewing something. 'Ow!' She pulled away. 'Stop eating my hair.' She tugged the clump from his mouth and moved back. He stepped forward, leaning against her legs and she caressed his silly floppy ears.

'Have you had breakfast? I take it not, as you were trying to eat my split ends.' He went to take a bite out of the chair leg. 'No! Don't eat that. Here, you can have the last of my baguette. It's stale anyway.' She never ate the rounded ends, preferring the centre sections where the outside was perfectly crisp but the inside was fluffy and chewy. He took it gently from her and trotted back out the door. One day she really would have to follow him and find out where he came from. Surely he didn't just roam free all the time.

After days of wearing her dungarees, it had been a pleasure to slip into a black and white polka-dot summer dress. It was one of her favourites, but not one she got to wear much in England. Scraping her hair back into a messy bun and adding her sunglasses, she grabbed the wicker basket and headed out the door.

The sun was still warm and golden, but it was cooler today with a stronger breeze that spread through the skirt of her dress. The last few days had been so hot she'd been dripping in sweat after performing even the easiest of tasks. The heat had zapped her energy and each evening when she'd sat down to write her article her eyes had grown heavy, and the words vanished from her brain. Today she was ready to sit in the fresh, clean air of the garden and write.

The route to the village had become familiar to her now with its dusty tracks and trodden pathways, and brought with it memories of Sarah. She'd been right before, she had walked this route with her, but when Lizzie thought back to it, she could only imagine trudging along behind as Sarah marched ahead. She'd paced liked a sergeant major, swinging her arms, her back straight, some enormous and brightly coloured kaftan wafting around her. In comparison, Lizzie's head had been down, staring at the ground, her hands in her pockets. No wonder Sarah had given up trying to chivvy her along. She'd spent far too long being miserable about being away from her friends. If only things had been different. Their final angry, resentful goodbye haunted Lizzie's thoughts. Suppressing the memories, she shook the misery away and focussed on the walk she had once found dull.

The lavender plants swaying in the breeze scented the air and Lizzie stopped to pick a few stems, holding them to her nose and taking in the dense floral scent. White clouds settled in the vast expanse of blue sky and far in the distance, the dark grey earth of the mountains covered in dense green shrubs towered upwards. The pace of life was so different in this place. Here they savoured every moment of every day. Lizzie liked that thought. It would be a good topic for her article.

Before long she was at the town, winding her way between the medieval houses and the uneven cobbled streets. She ran her fingers over the bumpy stone walls, which felt solid and sturdy under her fingers. The Sunday market was alive and buzzing as it had been the day after she'd arrived. She stopped to take even more photos, walking through the colourful vegetable stalls slowly, exploring all the things she hadn't had the chance to before. She'd been in such a rush that day, but today she had all the time in the world to shop.

After purchasing what she now termed 'the essentials', which included charcuterie, fresh fruit and vegetables, cheese and bread, she also treated herself to some olives and some apricot conserve sold by a smiling Frenchman with cloudlike white hair and a matching fluffy beard. Her basket weighed a ton but there were no shopping trolleys to load things in, no cans or garish wrappings. It was all so much more personal.

The handle bit into her fingers and she placed the basket on the ground. She had stopped next to a stall selling handmade sun hats. Choosing a tan-coloured floppy one with a wide brim, she placed it on her head to check the size.

'*Vous êtes belle, mademoiselle*,' called the owner.

Lizzie's French wasn't perfect, but it was getting better, and she was a little more confident in deciphering what he'd said. He'd said she looked beautiful, or something along those lines. 'I bet you say that to everyone,' she replied in English.

'*Non! Non!*' He placed his hand over his heart. 'I only say when it is true.'

She tossed her head back and laughed. 'Then I suppose I'd better buy it.'

'Don't believe him,' called the seller from the stall next door. 'He does say it to all the girls, but he is correct. It suits you.'

French men, it seemed, were very good for your self-esteem. She shouldn't be buying fripperies with everything else she needed to pay for, but really, in the Provençal heat a good hat was a necessity. She didn't want a sunburnt face and many times this week she would have liked something to shield her eyes and protect her nose. Lizzie handed over the money and placed the hat on her head. The cheeky owner blew her a kiss and before she picked up her basket and walked on, she gave him a wave.

The market was so crowded Lizzie was thankful to come to the end of the stalls and break free, but a familiar voice forced her to peer around. It was Luc, selling his wine, and the queue stood three people deep. The locals clearly liked it and as he laughed and joked with them, his beautiful accent knotted her stomach.

Over the last few days, he had relaxed in her company and hadn't gone back to the vineyard until late into the afternoon. She felt slightly guilty that he was working today while she was relaxing, but she reminded herself she'd be working later too when she typed up her article – albeit sat in the sun with a glass of wine.

Lizzie joined the back of the queue, holding her basket in front of her with both hands. When Luc spotted her, he did a double take. His eyes darted over her as if ensuring it was actually Lizzie, the crazy English lady, and when they settled on her face, something about his scrutiny set her on fire. Was there more than just recognising her? Did he like what he saw? Her heart gave a double beat at the idea, and she gave a shy wave, edging forwards.

'*Bonjour*, Luc. I thought you were having a day off today?'

'Market day is a good time to sell wine, remember? I nearly always sell out before lunchtime.'

'Then I better buy a couple of bottles before you do.' She cast her eye over the different labels. 'What would you recommend?'

Luc picked up a bottle and began explaining about the flavour and the grapes he used. She could have listened to him all day and would have bought a bottle of each type had she been able to carry them home. He was knowledgeable, but his eyes lacked the passion they'd had when talking about refurbishing the chateau.

'You must have a day off tomorrow and not come to the chateau,' she said, even though she'd be sad to miss him. 'You know, as you've had to work today.'

Luc shook his head, but before he could answer, they were interrupted by Sylvie.

'Élisabeth, I have been hoping to see you.'

Lizzie tore her eyes away from Luc. 'Hello, Sylvie. You look very well.'

'I have just eaten the most delicious fruit tart and it has energised me. I wanted to say how happy I am you are staying at the chateau. Sarah would have been so happy.'

Lizzie gave an awkward smile. The less she thought about Sarah the better at the moment. Every time she did, it stirred memories she wasn't entirely happy to recall, this time because of her own behaviour.

'Oh, I must rest my back,' Sylvie said, placing her numerous bags on the ground. She straightened up as much as she could but was still very hunched. A grimace passed over her face.

'Do you need some help, Sylvie? Would you like me to carry your bags for you?'

'Oh no. Henri will be here soon, and we don't live far. Now, did Sarah ever take you to the chocolatier on the edge of the town?'

'I think she must have done when I was younger, but I don't remember it.'

'She used to visit it almost every day.'

'Did she?'

'Of course. She'd buy a dozen dark chocolate truffles.'

'Every day?' Lizzie laughed. It was another thing Lizzie had forgotten.

'That is how she lived to such a good age. I do miss her, you know. We used to have lunch together at least once a week and she would reminisce about her travels and the great loves of her life.'

Lizzie's conscience rose, pressing on her heart. 'I wish I'd talked to her about them more. There's so much I didn't know.'

Sylvie brightened. 'Then you must come and see me, and I will tell you everything she told me.'

'That would be lovely, Sylvie.'

The old woman crinkled her nose in a warm, maternal way. 'Ah, Henri is here.'

But Henri was struggling under the weight of his own bags and there was no way Lizzie could watch them battle to their house. She turned to Luc.

'Luc, could I leave my basket behind your stall while I help Sylvie and Henri back to their house?'

'No!' shouted Sylvie, waving her arms around. 'No, no. You are busy.'

'I'm not too busy to help you. And I'm having a day off today anyway. Please, I'd like to help.'

Henri was puffing by the time he came to stand next to his wife. 'Let her help if she wants to. We are old, Sylvie. Though you do not want to admit it.'

Luc grinned and held out his hand to take Lizzie's basket. Again, his finger brushed hers as she handed it over, and a tingle shot through her arm. Once he'd taken it, she picked up Sylvie's bags and took the heaviest from Henri before walking with them to their house. It was only a couple of streets back from the market but even she found it hard in the heat and on the uneven cobbles. She made a mental note of the location for when she came to talk about Sarah, a conversation she was really looking forward to. They kissed her cheeks after she'd been forced to drop the bags on the step rather than in the kitchen to help them unpack. Sylvie claimed she hadn't tidied that day and the house was a mess. If the neat hallway was anything to go by Sylvie had better not come to the chateau. She'd have a heart attack.

When Lizzie returned to Luc, his stall was almost empty, and he was unloading the last few bottles from a heavy wooden crate.

'You're right, you won't be here long,' Lizzie said. 'I hope this means you can relax this afternoon.'

'I plan to read a good book in the sunshine.'

'Sounds perfect. I've got about three different books on the go at the moment.'

'How can you read three books at once?'

'It depends what mood I'm in. Don't tell me you only read one at a time.'

He nodded. 'Cover to cover.'

'That's crazy,' she replied, shaking her head.

The noise of the market disappeared. She hoped he was considering asking her to join him, she'd have accepted in an instant, but another customer came forward and the bubble around them burst, leaving Lizzie to take her basket and wave Luc goodbye, her heart ridiculously heavy. She had to stop imagining these moments between them. He'd probably wondered why she was still standing there, blocking his customers. There was no way Luc would be interested in her with all her baggage and craziness.

It seemed market day was the day to see everyone in

the town as she had barely gone ten yards before she ran into Margot and Amélie.

Margot, looking as chic as ever in navy wide-leg trousers, sandals and a loose T-shirt that draped attractively over her petite frame, waved enthusiastically. 'Lizzie! It is lovely to see you. I heard you had decided to stay. Amélie, do you remember Lizzie?'

Amélie lifted her head from her phone screen and nodded. Lizzie was sure she hadn't meant to sneer.

'Hello! Though I should really say *bonjour*, shouldn't I? It's lovely to see you again. How are you both?'

'Fine, fine,' Margot replied. 'You must come for lunch with us.'

Though Amélie's head had gone back to the screen it shot up at this request.

'That's so kind of you, but I should let you get on. You must be busy.'

Margot stepped closer to Lizzie, threading her arm through hers. 'I am not busy at all, and Amélie will be glad to not have me talking at her for a while. Not that she listens anyway. Come, we will have lunch at Café de France. It is not the most imaginative name, but it is exquisite. Come!'

Lizzie allowed herself to be enveloped by Margot as she led her out of the square and through small alleyways until they came to a tiny restaurant. Two small tables sat outside on the pavement, and a large red awning shaded them from the sun.

'Shall we sit outside?'

'Sure.'

Margot made herself comfortable on a chair and Amélie slid into the one next to her. 'This is my favourite café in the whole town. They serve the best *fleurs de courgettes farcies*. Have you had it yet? It is delicious. The best thing about Provence. Courgette flowers stuffed with goat's cheese. It makes my mouth water just thinking about it. And you can only get them at this time of year because they only use fresh ingredients.'

'They sound delicious. I'll try that.' The waiter came out dressed in a T-shirt and jeans but with a white apron tied around his waist. There must be something in the water in Provence as this was another handsome man, but Lizzie had to admit he had nothing on Luc.

'*Bonjour*, Hugo. This is my friend Lizzie. She has come to take over Sarah's chateau. Have you met yet?'

'No, I haven't had the pleasure. Welcome.' His surfer-blonde hair flopped into his eyes and he pushed it back.

'Thank you,' Lizzie replied awkwardly.

'Lizzie and I will have the *fleurs de courgettes farcies* and you already know my favourite wine. Amélie, what will you have?'

'Just a *pan bagnat*, please. And a Coke.'

The waiter left and seeing the chequered tablecloth and the single blooming stem in the vase, Lizzie took a photo. Amélie gazed at her in confusion. 'I'm a journalist,' Lizzie clarified. 'I'm just taking some photos for my articles. There's a lot of inspiration here.'

'You should see some of Amélie's photos,' Margot said. 'She is always taking them, and she is very good.'

'That's amazing, Amélie. This place must be quite

different from Paris,' Lizzie said, remembering Margot had mentioned before that she lived there, and they only came here for the summers. 'I've only been once, but I remember it being a beautiful city. Do you have any photos of it?'

Amélie nodded but when she didn't speak Margot stepped in. 'It is the best city in the world.'

'A bit busier than here, I imagine.'

'It is. The pace of life is so much slower here and you either love it or hate it. I hate it.' Amélie shot her mother a glance and a tension grew between them. Lizzie couldn't quite put a finger on what it was, and as being a teenager had been so prevalent in her mind lately, she smiled sympathetically at Amélie. Margot carried on. 'So I moved to Paris.'

'What do you do there?'

'I work in events.'

'That sounds fun.'

'It is, but it can be difficult with having Amélie to look after too. I have had to be very clear about what I will and won't do. She always comes first.' Margot rubbed her daughter's back, but Amélie kept her eyes down.

There was definitely an atmosphere, as if Margot's honesty was making Amélie uncomfortable, but she couldn't imagine Margot was any other way. There was an openness about her, and the lack of pretence was refreshing.

'I'd love to see your photos, Amélie, if you'd ever like to show me them. I'm looking for ones of the scenery around here and I'm documenting the changes to the chateau as I do it up.'

'That is so kind of you, isn't it, Amélie?'

Amélie nodded and her face lit up, but not at Lizzie's offer. 'There is Raphaël, *Maman*. May I go and say hello?'

'Of course, *chérie*.' Amélie ran over and began chatting to the young man. Margot turned back to Lizzie. 'I love that you are tackling the chateau by yourself.'

'Not entirely by myself,' Lizzie admitted. 'Luc has been helping me.

'Luc? Oh, I see.'

'He's very helpful, but . . .'

'But what?'

Lizzie blushed. 'Is he always so grumpy?'

Margot laughed. 'He can be sometimes, but he is not always so serious. We . . .' She hesitated and studied Lizzie as if deciding something. Lizzie wondered if she was uncertain of talking about Luc or was simply searching for the right word in English. As the pause grew, Lizzie prompted her.

'You?'

'We grew up together. But he can be fun sometimes.' A slight closedness passed over Margot's face but before Lizzie could wonder on it, it was gone. The waiter brought the wine in a small metal ice bucket and placed two glasses on the table. As they waited for the Coke to be delivered to Amélie, Margot poured them both a glass of wine. 'I'm sure he will be very helpful. He is a genius at fixing things.'

'That's what most of the village said when I asked.'

'Luc is very popular here. Have you tried his wine?'

'I have two bottles to try later.'

A burst of laughter escaped from Margot's mouth. 'We

are definitely going to be friends if you have two bottles of wine to drink this afternoon.'

When the waiter brought the food, Margot called Amélie over from her friend and Lizzie asked if she could snap some photos of Amélie's *pan bagnat*. All the food looked delicious. The delicate courgette flowers stuffed with goat's cheese were nestled on a green salad with purple edible flowers decorating the edge of the plate. This was something Lizzie would have expected in a top restaurant, not a small café on a side street in France.

Amélie's *pan bagnat*, which it turned out was a crusty roll stuffed full of all the ingredients that make a salad niçoise (bar the potatoes), looked incredibly appetising. The tuna was fresh and flaky, and in between the green of salad leaves and juicy sliced tomatoes were studs of black olive and the bright yellow yolk of an egg.

Lizzie picked up her knife and fork and tried the *fleurs de courgettes farcies*. It was divine. One of the most delicate yet perfectly balanced dishes she'd ever eaten in her life. The tang of the goat's cheese countered the floral courgette flowers and everything about it screamed summer. She could eat this every day for the rest of her life and never get bored. She was going to have to pitch a special feature on Provençal food, but she might have to wait a bit first. She didn't want to push her luck with Hilary.

'Now, tell me more about your life in England,' said Margot after she'd eaten some of her meal. 'Who have you left behind?'

Lizzie outlined everything that had happened recently. It was wonderful to be so open and honest about her past and the more she talked about it, the less pain it caused. Back home in England she'd told herself the wounds had healed, but they'd been open more than she realised. Having the space to really deal with them, the adventure of staying in France was helping her move on in a way she never would have at home.

Margot was a brilliant listener. She asked a few questions, made supportive noises in all the right places and called Will something in French that Lizzie couldn't understand but Amélie's reaction made her assume it was a rather strong swearword. Margot revealed little about herself, but Lizzie had done all the talking. She'd have to ask more questions the next time they met.

With lunch finished, and her article still to write, they paid the bill and made their goodbyes.

'You should swing by the chateau for lunch one day,' Lizzie said, lifting her basket. 'I have enough supplies to feed an army.'

'I'd like that very much.'

Margot kissed her on each cheek and Lizzie strolled back through the beautiful French town, snapping pictures of the gorgeous houses, eager to get to work on her article. Today she was bursting with love for life in France, even if it did mean living in a decrepit chateau, and she couldn't wait to convey that to her readers. She even had some ideas for freelance articles, which wasn't something she had ever considered before but might come in handy for extra money. Her brain was alive with creativity. That had to be a sign things were looking up.

Chapter Twelve

'Are you ready?' asked Luc.

Lizzie nodded. She wasn't sure that she was, but she couldn't turn back now. She opened the door to the living room and the two of them marched through. They'd been concentrating on this room for the last few days and boxes lined the far end. Most of them contained old paperwork of Sarah's Lizzie probably wouldn't need, but the others held more trophies from her adventures. They'd come across a strange kind of eggshell about the size of Lizzie's head, a beautiful blue geode, and numerous other tiny knickknacks. Lizzie had wrapped each one in newspaper and laid it carefully in the box. Luc had asked questions about them, but she was unable to answer, and it made her all the more determined to visit Sylvie and find out what she knew of Sarah's adventures.

The furniture, including the half-eaten sofa, had been covered with old sheets, and the wallpaper, which had been peeling from the walls, had been stripped, revealing crumbling plaster and numerous holes. Lizzie had told Luc she wanted to learn how to plaster herself, but now that she was faced with a bucket of pale pink goo and the large paddle he was holding out to her, she wondered if she was just a little bit out of her depth.

'Don't look so nervous,' he teased. 'It won't kill you.'

The large stone fireplace stood between them, and they each faced a section of wall.

'No, but it's a skill, isn't it? That's why people pay for it. I just think it's not going to be as easy as it looks.'

'You'll be fine. Here.' Using a trowel, he scooped out some plaster from the bucket and added a dollop to both his and her boards. 'Begin with the trowel,' he said, moving to the wall and adding a large splodge that he then effortlessly smoothed out.

On her side of the fireplace, Lizzie attempted to copy. The plaster fell from the side of the trowel onto the floor before she had the chance to do anything with it and she stared at it, hearing Luc chuckle. 'It's not funny. My trainers are ruined.'

'They were ruined before from you stomping through my vineyard in the middle of a thunderstorm.' He chuckled. 'You looked like a drowned cat.'

It was the first time he'd mentioned their first meeting and she'd been wondering what he'd made of her. 'Charming,' she replied with mock offence before bending down and trying to scrape the mess off the floor tiles. 'I thought you Frenchmen were supposed to be the kings of charm and romance and . . . that sort of thing.' She wasn't normally prim, but with how attractive he was looking today – a T-shirt stretched over his chest and a checked shirt tied around his waist – she didn't know what would happen if she said the word sexy out loud. No doubt her face was already pink.

'We are.'

'By saying I looked like a drowned cat?'

'You did.' He smiled and she turned back to the wall, warming inside.

'Then I have no idea how you have that reputation.'

'We are taught to be more aware of women's emotions.'

'Really? And how is describing me as a drowned cat supposed to make me feel?

'It is factually correct.'

'Hmm.' She went back to racing the wet plaster onto the wall before it fell off again. 'And what can you tell about my emotions right now if you're so aware of how we're feeling?'

He glanced over at her, his dark hair curling in front of his face. Lizzie wished she hadn't asked. She'd be mortified if he could actually tell. Her thoughts and emotions were distinctly X-rated right now. She pictured Mother Teresa instead.

'You are annoyed that you cannot master this first time. I think you have always understood things quickly and you don't like to look stupid in front of other people. Not that you do look stupid,' he added quickly.

Wow. Was that true? It was when it came to work, certainly, and now she came to think about it, it had been the thing she'd found hardest about her breakup with Will. The whole thing had been a painful mess, but it had been the idea that people thought she was somehow bad at relationships and had caused it to happen that hurt most.

'But you must not be upset. Plastering is a skill that can take lots of practice.'

'You must have thought I was crazy turning up in your vineyard like that,' she said, trying to change the subject.

'It was an unusual way to meet,' he admitted. Again, there was that glint of mischief that brightened his eyes. 'I don't get many women crawling through the undergrowth. If a woman wants to speak to me, she normally just knocks on the door.'

'Haha. And I would have knocked on the door once I'd found it. It's just you came out and shouted at me first.'

'I didn't shout at you.'

'Maybe not, but you weren't exactly pleased.'

'I had to go out into the storm and get wet, of course I wasn't pleased. Plus, I didn't know who you were then.'

Would he mind if it happened now? What had he meant by that?

'Try again,' Luc said gently, nodding at the bucket of plaster.

She did, and though she got it onto the wall, it wasn't long before the dollop hit the floor. Lizzie groaned. 'What am I doing wrong?'

'It is the angle of your wrist. Here.'

He came over and stood behind her, taking her wrist and adeptly tilting it. She didn't resist and though his body wasn't exactly pressing against hers, she could feel the sturdiness of him behind her, the strength of his hand and the smell of his aftershave. Unable to stop herself, she turned her head slightly towards his. His soft, full lips were tantalisingly close to hers. He could feel it too, she was sure. There was a pull between them. Something undefined but present in the air. He dipped his head. Was he going to kiss her? Did he want this as much as she did? But then he turned away. The plaster stayed on the wall, but Lizzie was too wrapped up in his proximity and too confused at his reaction to notice.

Luc let go of her wrist and stepped away. 'There, you did it. Now all you need to do is gently spread it out.'

Heat rose up her back and she was sure it had set her face alight.

'You need to use the scraper and go over it like this.' He moved it at different angles, smoothing out the surface as if nothing had happened. With no other option, Lizzie did the same, following his instructions. 'Don't be so heavy-handed.'

'I'm not heavy-handed,' she replied defensively. She felt exposed by the moment that had passed between them. Vulnerable, and it had to be said, rejected. Will's departure had signalled the arrival of insecurities she found hard to deal with. Could a man like Luc be attracted to her? Not how she was dressed at the moment, she was sure. She was reading too much into everything.

'You are smashing at the wall like a killer in a bad horror movie.'

Taken from her thoughts, she couldn't help but laugh at his analogy. 'I am not!'

'Look, like this.' He moved back to his side of the wall and showed her again. It looked far nicer than hers. 'You see. Gentle. Soft. Not like a psycho.'

Part of her knew he'd meant it as a joke, but the word caused a wave of emotion to hit her. Will, who at one time would never have called her such a thing, had used the same word on a few of her drunk-dialling episodes and though it had been a bit true then, for some reason she didn't like the reminder of it now. Pain and embarrassment shot up at the memory and formed a shield around her. Perhaps knowing Will had moved on with someone else had caused it. She wasn't being hypocritical. It was clear that she was developing feelings for Luc, even if he was one of the grumpiest men on the planet. But it was more that in the time she had healed enough to have a fluttery tummy near a handsome Frenchman, he'd met someone, been on multiple dates, changed his status to 'In a relationship', and plastered it all over Instagram.

'Can you not call me that, please?' Lizzie's tone was harder than she'd intended, and Luc's face became stern.

'Of course, but it was only a joke.'

'I know, it's just . . . I—' How did she explain without admitting to some of the more humiliating moments of her breakup? 'I just don't find it that funny.' There, that should do.

But any hint of fun and flirting had vanished. Luc retreated into himself again and they worked on in a cold, stony silence. She just couldn't be that honest with him yet.

An hour later, her side of the wall was still nothing like his and humiliation prickled her skin. She glanced at her reflection in the large mirror leaning against the wall, taken down before they began work and sure enough, her face was a violent shade of red, as if she'd just dragged her carcass over the finish line of one of those sporting events where you cycle, run and swim. Torture. Unsurprisingly, seeing her reflection only added to her embarrassment.

'Why does mine look so different to yours? I did exactly what you told me.'

'You did not,' he said calmly, stopping work. 'You used too much plaster and you did not smooth it out enough.'

From the lumps and bobbles of the uneven surface he was right, even though she'd regularly stood back and checked it.

'If you saw I was doing it wrong, why didn't you say anything?'

He shrugged. 'You were annoyed already.'

That was no reason to let her continue doing it wrong. 'I was a bit miffed you called me a psycho but you're the one who stopped talking.'

'I was not. You did.'

They sounded like bickering children and her frustration grew. 'If you saw me doing it wrong, you should have said. I've wasted all this time and now I have to do it all again. I can't believe you didn't say anything. Or you could have helped me.'

'I didn't think you would want me to.' His voice was low and edgy. 'And you wouldn't have listened. You would have bitten my head off. You city girls are all the same.'

Lizzie felt her anger rise. Who was he to judge her so harshly? She might have judged him as being rude and grumpy when they first met but she hadn't let that be her only opinion of him. Regardless of his comment earlier he clearly didn't know her at all. 'City girl? What's that supposed to mean? There's nothing wrong with living and working in a city.'

'Isn't there? Besides, you know what I mean.'

'No, I don't.' Her voice had risen, and she made an effort to bring it down. 'What does coming from a city have to do with anything?'

He turned to face her, and his eyes blazed as he waved his hand around as he spoke. 'It is not coming from a city that is the problem. It is the attitude that you city girls have that out here in the countryside, we have no idea about how life works. That we are all stupid and you can do things so much better than we can—'

'I've never said anything like that!' Lizzie exclaimed.

'You think that being busy all the time is something to aim for. A badge of honour of how successful you are. You think that relaxing and enjoying life and not wanting to change the world is a terrible thing. Boring.'

'I have no idea what you're talking about.' Lizzie put her tools down, though Luc was still holding his. 'I'm just upset you didn't tell me I was doing the plastering wrong.'

'You would never have listened because you think you know best.'

'Oh, do I?' That was enough. She wasn't putting up with this. 'Well, if I know best about everything then I don't need you, do I? So maybe you should go.'

'Gladly.'

He threw his trowel into the tub of plaster and stalked out of the room. A second later she watched him pass the window, head down, hands in his pockets.

What the hell had just happened?

Chapter Thirteen

Lizzie threw her trowel down and went to the kitchen to wash her hands.

How dare he? Who was he to make judgements about her? Especially when she'd never (as far as she was concerned) acted like an all-knowing city girl. She'd been a bit annoyed that he hadn't told her she was doing it wrong, but what was all that other stuff about? Was that what he really thought of her? No wonder he hadn't seemed to reciprocate her feelings. But if he didn't, then why had he nearly kissed her? She hadn't imagined that. Had she?

Men were utterly confusing. Laws unto themselves. She had no idea what went through their heads. She angrily washed her hands, rubbing and scrubbing the dried plaster off her fingers. She leaned her wet hands on the edge of the sink and took a breath. Her heart rate was slowly returning to normal, but her chest pulsed with her uneven breaths. As much as she wanted to finish the job, she needed to do something else – anything else – to take her mind off her and Luc's heated exchange.

Lizzie paced aimlessly around the house, pausing at Sarah's study. She glanced at the door, dust-coated and bleak, then moved on. There was no way going in there was going to calm her down. If anything, reliving some of the awful memories would do the opposite. She moved to a room of the house she'd hadn't paid much attention to since returning: the dining room. Swinging the door open, the musty, dust-ridden air hit her and she traipsed over to the windows, casting them wide open. When her phone began to ring, she jumped in surprise. Why did she have signal in here when everywhere else was so patchy? She checked the screen, hoping it was Luc apologising. Disappointed to see it wasn't, she accepted the call.

'Hilary, hi, how are you?'

'Good. Really good. Is now a good time to talk?'

'As good as any. I was just plastering the living room.'

'Wow, that's amazing. Are you enjoying getting your hands dirty?'

Lizzie thought back to being pressed against Luc. At that point she had, but after his bad temper, not quite so much. 'It's very hard, as it turns out, and I'm terrible at it,' she answered, keeping her voice light. 'So what's happening your end?'

'I just wanted to ring to say how much I loved your first article. Honestly, I was crying with laughter.' Lizzie glowed with pride at the compliment and reminded herself that when she went home, she'd be in a really good position to secure a promotion. 'Did all of that really happen to you on your first day there?'

'It really did.'

'Incredible.' Hilary chuckled. 'And Gary the goat?'

'I haven't seen him today but yep, he's real and loves chewing my furniture.'

'Comedy gold. What sort of things will you include in your second piece? I loved the first, but we need to keep up the momentum for the readers.'

Lizzie sat down on one of the formal dining chairs surrounding the huge length of table. More of Sarah's treasures lined the walls, stored under a layer of dirt in heavy wood and glass cabinets. Fossils, a tiny gold teapot and a strange musical instrument like nothing Lizzie had ever seen before were huddled together in the one closest to her.

In here, the cornicing around the edges and circling the main light were all intact. The room was so grand, yet this had always been a room Sarah hadn't really bothered with. It was only used for parties and large gatherings, most of which had been held at Christmas when Lizzie wasn't there. In the summer, everyone congregated outside. A memory of the two of them enjoying late-evening picnics formed in her mind. Sarah lying on her back, staring at the dusky pink sky as they ate fresh apricots and juicy peaches. Lizzie had been so young then. Still so in love with the magical chateau and yet, she suddenly remembered nights when she was older, when she'd been allowed to stay up till whatever she time she wanted, lying on the grass on a sultry summer's evening because it was too hot to try and sleep. Her fear of missing out hadn't bothered her then. She shook the unsettled feeling away.

'I was thinking I'd detail my plastering disasters of today in the next one.'

'There is a reason people pay for someone else to do it.'

'That's exactly what I said to Luc.'

'Luc?' Her voice had gone up an octave. 'And who's Luc? Have you told me about him before? Is he handsome?'

'Hilary!' *He's handsome and sexy and . . . infuriating*, she thought. 'He's my neighbour. I think I mentioned him before. He owns the vineyard. He's been helping me with some of the work. According to the town he's a dab hand at all things DIY.'

'That still doesn't answer my question as to whether he's handsome or not.'

'He is,' she admitted, feeling a warmth inside. 'But I am not in the slightest bit interested. I'm still not ready.' For such a short statement it carried so much truth and so much confusion.

'Is he going to feature?' Hilary asked, her tone losing the teasing edge.

'I doubt it. Maybe only as a nameless accomplice. I don't think he'd like to be included by name.'

'Fair enough, but that might be another good hook for the readers. It sounds like you've got a lot to talk about, which is great. Send me the second one soon, won't you? I don't know about our readers, but I'm absolutely hooked. I'm sure they will be too. And that's why I called – I'm happy to say that the money we promised should be in your bank by the end of this week. Like I said, it's not a lot but hopefully five thousand pounds will help with something.'

'Hilary, that's amazing!' Lizzie replied with a smile. 'Thank you so much! It'll definitely help.'

'I'm glad to hear it. You know I had some concerns at the beginning, but I'm glad to see it going down so well.'

'I can't tell you how grateful I am, Hilary. And I promise I won't forget my deadlines in all the excitement of scrubbing plaster off the floor.'

'Keep well, Lizzie. Speak soon.'

Hilary rang off and Lizzie stared at her phone. Did she have enough signal to watch some YouTube tutorials? Surely there'd be something on there that could help with the plastering disaster in the living room. She tapped away and watched a series of videos from builders and DIY enthusiasts. One tip was to wet it all to smooth it out. She stomped to the kitchen and found a sponge by the sink and an old plastic bowl that she filled with water. She'd show Luc. Maybe she didn't need him at all.

Back in the living room she scraped her trowel to clear as much of the old, tacky plaster as she could and dipped the sponge in water. Unsure how wet it should be, she wrung it out till it was almost dry, but all this did was make bits of the sponge and a few crumbs she hadn't noticed stick to the wall. Muttering, she tried again, this time leaving the sponge wetter. Too wet, as it turned out. The grubby liquid ran down her arm and when she applied the sponge to the plaster, giant rivulets of water chased each other down the wall. Lumps of the plaster she'd only just applied began to fall off, gathering on the floor.

This was hopeless.

She'd just have to let it dry and then sand it down. That was the other option, according to YouTube. Maybe if she started on a different area, she'd make a better go of it. Luc had been right. She didn't like being bad at things, but she was far too stubborn to give up. Wiping her arm and hands she took up her tools once more, positive that she'd pick it up if she just kept going. She'd just have to use less plaster this time and be gentler.

Another hour later and this section of wall looked even worse than the one before. Lizzie snarled at it while dots of plaster covered her clothes and hung from her hair. Trying to use less plaster had somehow ended up in making the holes bigger as she tried to scrape it around and fill the gaps. Maybe she had been hacking at the walls that time. While Luc had made her cross with his accusations of being a clueless city girl, she had to admit defeat when it came to plastering. It had been far too ambitious for her first solo DIY job.

Retreating to the sofa, she tucked her knees up and cradled them. It looked truly, truly awful. There was no way she could paint over it or cover it with wallpaper. Every lump and bump would show underneath and if she sanded it, she had a feeling more holes would appear, creating more problems than she solved. A sinking feeling hit her stomach. She was going to have to call Luc. This needed fixing before it dried too much, and she clearly didn't have the skills to do it herself.

She gazed out of the window at the early-evening sky. The view was instantly calming. Sometimes the sun shone for so long it was difficult to tell what time it was. As the bright sun sank a little lower, the long grass in the fields around the house swung gently in the breeze. Lizzie checked her watch. It had been hours since Luc had left and with her appetite killed by stress, she hadn't noticed the time go by. Would he have calmed down by now? She thought of her relationships with Sarah, and now Luc, and it seemed as though unresolved conflicts ran in the water here. But she wasn't going to let things linger on. They were both adults after all.

Gritting her teeth, she pulled out her mobile and was about to dial his number when there was a knock on the kitchen door. Lizzie rose to answer it. Perhaps it was Margot and Amélie stopping by. As everyone knew Sarah, she hadn't bothered giving her address. Everyone seemed to know it already.

'Luc!'

'Lizzie.'

'Hi.'

Whenever she and Will had a fight, he'd let his phone go to voicemail and sometimes even stay at his mates'. He'd ignore her for ages no matter who was at fault or how silly the argument had been. It hadn't been his most attractive feature and one she was pleased to be away from. She wondered if he did that to his new girlfriend. Maybe not right now, when everything was shiny and new, but the gloss would wear off soon and he'd begin walking around in his pants and sulking when things didn't go his way. Maybe she was better off without him after all.

'I was just about to call you,' she said, quietly.

'You were?' Luc shuffled on the spot, stubbing the toe of his boot into the ground. Why did he have to look so bloody gorgeous all the time? Especially leaning against the door frame like that. He was wearing the checked shirt that matched the blue of his eyes.

'Lizzie, I—' He sighed, keeping his eyes down. 'I owe you an apology.'

She paused. Will would never have said that. Not straight up just hours after an argument. He'd apologise eventually but never so clearly and so soon. It threw her.

'I should not have said the things I said. They were . . .' She waited, eager for him to spell out what exactly it had all been about. 'Unfair.'

Unfair? Was that it? She didn't want more of an apology, he'd been gracious and to the point, but she had wanted to learn a little more about the whole city girl thing. Who had he been talking about? Now Lizzie had calmed down a little, she was sure it wasn't her.

'I'm sorry. Being in the city was hard for me. I met people I didn't like and it affected my relationship.' His voice was low and loaded with emotion. The tingling started again in Lizzie's body, and she ignored it.

'I'm sorry too. I obviously didn't make it easy for you to let me know I was doing something wrong. Please always feel free to be honest. My editor's not backward in coming forward, she'll—'

'Backward in coming forward?'

His confused expression was almost comical. 'She always gives criticism. It's kind of her job, so I've got used to it.

Don't ever feel like you can't give me advice. I won't mind, I promise.'

'Okay.' He nodded. 'It's a deal. So, you were about to call me?'

Here goes. Humiliation rose red hot up her back, prickling her hairline. 'Right. So, this is sort of a bit embarrassing but—'

'You haven't covered this Gary the goat in plaster, have you?'

'No, but there is more on the floor than the walls.' Relaxing as he grinned, she let her guard down. 'Oh, Luc, I've done such an awful job. After you left, I decided to start on a new patch, determined to prove you wrong, but it's ended up even worse than the other bit and I have no idea what to do.'

'Is it still wet?'

'Kind of.'

'As long as it hasn't dried, we should be able to smooth it out a bit.'

A bit was about all she was going to get but she liked that he said 'we'.

Lizzie followed him through to the living room and watched as his eyes widened, registering the mild panic at the mess she'd made.

'Don't say anything,' she warned him playfully.

'I wouldn't dream of it.' He undid the shirt and shook it from his shoulders. Lizzie caught a glimpse of the muscles of his arms tensing with each action. After tying it, he stood beside Lizzie, placing a hand gently in the small of her back. Had he detected the note of vulnerability in her voice? It had rung as clear as a bell to her. Lizzie swallowed, heat radiating from where his hand sat. 'I will see what I can do.'

'Shall I help?' He turned to her, raising one eyebrow in question. 'Probably not, hey? How about a cup of tea?' She asked with a smirk.

'Tea would be good. I like how you make tea.'

Glowing from the compliment, she went to the kitchen. He liked the way she made tea and she liked the way he made her feel. But after longing for that kiss earlier, she was careful not to get too overexcited; her heart had been damaged almost beyond repair, and whoever the city girl was that Luc had referred to earlier had clearly damaged his too.

Chapter Fourteen

After the plastering debacle, Luc had work to catch up on at the vineyard, which left Lizzie free to clear some more rooms and take things at a slightly slower pace. They still needed to re-plaster another wall of the living room, but she was reticent to do that without Luc around. As she'd proved, it wasn't her strong point.

So much was yet to be done. She was never going to sell the place with holes in the roof, never mind the less chic and more 1970s B&B-style decor. As much as she was growing to like the town and the people, Lizzie reminded herself this was only a temporary home and she'd be leaving again to get her life back on track in London. So why did the idea cause a hollow feeling in her chest? She shook it off. It was probably some kind of asthma caused by the dust and debris.

The bedroom Lizzie had commandeered on her first night wasn't the one she'd had as a child. That one had a dirty great hole in the ceiling and a bucket strategically placed beneath it in case it rained again. The one that she'd chosen now had been the freshest smelling, though it still had mildew climbing into the corners. Old flowery wallpaper peeled from the walls, but after a couple of weeks of opening the windows, the air was clearer. Lizzie had even picked some wildflowers from the back of the chateau and placed them in a vase on the windowsill. A subtle floral scent now perfumed the air and some of the dowdiness of the chateau had been shaken from the room. As Lizzie stared out of the large window, she could see the grounds that surrounded the back of the chateau. Fields that had once seemed endless and acted as her playground were full of overgrown grass, and the flowers that punctured the dense greenery barely moved in today's still, sunny weather. Wild blooms reached their heads towards the strong sun that bathed everything in a warm, golden light. It still felt like she was living in a painting: a Monet or a Cézanne. Every colour vivid and bold.

Having changed out of her work clothes for the day, Lizzie was just about to make some lunch when a knock on the front door echoed through the house. There were so many comings and goings in this little French town. Back in London, her doorbell only ever rang for takeaway deliveries and parcels. That was when she'd lived with Will. All the while she'd been bunking with her friend, in the rugby fanatic's room, the doorbell had never rung for her.

Lizzie found Margot and Amélie on her doorstep.

'Lizzie!' Margot cried, leaping forward and wrapping her arms around Lizzie's shoulders, pulling her in for a hug.

Lizzie responded just as warmly. 'It's so lovely to see you. Come in, come in.'

Margot strode through while Amélie hesitated before her mother ushered her inside. 'We have decided to take you up on your offer of lunch. Haven't we, Amélie? That's if you are not busy with the refurbishment.'

Amélie took out her phone. As much as Lizzie wanted to believe all tweens were like this, she was getting the distinct impression that Amélie really didn't like her.

'No, no,' Lizzie cried, happy to see her friend. 'He had to work on the vineyard today which is fine, because I've got lots to be getting on with. Come through to the kitchen.'

It was by far the nicest room for visitors, which spoke to how much more work she had to do before she could even think about selling the place.

'Were you nearby?' Lizzie asked.

The only place nearby, as far as she knew, was Luc's vineyard.

'Something like that,' Margot replied. 'You are making progress, I see.' She pointed to the boxes lining a wall.

'Yes, slowly. How are you, Amélie?' Lizzie asked, eager to include her in the conversation.

The young girl looked up and for the first time Lizzie realised how unlike Margot she was. While Margot had long blonde hair and brown eyes, the girl had thick dark hair and blue eyes. Amélie brushed a curl behind her ear, flattening the rest with the palm of her hand, and Lizzie felt a pang of sympathy. When she'd been twelve, she'd been too scared of straightening irons to use them, and her hair had been a helmet of frizz in every school photo ever taken. It wasn't until she'd found a hairdresser who understood her vague and unhelpful descriptions that her hair had become manageable. Growing up was such hard work.

'I'm fine,' the girl replied, scanning the room. Without realising it, her eyebrows had pulled together, and she seemed dismayed. If she was used to living in Paris, the state of the decrepit chateau was probably off-putting, but Lizzie tried to make her feel at home.

'Please sit down, both of you. I'll make some drinks and then we can have a picnic on the lawn outside, if you like.'

'Doesn't that sound wonderful, Amélie?' Amélie's expression didn't change. If anything, she looked even more annoyed.

'Have you taken any more photographs?' Lizzie asked her.

'Not really.' Her eyes flicked momentarily to Lizzie's before she began to type on the phone that had remained firmly in her hand.

Margot rolled her eyes and Lizzie smiled as she began to gather together everything she could find to make a delicious lunch.

'What can I do to help?'

'No, sit, you're my guest.'

'Nonsense,' Margot said. 'We are friends. Let me help you.'

Margot went to the fridge and took out an opened bottle of Luc's wine, shaking it at Lizzie for confirmation. Lizzie giggled as she nodded, and Margot found two glasses.

'There's pop in the fridge if you'd like some, Amélie.'

'Pop?' Margot asked and the way she said it made Lizzie chuckle again.

'Coca-Cola – or there's some fizzy orange.'

'Ah, I see. Cola, Amélie?'

Even this exchange didn't raise a smile from Amélie as she nodded her consent. Was she finding it as hard to be here in the depths of the countryside and away from her normal life as Lizzie had? Or did she just dislike being around grown-ups like Lizzie? She certainly did not seem keen to be around her.

Margot got her daughter a drink and Lizzie found the sheet she and Luc had used as a picnic rug the other day, opening it out on the grass. Together they assembled the food and cajoled Amélie into helping them carry everything into the garden.

Soon they were settled in the shade of a large, leafy tree, and the sun dappled through its thick branches onto their shoulders as it made its way across the sky. Lizzie and Margot talked incessantly about food, fashion, movies and music while Amélie made one or two comments but mostly nibbled food and played on her phone. Lizzie didn't mind at all as long as the girl was happy, but she wasn't sure she was. Once or twice, she'd caught her staring at the house, no doubt eager to leave.

'What did your editor think of your article?' Margot asked, curling her legs underneath her.

'She loved it. She thinks it's going to be a great series and it's doing a lot for my career prospects, so as long as readers don't get bored, things are looking good.'

'It is hard to be ambitious and a woman,' Margot added

somewhat sadly. The comment sparked some tension in the air and Amélie turned away from her mother. A moment later, she said something in French, but Margot answered in English.

'Of course, *ma chérie*, but stay near the chateau please.' She'd clearly asked to go for a walk and after Amélie had left, Margot rolled her eyes. 'It is so hard being a child today. So much on the phone and she gets bored here when she is away from her friends in Paris.'

'I used to get bored as well. I'm happy to speak to her if you like. Tell her I used to feel the same way but actually it's wonderful here, if you only let yourself feel it.'

'Perhaps,' Margot said. But as usual, she shook off the sadness that had lingered over her words. 'So, what are you up to today? Tell me how the chateau is going.'

'It's funny but sometimes I seem to make lots of progress and then other days I work from dawn till dusk, and nothing changes.' She looked over her shoulder to stare at the building. If only it could take her words as a warning to shape up. 'The electrics and roof are the next two big things to sort, but as I clear more rooms, I'm able to do some bits for myself. At the moment, I clear a room as much as possible, strip the wallpaper, then see what else I need to do. I'm afraid I haven't been very organised about it, and I deal with whichever room takes my fancy. I should probably try and do it floor by floor or something.'

'Why must you work in a certain way? It is your chateau, your life. You don't have to answer to anyone, so you should work how you want.'

'Do you really think so?'

'Of course!' Margot's long blonde hair, impressively soft, had fallen on her shoulder and she flicked it back. She seemed to have no idea how chic she looked, and it only added to her charm. 'It will all get done in the end. I hate it when people tell me I should be doing something a certain way. I work how I work, and my events are always successful. And in life, you cannot follow the same formula as everyone else.'

That was true. Lizzie toyed with a piece of grass. 'It's funny you should say that. For the last few months, I've felt like I've been doing life all wrong. After Will left, I felt like a failure at relationships and at life in general. I've been living in a friend's spare room while her usual roomie is out in Australia and I won't have a home to go to when I go back.' God, that sounded awful. Her life back home was a complete dumpster fire. It certainly wasn't where she'd hoped to be in her early thirties. She hadn't exactly planned for a car, a house and 2.4 kids, but she had thought her life would have more permanence by now. 'It's been good to focus on my career, though. I mean, I've always worked hard and wanted to do well but it became more of a priority after Will left. A coping strategy, I suppose.'

'We all have them,' Margot said softly. 'My career was always important to me, even when I was growing up here.' Lizzie was just about to ask about Amélie's father as Margot hadn't mentioned him in any of their conversations so far, and while Lizzie didn't want to pry, she was curious about her new friend. But Margot was too quick for her and changed the topic back to Lizzie. 'You must miss Sarah terribly.'

'Sarah and I never really got on, but yes, I do. More and more, actually. My parents used to send me here because we couldn't afford holidays and because all my friends would go away for the summer, they wanted me to have something too. The trouble was, as I got older, Sarah and I just seemed to rub each other up the wrong way. I wasn't like her at all. Not adventurous or brave, especially not as a teenager—'

'Who is? As a teenager I was certain I would never be brave enough to leave my town, especially not for Paris. I dreamed of being a successful woman, but back then . . .'

When Margot didn't continue, Lizzie took a sip of wine. Perhaps it had gone to her head, or maybe the heat had got to her as she suddenly blurted out, 'Did *you* like Sarah?'

'Yes, very much, but maybe she was different with me than she was with you. I do think she may have changed with age, according to some people in the town.'

Lizzie didn't want to know what some people in town thought of Sarah. After what had happened, she was sure there were many who didn't like her one bit. But then, those she'd met had all spoken so kindly of her. Had they forgiven and forgotten? Had they not cared as much as Lizzie had? She was beginning to think that as a teenager she'd overreacted and now it was too late to turn the clock back.

'You think she'd mellowed?' Lizzie asked. Margot nodded. 'When I was younger, she was always very passionate. She always wanted me to grab life and wrestle it into submission. She'd ask if I had a boyfriend yet and

I'd just say no and walk on, head down. At the time I felt like I was failing at getting out there like she wanted.' Lizzie thought about mentioning the last time she'd seen Sarah and the words exchanged between them, but she didn't want to spoil the lunch by dragging up painful memories. 'Did she ever tell you about her travels?'

'Many times. She lived a very exciting life from what she told me. She travelled the Nile and explored the Pyramids. Went to tiny villages in the rainforests. She was extraordinary in many ways and that was before she moved here. She was so brave to leave her country behind and everyone she knew. Did you know she spoke seven languages?'

No, Lizzie hadn't known that. She shook her head, unable to speak. There was so much more to Sarah, and she'd never get to know that now. A vague memory of Sarah telling her bedtime stories when she was younger came to mind. Lizzie could only have been eight or nine. She hadn't stayed for whole summers then. Just a week or two. At the time, Lizzie had believed she was just telling a story she knew, but what if the tale of lions and tigers had been real and one of her own adventures?

Amélie rounded the corner of the chateau with an unexpected companion and the conversation came to a natural conclusion.

'Gary!' Lizzie cried. 'Back again, are you?' The goat trotted along beside Amélie, casting glances at her as if she were Little Bo Peep and he one of her sheep.

Margot turned, a grin taking over her face. 'So, this is Gary.' She rolled the 'r' in that exquisite way the French do.

'I hope he hasn't been a pain, Amélie?' Lizzie asked, sipping from the water bottle she'd brought out but left untouched.

The girl was smiling, a wide, happy grin that lit her eyes and transformed her face. She seemed younger, more innocent and content. It was something Lizzie hoped to see more of as she felt a strange affinity with her.

'He's very sweet,' Amélie replied, sitting back down on the rug. It was the first conversational sentence Lizzie had heard from her. Gary stopped by Amélie's side and after she'd fed him a little of the leftover bread, sat down next to her.

'You certainly have a way with animals.'

'I keep asking *Maman* for a puppy, but she won't let me have one.' Cue an evil glance at Margot, who remained unfazed.

'In our apartment in Paris? It would be on its own all day and that is not fair.'

'Papa could get one.'

It was the first mention of Amélie's father and Lizzie's natural inquisitiveness piqued.

Margot shook her head. 'Papa is too busy.'

Amélie gave Margot the same puppy-dog eyes Lizzie had given her mum and dad when she'd begged for a puppy as a child. They never got one either. Mum hadn't been in favour, though her dad had wavered on occasion. For a second, Lizzie thought what a shame it was she wasn't staying here. She could finally get one. Will hadn't wanted one for the same reason as Margot mentioned, but as she was, for all intents and purposes, working from home at the moment, it would be lovely to have a companion around. Though Gary might not be too impressed by the idea.

'I don't suppose you know where Gary comes from, do you?' Lizzie asked Amélie. 'I keep meaning to follow him and find out, but I haven't had the chance yet and every time he disappears, I start to worry something terrible has happened to him.'

'Maybe. *Maman*, do you think he could belong to Monsieur Mercier?' Margot nodded and Amélie turned to Lizzie. 'His farm is that way. He keeps goats.' She pointed in the opposite direction to Luc's vineyard.

So he was her neighbour on the other side. She had no recollection of him from her days here with Sarah but there was a lot she'd forgotten about those summers.

'I'll have to take Gary over the next time he breaks in. I'm still not sure how exactly he gets in the chateau. He's like Houdini – only he breaks in rather than out! He likes you though, Amélie. Normally he's trying to eat everything in sight, not sitting there looking cute like he is now.'

Amélie couldn't help but smile.

'Right, I think we should go,' Margot said, unfurling her legs and standing up. 'Before Amélie starts asking me for a puppy again. Come, *ma chérie*. Let us go. We are heading back to Paris for the weekend, and I have some things to do before we leave. But we will be back on Monday. I will come and see you next week, Lizzie.'

'Or we could meet in town for lunch? You don't always have to come out here, especially if it's out of your way.'

Margot waved the suggestion away. 'I will call you and

we can arrange. *Au revoir*, *mon amie*. Do not work too hard. And remember, work your own way. This is your house, you may do what you like.'

Lizzie kissed Margot's cheeks, assuring her she would call. She watched her and Amélie walk around the side of the chateau, taking the shortcut back to town.

Margot's words resounded in her head and after giving Gary another chunk of bread to eat, Lizzie sat back down on the picnic rug and stretched out her legs. Overcome by a sense of relaxation, she lay down, feeling the breeze tickle her cheeks, her breathing slow and quiet.

Her friend was absolutely right, life didn't follow a formula. If it did, everyone would be doing the same thing and that would be incredibly boring. Lizzie's life hadn't quite turned out how she'd imagined it, but that didn't mean she was doing something wrong. She was proud of herself for undertaking this adventure, for tackling things she'd never have dreamed of, even if she was spending her days rolling out of someone else's bed (in the most boring way possible), commuting into London and enduring the office whispers. Maybe Sarah would have been proud too. Lizzie was certainly taking hold of this opportunity and wrestling it to the ground.

Gary sat down beside her, resting his head on her stomach. Her mind wandered to Luc, and she imagined his head resting there, her fingers curling into his thick dark hair as they chatted and laughed. But beggars couldn't be choosers, and at least Gary wasn't going to eat the last of her favourite cheese. She remembered the special box she and Will would buy at Christmas. They'd loved tasting and sharing it, but Will wouldn't always think of saving some for her when her appetite ran out. These annoyances had never been deal-breakers to Lizzie, but now she thought of it he'd had quite a lot of irritating habits she was happy to be shot of.

Listening to the birds singing in the bushy trees and the chirping of crickets in the long grass, Lizzie tucked her arm under her head. She'd just lie here for a little while longer. After all, the chateau wasn't going anywhere.

Chapter Fifteen

It was Saturday morning and the electrician had finally arrived to quote for the re-wiring of the house. Lizzie skittered around after him, tidying random areas (like that would make a difference!) and nervously waiting for the verdict. Luc had paused in between fitting some of the new windows now the glass had arrived. Victor, the electrician, spoke very quickly and Lizzie couldn't decipher more than one or two words, and by the time she'd figured out those, he'd moved on to another room or another topic. His English wasn't very good either, but Lizzie was thankful for Luc's reassuring presence, and his very practical French language skills.

Nerves bit hard at her stomach. What if it was more money than she had? The simple answer was that she'd just have to keep working until she made enough. She might have to talk to Hilary and take on some extra freelance work. The money from Sarah's will still hadn't come through but her mum had assured her it would only be a few more weeks. That's what Mr Devlin, the solicitor, had said anyway.

After following Victor around the house, he and Luc paused in the hallway. Lizzie watched in wonder as they spoke, wishing she'd paid more attention in her youth and learned the language. Luc and Victor's conversation ended with a slight nod from Luc and a resigned shrug, but Lizzie still didn't know if they were talking about the chateau or something else. She hoped from their dour expressions they were discussing the football, but the way Victor wouldn't meet her eye made her anxious.

'So?' she asked.

'I'll just see Victor out,' said Luc and Lizzie's stomach roiled.

Was it so bad he feared her reaction in front of him?

Luc bid his friend goodbye, as did Lizzie, thanking him for coming, and Luc shut the heavy front door behind him. 'It's a lot of money.'

'How much?' A lump formed in her throat.

He named a sum that was eye-wateringly high. 'Nearly twenty thousand euros? That'll wipe out everything I've got left. And more.' It would use the money Hilary had given, clear out the little that remained in her current account, and still leave her short. She'd need a loan and she'd been living paycheck to paycheck already. But what other option did she have?

'He also said that you might want to get the electrics done after you've fixed the roof. With leaks in some of the rooms, he doesn't want to do the electrics for there to be problems with water intrusion after.'

'So the roof has to be the first priority?' she asked, her voice weighty with stress. 'I suppose that makes sense.'

'He doesn't think you're in any imminent danger. It's not as if the wiring is going to explode or cause a fire.'

That thought hadn't actually occurred to her before, but now he'd said it, her eyes widened in panic. Was she going to burn to death in her sleep or lose the entire chateau in some awful fire?

Luc reached a hand out and touched her arm. The warmth flowed through her body like a salve. 'Don't look so worried. He said that's *not* going to happen.'

'Why did you mention it then?' She injected some life into her voice to show she wasn't annoyed. 'I'm not sure I'm going to sleep tonight now.'

'Yes, you will. I am going to tire you out – I mean—' He glanced away, his cheeks colouring above the line of his neatly trimmed beard. 'There is a get-together in town tonight. I thought we deserved a break, and we might go.'

'A get-together? What for? Is there a festival or something?'

'No reason. It just happens like that sometimes. Someone says they are going for a drink or dinner, then someone else says they will too and before you know it, the whole town has decided to meet. It will be nice to relax. You – we – have both been working too hard. In Provence, you must slow down or life will pass you by.'

Lizzie smiled, her body fizzing at the idea of spending the evening with Luc. His consideration was sweet, as was the way he hadn't quite met her eye as he'd spoken. A shyness had come over him and she found it incredibly endearing. 'Is that a rule here?'

'It is.'

'It sounds wonderful.'

He smiled widely. 'The rule or the party?'

'Both.'

'Good.' He met her eye fully this time. 'Shall I meet you here at seven and we will walk to town together? We can have dinner.'

'Sure. That'd be great,' she said coolly.

From the way her heart was racing, it was going to be more than great. Her stomach filled with an unexpected and altogether unsettling feeling. Her feelings for Luc were definitely growing stronger, but her heart was still bruised and battered from Will's treatment of her. She'd have to play it safe this time.

Luc and Lizzie tackled plastering the last wall in the living room. It had been much less of a disaster this time with nothing but teasing and laughter as their soundtrack. With that done, Luc had disappeared for his vineyard duties and Lizzie had fussed and worried over what to wear for her 'date' with Luc.

Her stomach somersaulted, sending ripples through her body. She didn't want to dress up too much, not that she had anything really dressy anyway, but there was nothing worse than turning up to an event over – or under – dressed. She thought about texting Margot and asking her advice, but Margot had said they were in Paris for the weekend and Lizzie didn't want to disturb them. She'd just have to figure it out on her own. She only had three dresses to choose from and it wasn't like she could afford to buy a new one, so it wasn't going to be a difficult decision.

After a refreshing bath and applying her make-up with a lot more care than normal, she was ready to go. Her long blonde hair fell around her shoulders, already curling in the heat. She took a hair-band and threaded it onto her wrist in case her hair continued to puff. The last thing she needed was a frizzy mess by the end of the night.

The last time Luc had seen her in a dress was when she'd worn her favourite black and white polka-dot one, so today she'd opted for a deep burgundy dress with tiny white love hearts on it. She paired it with her second favourite pair of trainers, which were thankfully still white because she hadn't trampled through any muddy fields or plastered walls in them. She looked understated and, dare she say it, pretty. She hadn't felt pretty in a long time, and it had been a while since anyone had told her so. Will had been full of compliments at first, but over the years they'd faded. She wouldn't let thoughts of him spoil her good mood and pushing him out of her mind, she went to meet Luc.

He appeared at the door moments later, blue eyes popping between the darkness of his hair and a black shirt fitted to his frame. As usual, he'd rolled the sleeves up to the elbow and as he brushed his hair back, Lizzie's heart almost burst out of her chest. Luc didn't seem to have any idea how attractive he was. He never posed and rarely smiled, though Lizzie was pleased to admit he'd been smiling more every time she'd seen him lately.

'Ready?' he asked.

'Ready.' She told the butterflies in her stomach to calm down as she grabbed her bag and sunglasses.

They walked in silence at first, winding their way around the chateau out to the dust track and lavender fields. The purple horizon was as dazzling as always and bees buzzed around the flowers, searching for pollen, adding a gentle hum to the evening soundtrack.

'I have lived here nearly all of my life and every time I see these, I feel calm,' he said, breaking the silence.

She pulled a single stem from a stubby lavender bush and took a breath. 'It really is a beautiful smell. I don't think I'll ever get tired of it.' He glanced at her for a moment as if something she'd said struck a chord, but he didn't respond. 'So, what's it like owning a vineyard?'

Luc shook his head. 'I don't own it. I run it for someone else.'

'Oh, right. Do they come down much or just leave you to it?'

'They are a silent owner, but I like it that way. I don't like being watched or managed. I like being my own boss.'

'There is something quite freeing about being able to do things your own way. I never realised it myself until now. Do you like being a vintner?'

'I do, but there are other things I like more. I have always liked working with my hands, but it is hard to find the time to pursue other hobbies.'

Lizzie glanced at him, concern pulling at her thoughts. 'If the chateau is taking up too much time, you must tell me. I completely understand if you have other things you need to do.'

'*Non*, it is fine. The other hobby I would like to pursue, it – it requires more than just time.'

'Right.' She wanted to ask more but couldn't think how to without being pushy.

'But I do like working here in Provence. I love the town and the people and the way of life.'

'I gathered you're not a fan of city life.' She said it jokingly but held her breath as she waited for his response. If her light-hearted reference to their row didn't land, the evening would be ruined before it had even begun. To her delight, Luc laughed.

'You picked that up, did you? No. I'm definitely not cut out for the city. I tried once, but it didn't work.'

'How long were you there for?'

'A few years. I moved there for someone but . . .'

Though he'd answered her question, a subtle shift in his body language, putting his hands in his pockets, told her the subject was uncomfortable.

'I was introduced to *fleurs de courgettes farcies* the other day and it was divine – what would you recommend I have tonight?'

'We are going to La Maison Café—'

Lizzie interrupted, unable to contain her excitement. 'The café in the corner of the market square?'

'You know it?'

'I had a coffee there the day after I arrived, but I remember seeing the lights strung in the courtyard and wanting to see it all lit up. Now I will. I'll have to take some photos for future articles. I just know it's going to look beautiful.'

Luc chuckled. 'You are a very strange woman.'

'Crazy English lady. I know.'

His hand brushed hers, but he didn't pull away. She wanted him to hold hers and disappointment tinged her mood when he didn't. She chastised herself for being led by the romantic scenery and she definitely needed to curb this crush sooner rather than later.

'You seemed so serious when you arrived, but there is a part of you that is almost . . .'

She waited as he searched for the word. 'Almost what?'

'French.'

'French?'

'Yes. I feel that you could be French if you just relaxed a little bit more. You see beauty in the world, as we do. You enjoy the life we have here. You have not freaked out about the chateau like some people would have.' He met her gaze and a fire started inside her.

'There's a lot here to appreciate,' she mumbled, heat rising up her neck and onto her cheeks. 'I feel like I've left a lot of my troubles behind.'

'You refer to your ex?'

She nodded. 'I was so stuck back home in England. Trapped, feeling sorry for myself, but now I feel freer.'

So often she'd told herself she was over the breakup, had tried to convince herself that was the case, but now maybe she was actually moving on, leaving thoughts of Will behind. Even news of his relationship hurt, but not enough to send her on a downward spiral.

'He's seeing someone else now. I found out recently.'

'Was that the day we delivered your car?'

How had he known? 'Yes. Sorry if I was rude. It was a bit of a shock.'

'It always is,' he replied. 'But you are okay now?'

Was it her imagination or was there more to his question? No, just wishful thinking on her part. 'I'm good. I'm actually really, really good.'

'I'm glad.'

She glanced around, worried she was blushing. The sky above was astonishing: a painting of such dazzling colours she could hardly believe it was real. The sun settled lower like a bright orange orb, and from it streaks of pink, tangerine and mauve were slashed from one vista to another. The green stems of the lavender plants and their bushy purple tops were something from a Van Gogh and in the very far distance the hills and mountains rose, watching over the town.

They continued into town and out into the market square. Lizzie gasped as she saw the café and the sheer number of people who had gathered for this impromptu party. Because that's what it was: a party. The fairy lights she'd seen strung up were lit, swaying gently in the warm evening breeze. The medieval buildings had been brought to life once more and the atmosphere was one of fun. More bottles of wine than she could count were strewn on the tables and several of the townsfolk were playing musical instruments. The café overflowed with people onto the benches of the market square, everyone laughing and joking. The whole town had come out to join them.

'It's wonderful!' she cried, joy filling her body. 'I can't believe this is just a . . . a gathering.'

Luc smiled, as happy to see it as she was. 'Someone says

they will bring their accordion and someone else brings their guitar and before you know it you have this.' He held his hands out in front of him, gesturing to everyone.

'Magical,' she breathed.

'Come, let us find a seat and order some food. I'm starving.'

'Me too, and whatever they're cooking smells delicious.'

Luc placed his hand on the small of her back as he guided her forward and Lizzie tried not to show how much it affected her. He pulled a seat out for her, and she sat. When he snuggled in, his leg touched hers, but he didn't pull away and she let her knee rest against his, excitement building inside her.

Sylvie and Henri were at the table next to them.

'*Bonsoir*, Henri. *Bonsoir*, Sylvie,' Lizzie said.

Sylvie looked resplendent in linen trousers and a loose pale pink shirt, while Henri was dapper in a cream summer suit. Her silver hair shone in the golden evening light and Henri's had been slicked down, though the skin of his scalp could be seen between the combed dark grey strands.

'*Bonsoir*, Élisabeth. It is lovely to see you. I did not know you were coming.'

'Luc suggested we kick back and relax after working so hard on the chateau, and it's such a wonderful evening. I'm very glad we came.'

'So am I. You must come and sit here. Join us, please?'

Though she was looking forward to eating with Luc, she couldn't refuse the lovely old woman and shuffled over to their table. As soon as they'd moved, the space was filled as more and more townspeople joined the party. It seemed they were sitting with Henri and Sylvie for the evening. Regret danced on the outskirts of her thoughts but was quickly replaced by excitement as the waiter brought out two plates piled high with ratatouille followed swiftly by a basket of crusty bread cut into rounds. Lizzie's mouth watered.

'It looks good, doesn't it?' Sylvie said, seeing her expression. 'Here. Try some?'

'No, no. I couldn't. You enjoy it. I'll order something in a minute.'

'I insist.' Sylvie manoeuvred her fork towards Lizzie like a mother feeding a baby. Lizzie shrank but then the flavours hit her mouth. She'd never had ratatouille like it.

'Oh my god, that's amazing!'

Luc signalled to the waiter and asked for two menus.

'I don't think I need one,' Lizzie replied when she'd finished her mouthful. 'I'm having that. It's sublime.'

Sylvie grinned as she used the bread to soak up the rich tomatoey juice coming off the vegetables. 'It is the best ratatouille in the whole of the world. And you should drink some pastis. Sarah loved it. Though it took some getting used to.'

Luc requested two glasses of pastis and the waiter brought them out with a large carafe of water. Eager to see what it tasted like, Lizzie took a sip of her drink and spluttered. The aniseed flavour hit her tastebuds so hard her eyes watered, and the fiery alcohol made her cough. She dabbed at her eyes.

'You're supposed to water it down,' Luc said gently, pouring a hefty measure from the carafe into her glass, then filling his.

Embarrassment coloured her cheeks and she glanced away. Sylvie's small hand pressed gently on her arm. 'Sarah did exactly the same thing when she first tried it.'

Lizzie relaxed. Had Sarah really made the same mistake? Would she have laughed at her? Before, Lizzie would have been sure she would have, but now she wondered if Sarah would have laughed at her expression, just as her mum and dad would have, rather than the mistake itself. Sylvie's warm, maternal smile showed they didn't think badly of her for getting it wrong.

Luc took a drink of his pastis and caught her eye. 'Try again. It is much nicer now.'

She did as instructed, and this time the aniseed flavour was subtle and the drink pleasant on such a hot summer evening.

'Much better,' she joked and Luc grinned, his eyes remaining on her as Sylvie ate and talked.

Their meals arrived and conversation turned to the wonderful food of Provence, the beautiful countryside and eventually towards Sarah.

'Did she ever tell you that she rode the Orient Express all the way to Venice?' Sylvie asked.

'On her own?'

'I believe so. She never mentioned travelling with anyone when she told the story.'

Lizzie checked around. She knew who she was looking for, though she had no idea what he'd look like now.

Sylvie followed her gaze. 'If you are looking for Guillaume, he died many years ago.'

It was the first time Sylvie had mentioned him and Lizzie's

skin prickled. She and Sarah had been close but Lizzie didn't know how much she knew. Did she know all of it? 'He did?' She felt a stab of sadness at hearing that. 'I'm sorry.'

'And his wife moved away. She lives with her second husband many miles from here.'

Luc leaned forward. 'Guillaume Tremblay? How was he connected with Sarah?'

Lizzie shot Sylvie a panicked glance, but Sylvie, unruffled, waved her napkin at him, brushing his enquiry aside. 'Everyone has known each other in this town since forever. Since before you were born. Everyone's history is wrapped around someone else's here. You remember them being friends. Now, who is going to have some dessert with me? I cannot possibly eat on my own. You will make me feel fat.'

Lizzie laughed as the tension dissipated, but a wariness had come into Luc's eyes. He knew she was hiding something, but she didn't want to bring up the past tonight. She'd always felt justified in her actions but had Sarah come to regret hers? She was beginning to see she hadn't known her great-aunt very well at all, and that opened the door to doubt.

'Lizzie, what will you have?'

She perused the menu and they both ordered *poires belle Hélène*, poached pears, something Lizzie remembered Sarah cooking from time to time. The pears, simmered in sugar syrup, were soft and sweet, and drizzled with melted chocolate. They had worked together in the kitchen to make it, laughing and joking, but Lizzie pushed the memory down. The past was going to have to stay away from the present for tonight.

'What did she tell you about the Orient Express?' Lizzie asked Sylvie.

'It was something she always wanted to do, and you know Sarah. She was never going to wait for a man to accompany her. She wanted to go, so she did. She got on after visiting your family. This was before you were born, I think. She boarded at London and travelled through Paris, then onto Venice. I've never been, but Sarah said Venice was one of the most beautiful cities she had ever visited. I believe she met a rather nice Italian man there and broke his heart when she left. He even proposed to her, I believe, in an attempt to get her to stay, but she said no. She had more adventures to have.'

'It sounds wonderful,' Lizzie replied. 'Like something from a fairy-tale. Was she quite young at the time?'

'About your age, I think. She said the train was exquisite. The service perfect. She felt like a princess. They drank cocktails and ate fancy midnight snacks. It sounds far too extravagant to me, but apparently it is the done thing on the Orient Express.'

'What did she do after that?'

'I believe she came home to the chateau for a while and then went off somewhere else. Do you remember where it was, Henri?'

The old man turned from his own conversation with a friend. 'Africa somewhere, to help build a school or an orphanage or something.'

'Oh yes,' Sylvie nodded as the memory came back to

her. 'She always tried to do something for fun and something with meaning. I remember that. She wasn't always about gallivanting around enjoying herself. She would sometimes combine trips with something she felt passionate about. Something she could do to help others. There are probably photographs at the chateau somewhere.'

'There are quite a few trinkets and souvenirs, but I haven't got round to clearing her study yet. Was there anything you wanted of hers, Sylvie? You were friends for such a long time. I'll have to check if there was anything specific she wanted you to have in her will.'

She'd been putting off clearing the study ever since she'd arrived. Too worried about the feelings she'd have to confront if she opened the door. It was where they'd had their last horrible argument and she had no wish to relive it.

'Oh, how kind of you to ask, Élisabeth. I would love something to remember her by. But you choose. It will be a lovely surprise.'

The man Henri had been chatting with at the table behind called out. 'Henri! So, this is Sarah's niece?'

Sylvie nodded and Lizzie turned to face him. He had a long white beard but was completely bald. If Lizzie remembered rightly, he had been sat on the bench with Henri when she'd first met Sylvie in town.

'I am very pleased to meet you,' he said, holding out his hand. 'Sarah was quite wonderful. I'm very sorry.'

'We were just talking about her travels,' Henri said before sipping his pastis.

'I heard. I'm sorry for listening.' He held his hand to his heart in apology. 'That's why I had to speak to you.

She once told me all about a trip to Greece where she volunteered on an archaeological dig. She shouldn't have, but she stole a little something. A coin or something like that, nothing too important. She could be very naughty sometimes.'

Lizzie could just imagine Sarah thinking she was Indiana Jones. But all these stories . . . She really hadn't known her at all.

The tables were cleared, and the pastis changed for wine. Lizzie sipped, watching the sun disappear behind the tall white stone buildings of the square. The fairy lights grew brighter against the darkening sky, suddenly ablaze with velvety blues and lilacs. It was almost too much to look at. She took a snap with her phone, happy that she hadn't really looked at it for hours. It had sat on the table, turned over and untouched. She'd been far too busy living in the moment.

A quick glance now showed no calls, no new emails, or messages. Before, that realisation would have upset her. Where were the friends she'd shared with Will? She'd been consumed by a fear of missing out while she'd been mourning their relationship but hadn't been able to drag herself off the sofa and go outside. When work had become everything, it had filled a void. Now she was sat here with friends (Sylvie would have been upset if she'd called her anything else), Henri was chatting with Luc, and more and more townspeople were joining them, coming to say hello, chatting and laughing. There was such a sense of friendship here, of acceptance. She'd miss it when she left.

The music grew louder and changed from soft background thrumming to a lively tune. Henri stood and offered his hand to Sylvie, who smiled adoringly, and they walked out of the café into the square and began to dance. Others joined them and then the singing began. Lizzie wished she knew the words and longed to join in, but it was beyond her. She sat back and revelled in the atmosphere, soaking up the fun and enjoying the spontaneity of it all.

Luc moved into the chair Sylvie had left and leaned in to speak over the music. 'Sarah loved this dance.'

'Did she? I didn't know she was much of a dancer.'

'She would dance with whoever asked her. She said it was rude not to. She even danced with me once.'

'You?'

'Why do you sound so surprised? I can dance.' He sat back and crossed his arms over his chest.

'Sorry, I didn't mean to sound so shocked. I'm sure you're an amazing dancer, but I'm not. Pretty sure I have two left feet, or at least a right and left that don't get on.'

Luc laughed, then stood holding out his hand. 'Come. I will show you.'

'Are you sure you want to take the risk? I have no idea what I'm doing.'

'*Oui*, *Mademoiselle*. Come.' He bowed and signalled the way with his other hand.

The way he'd said *mademoiselle* sent her senses fizzing and when she placed her hand in his, every nerve in her body jolted into life. On the dancefloor, his hand rested gently on her waist while the other held hers out. He didn't try any fancy spins like Sylvie and Henri were doing and instead led her gently around the floor.

Will had hated dancing and when forced to, grabbed her hands so tightly her fingers ended up squished together. Then they'd slowly move in a tiny circle, rocking side to side. She'd never felt comfortable like that. It made her dizzy. Luc was leading them in an arc around the floor, dodging in and out of the others.

After a while, when she seemed more comfortable, he opened his arm and she instinctively turned underneath it, then he took her in again at the waist. Her body moved closer to his, pressing against him and the atmosphere between them boiled with emotion. Even the look in his eyes told her something was happening. She wasn't imagining it and it wasn't just a physical reaction, something unexpected was stirring for them both. There was a tug at her heart, a feeling deep down inside that this was more.

Wasn't it too soon to feel anything for someone else? Obviously not for Will, given his recent Instagram post, but for her? She looked up into Luc's face, hoping it would answer her question or give her some clarity on what she should be feeling, but all it did was send her senses into overdrive. There was a connection between them. Something she couldn't quite put her finger on, but something bound them together. She could feel it deep within her heart, in a place she'd reserved for love but had locked away after Will had left. Whatever it was, she was sure he could feel it too.

She was so close to him, to his lips, that she would have succumbed had he brushed his against hers. She longed for a kiss and the gentle strength with which he held her only intensified that feeling.

The song finished and everyone stepped away from their partners, applauding the musicians who launched straight into another tune. Her legs were like jelly as she battled feelings of intense desire, which was immediately followed by disappointment as Luc stepped away from her.

'Shall we get a drink?' he asked, backing away towards their table.

'Yes,' she replied, breathlessly. But no break was going to help bring her breath back. Luc Allard had taken that from her whether she was ready for it or not.

Chapter Sixteen

The next day, Lizzie still felt breathless. Luc had overtaken her thoughts throughout the night and today, more than anything, she wanted to be in his company. Even now she couldn't stop thinking about him and his name skipped on the tip of her tongue. Had she had someone to talk to, she would have felt the need to bring him into the conversation, to say his name out loud. As it was, Lizzie contented herself with daydreaming about the dance and the feel of his hands on her body. She wasn't supposed to see him today. They had decided not to work on the chateau as it was a Sunday and because they hadn't made it home until three in the morning the previous evening.

The restaurant had stayed open, the wine flowing, and Lizzie had chatted to more and more people about Sarah. It seemed she really would be missed by all who knew her. The familiar jab of remorse hit Lizzie, but she reminded herself of how Sarah should never have asked her to get involved in the mess she herself had created. She owed

Sarah's memory something, as a thank you for the happier summers of her childhood, and she was repaying that debt by fixing up the chateau so it could be lived in and loved once more. The shadow of her return to London lingered in her mind, asking her what that meant for her budding feelings for Luc, but she ignored it. She wouldn't think about anything else right now. She had something far nicer on her mind.

Lizzie toyed with various ideas as to how she could run into Luc but none of the scenarios she'd played out throughout the morning had been feasible and some had been downright bonkers. Eventually, she'd settled on simply walking over with a picnic and asking if he wanted to join her for lunch.

With the picnic packed, Lizzie took the chilled wine from the fridge. It was from Luc's vineyard, and she hoped they'd sit and drink it in the shade of the grapevines, snuggled on a picnic rug.

The midday heat pounded down, and Lizzie adjusted her sun hat to ensure it covered her head and shoulders. Not a single cloud marred the view and the bright cornflower blue sky stretched out before her. She took a breath of the floral scented air, allowing it to fill her senses.

Her feelings for Luc had confused her yesterday, but today she refused to over-analyse them. What would be, would be. There had been more hints in his looks and manner to suggest that he at least found her attractive and though she wasn't quite ready to dive headfirst into a new relationship, she couldn't bring herself to push him away. If he said yes to this impromptu date, it would be a sign and they could then take things slowly and see where life took them.

Her phone rang, bringing her thoughts back to the present and she answered it.

'Hi, Mum.'

'Hello, darling. How are you getting on with the chateau?'

The last time they'd spoken her mum had been ecstatic at the prosect of Lizzie staying for a while and fixing the place up, even if it was to sell it to a family. As long as it would be loved by someone, her mum was happy.

'They're going okay. How are things back home?'

'Oh, you know your father, he's as annoying as ever.'

'I am not!' came a faint voice in the background. Lizzie smiled.

'You're sounding decidedly chipper,' her mum said. 'It's so wonderful to hear you happier.'

'Thanks Mum.'

'What are you up to today?'

She glanced at the picnic basket in her hand. She wasn't quite ready to talk about last night or Luc yet. 'Just this and that. I'm taking a walk at the moment. Enjoying the scenery.'

'So you should. It's important you have fun as well as work. Well, I'll let you get on. Your dad will be wanting his lunch soon or he'll moan I'm starving him.'

'She is starving me, Lizzie. She won't let me have another biscuit!'

She giggled at her dad's silly joke and bid them farewell before shifting the basket to her other hand.

The heavy lavender scent from the fields around the

house began to give way and as she approached the vineyard, the smell of fresh grapes overtook the floral notes. Where Luc had watered the vines, a hint of damp earth underpinned everything like a multi-layered perfume. The regimented rows of grapevines with their thick leafy covers signalled she had arrived faster than expected, so Lizzie slowed her pace and began to weave between them on her way to the farmhouse.

Lost in the fairy-tale nature of her surroundings, she barely noticed the voices that carried towards her. She approached the house, turned the corner and halted, her grip tightening on the picnic basket.

Margot and Luc were at the farmhouse, framed between two lengths of vines. They hadn't noticed her, and their bodies were almost touching. They were standing very close together. *Too* close together. Not like strangers or neighbours, like a couple. Like lovers.

Margot, ever beautiful, toyed with a leaf, twisting and bending it in her slim fingers. Luc took it from her and tossed it onto the ground before holding her hands gently in his. He was as handsome as he'd been last night. Maybe more so now. Lizzie's heart seized in pain. His head bent towards Margot's just as Lizzie had longed for his to dip towards hers last night. Would he kiss her? She couldn't bear to watch.

Hurt and humiliation, white hot and all-consuming, engulfed her. Were they together? Had they been together all this time and she'd not noticed? Why was Margot even here? She'd said she'd be in Paris till Monday.

Lizzie stepped backwards, hiding herself behind the

shaggy leaves. She had no intention of staying to pry, she just didn't want to make a noise that would draw attention to herself. They couldn't find her there. She was too upset, too shaken to speak to them, but unable to draw her eyes away she watched through the leaves as Luc wrapped his arm around Margot's shoulders and pulled her in for a hug. Had they kissed in that moment she hadn't been looking? She wished now that she knew. Margot's head pressed into Luc's chest and his hand cupped the back of her head, his fingers curled into her hair. It was so intimate and despite her pain, Lizzie felt a pang of guilt for intruding. They stayed like that for a moment, then Margot stepped back and looked up at Luc. Surely, they were going to kiss? The intensity of their gaze, the heightened emotion radiating off them. She could feel it all the way down to where she was hidden.

Turning her head, Lizzie squeezed her eyes shut. She stifled the sob pushing up through her throat. She'd got it wrong again. Just like Will. An agonising tightness squeezed her ribs, suffocating her voice and heart. She headed off, running with the heavy picnic basket in her hands. As her muscles burned, she forced her legs on, her body collapsing in on itself. She'd been so stupid. She glanced behind her to make sure they hadn't spotted her, but of course they hadn't. Why should they? They were wrapped up in each other and wouldn't have noticed if she'd walked past wearing nothing but a thong or one of those massive inflatable dinosaur suits.

Margot had made such an effort to befriend her; Luc too. Why had neither mentioned the other? Or at least mentioned they were in a relationship? Was it to protect Amélie? Perhaps after the divorce, Margot didn't know if Amélie was ready for someone new to enter her life. Lizzie mentally scanned their conversations, looking for clues. Clues she'd obviously missed. Margot had seemed surprised when Lizzie had mentioned Luc was working on the chateau, but she hadn't said anything. All she'd said was that they grew up together. Now she came to think of it, when she'd mentioned Margot to Luc, he'd looked at her suspiciously too, but she'd thought he was just surprised she was making a new friend already. Was it that he was surprised she was making friends with his girlfriend?

Sweat dripped down her temple. She'd been running so fast her heart pounded. Far enough away now, she slowed and caught her breath. Why did this hurt so much? Humiliation was the only answer she could come up with, and that ever-present feeling of rejection since Will had left her. If Luc was with Margot, then everything that had happened last night could only have been done as a friend. Perhaps Margot had asked him to take Lizzie to the party because she was out of town? Luc must have thought she was throwing herself at him. Unable to keep quiet any longer, Lizzie let out a half-groan, half-cry. She wanted to hide in the chateau and never see anyone again. No one in town had mentioned Luc and Margot being a couple, but then, she hadn't walked in and directly asked anyone. And as Sylvie had said, everyone's history was wrapped around someone else's here. Did they all just assume she knew? Whatever it was, it proved she couldn't trust her own judgement and she should have known that, after standing at the church on her wedding day, arguing with her dad that he must have misunderstood Will's phone call. He was coming. He couldn't possibly have said he wasn't.

She'd been so happy to stay here, to leave Will and his ability to move on behind, and to build her career so that when she returned the whispers wouldn't be so hurtful. But now she was stuck here with the whole town thinking she was a tart, throwing herself at a handsome man as soon as his girlfriend was out of town.

They'd think she was just like Sarah.

Just as the chateau came back into view, she saw Amélie wandering aimlessly, then, a moment later, plonk herself on the ground. Though Lizzie couldn't really bear the thought of seeing anyone, she had to check on the girl. What if she was ill? Lizzie dried her eyes and made her way towards her.

'Amélie? Are you okay?' The girl looked up, surrounded by the long grass, her face tear-stained. She wiped at her cheeks and Lizzie lowered herself down beside her. 'What's happened?'

'Nothing.'

'It doesn't look like nothing. You're upset. Something must have happened.' Amélie shrugged in reply. 'If you don't want to tell me, that's fine, but can I walk with you back to town, to your mum's, then you can tell her.'

Amélie looked at Lizzie for a moment then drew her knees up, resting her chin on them.

Lizzie's eyes fell to the picnic basket. She wouldn't be sharing that with Luc now. 'Would you like an apple?'

Amélie eyed it for a moment then took it, but didn't bite.

'Are you sure you're okay?'

Amélie sniffed and wiped her cheeks. 'My friends are all sharing messages and videos of what they're doing in Paris. It's not fair.'

'You feel left out?' Amélie nodded. 'I'm sorry. I remember how tough that was. Have you asked them not to?'

'Yes. They said they can't pretend not to be having fun just because I'm not with them.'

'I see. It must be difficult for them too, I suppose.' She didn't really have any more advice to offer. She hadn't had that much experience with teenage girls recently. She thought about suggesting Amélie come off her phone for a while but didn't get the impression that would go down well. Lizzie searched for something reassuring to say. 'I'm sure they don't mean to hurt you. They probably don't realise how much it upsets you.'

'They do. They just say it's not their fault and I shouldn't get angry at them. They're not doing it on purpose to upset me.' She gave a heavy sigh, which Lizzie echoed. It wasn't Margot and Luc's fault they'd upset her so much either, but it didn't stop it hurting. 'Sometimes life sucks,' Amélie declared before biting into the apple.

Lizzie glanced at her then turned her gaze first to the chateau, and then to the direction of Luc's vineyard. She took an apple from the picnic basket too. 'Unfortunately, Amélie, sometimes it really does.'

Chapter Seventeen

When Monday morning rolled around, Lizzie was incapable of being in the same room as Luc without feeling debilitating embarrassment or anger at how he'd made a fool of her. She decided the best thing was to work in separate areas of the house. That didn't include Sarah's study. She still wasn't quite ready to go in there, but there was plenty Luc could be getting on with while she tackled one of the bedrooms.

Lizzie bit into a croissant, ripping it angrily from her mouth as she moaned on at Gary the goat who'd decided to join her for breakfast.

'I just don't get it. Why would he invite me to the party, not to mention dance with me the way he did, when all the time he's been with Margot?' She took another bite and raged through the mouthful of food. 'I mean, what's with that? Is he a cheater or did I misread all the signals?' She sighed, tossing her head back. 'I must have misread *all* the signals. He probably pitied me knowing the way I feel about him. Felt about him, I should say, because clearly nothing's going to happen now. I mean, he seemed so honest. I must have imagined that whole nearly-kiss thing in the living room, and the dance can't have meant anything at all. Maybe I'm just desperate and seeing things that aren't there?'

Gary didn't respond.

'Is that it? I'm sex-starved and still so broken from the breakup with Will I'm imagining romantic gestures and flirting when really, it's nothing. That's a depressing thought.'

A few minutes later, Luc knocked at the open kitchen door and walked in. He smiled and though she didn't want it to, her body gave its usual fizz at the sight of him. Why did he always have to look so good? Not that it mattered. It was definitely a look but don't touch situation now.

'*Bonjour*, Lizzie. Ah, this is the goat you've been telling me about? I cannot believe I haven't met him until now. I was starting to think he was a figment of your imagination.'

'Yep. This is Gary,' she said, feeding him some of her croissant. She wasn't that hungry anymore. A hostile note had penetrated her voice where her bruised feelings were forcing themselves to the surface and she pushed them away.

Luc chuckled. 'Where has he come from?'

'Amélie thought he might belong to a farm on the other side of the chateau.'

Lizzie watched carefully for a reaction from him at the mention of Margot's daughter. She hadn't expected him to fall to his knees admitting that he and Margot were a couple, but there wasn't even a flicker of an eyelid. He petted the goat, who had become a lot more friendly since

Lizzie had stopped chasing him around the chateau. She did the same when he came to her, though her eyes kept shifting towards Luc.

'Ow!' Lizzie pulled her hand back as an eager Gary had tried to lick the smell of croissant from her fingers but had nibbled her instead. 'Gary, no!' She waggled her finger at him. 'No. Bad goat. Bad!'

'Lizzie, you know he's not a dog, don't you?'

'Yes,' she said, trying hard not to laugh at his tone. 'I am aware of that. But he needs to know he can't just try and eat people's fingers.'

'That is true. Gary, bad goat.' He mimicked her gesture from moments before and Lizzie repressed a giggle. 'So, what are we working on today?'

He took a croissant from the basket on the table and then leaned against the sink. They had been having breakfast together since starting work on the chateau.

'Would you mind carrying on with the windows? I was going to crack on upstairs.'

'Oh? Yes, sure, if that is what you want.'

'Yes,' she said, more confidently than she felt. Truth be told, she'd rather have continued to work with Luc. She'd much rather she'd never seen him and Margot cosying up in the vineyard and would love to turn the clock back and live in the buzz of Saturday night forever. But life didn't work like that, and she had a chateau to get ready for sale. Perhaps it was a good thing her crush was being well and truly squashed; it could never have worked out between them anyway, with her returning to England. 'I thought it would speed things up a bit.'

'Very well. I might need some help though. Some of the panes are quite big.'

'Of course.' She smiled, hoping it was convincing. 'No problem.'

Seeing Luc's face, which for some reason showed hurt as well as surprise, she softened a little. 'Just give me a shout when you need me.' The smile he gave her made her even sadder knowing it would never mean more than friendship. She'd never expected to feel this way so soon after Will. Lizzie stood. 'Right, out you go, Gary. You're not staying here and eating the chairs. I've got work to do.' She gently shoed the animal outside. Once she'd shut the back door, she said, 'You know where everything is, don't you? I'm going to get started.'

Shuffling past Luc, who hadn't even finished his breakfast, she skedaddled upstairs to hide.

Later that afternoon, Luc's friend, the roofer, pulled into the driveway and climbed out of his car. Lizzie saw him arrive from the bedroom window and ran downstairs where Luc met her in the hallway.

'Ready?' he asked as they stood side by side, facing the closed front door.

'Ready.'

Was it her imagination or had his hand touched hers? It could only have been an accident, but it still sent her pulse racing. The night at the dance had changed everything for her. She'd suddenly realised she was capable of feeling again: real feelings, not just the pain, hurt and occasional anger that had existed since Will left her. She was edging ever closer to being almost ready to open her heart to the prospect of someone new. She still couldn't imagine diving headfirst into a new relationship, but she couldn't deny something had happened inside her when she'd danced with Luc, even though that relationship was clearly a dead end. It was progress at least. However painful.

The heavy knock on the front door startled her from her wandering thoughts and she rushed forward to open it.

The man in front of her didn't look like the owner of a construction firm, he looked like some sort of gangster. His fingers were covered in skull rings and his arms were tattooed from the backs of his hands all the way up to the edge of his T-shirt sleeve.

Lizzie greeted him and stepped out into the sunshine. The two men, who were actually about the same age, hugged like old friends.

'This is Sébastien,' Luc said. 'We have been friends a long, long time.'

'A long time,' his friend echoed in perfect English. 'You are Lizzie! I've heard a lot about you.' Luc looked away and Lizzie felt her cheeks burn. 'It is a pleasure to meet you.'

'And you. So, this is the chateau and that's my terribly leaky roof.' She pointed to the roof, not that she needed to. He was already peering at it and frowning.

'Hmm. May I look around the outside?'

'Sure. I'll leave you to it – I'll be in the kitchen if you need me.'

Sébastien went off with Luc and Lizzie made her way to the kitchen to make a cup of tea. About ten minutes later, Luc joined her.

'I left him to get on. He is getting his ladders and just seeing them made me feel sick.'

She wanted to laugh at his joke but the nerves balling in her stomach wouldn't let her.

Half an hour later and Sébastien had finished. Lizzie handed him a cup of coffee. Luc already had one and was nervously shifting from foot to foot.

'So, Sébastien, how bad are we talking?'

'*Excusez-moi*, *mademoiselle*, but I'm afraid it is very bad. The entire roof needs replacing as well as some of the roof joists. It is a very expensive job. I hate to tell you how much but . . .'

Lizzie thought she might pass out, the sum had so many digits. The shock must have registered on her face as Luc took a step towards her while Sébastien began to study the floor. It wasn't his fault, of course, he hadn't damaged the roof, but it did leave her in a pickle.

'Is there any way we can do small areas of the roof at a time? Then I won't have to pay it all in a lump sum.'

'Yes and no,' he replied, tipping his head from side to side. 'We could do the turrets separately, but when it comes to the main part of the house, as we have to replace the joists, we will have to do very large areas. It is impossible to do only one small area then another.'

'Yes,' she said with a sigh. 'I suppose that makes sense. I have to be honest with you, Sébastien, I just can't afford it. I—' She shook her head. 'I don't really know what I'm going to do.' And that wasn't in any way an understatement. 'I'm sorry to have wasted your time.'

'Not at all, *Mademoiselle*.'

She showed Sébastien out, who to his credit wasn't at all annoyed.

All the resolve and resolute spirit she'd shown so far began to dissolve. What was she going to do now? Not only could she not afford to fix the roof, it would also mean an end to her regular feature. There was no point in doing the electrics or decorating anymore until the roof was fixed and if she couldn't afford to do that, her only option was to sell it. Even if it meant selling it to knock it down. Then it wouldn't be long until she had nothing to write about. At least, not anything her readers would actually like to hear. The prospect of all her work so far being wasted as selling seemed again to be the only option was like a giant punch in the gut that sent her backwards. Right back to where she started.

She rounded the kitchen door, trying not to cry. Luc immediately jumped forward, placing a hand on her shoulder.

'It will be okay, Lizzie. We can figure something out. Maybe you could get a loan from the bank or . . . something.'

The yearning she normally felt when his skin touched hers failed to materialise. Whether it was pure devastation at the end of her French adventure or the thought of his belonging to Margot, her body couldn't muster the energy to tingle at his touch. She grabbed a tissue from her pocket and wiped her nose.

'There's nothing I can do. I don't think I can get a loan for that amount of money. It would take me the rest of my life to pay it off. The wage from the magazine isn't enough to cover it and I'd ringfenced that for the electrics. Even if I did put that towards it, how will I pay for the next job, and the one after that? This place is a money pit and I've run out.'

She plonked herself into a chair and Luc knelt down in front of her. His hand covered hers. If only she could allow him to comfort her. She didn't move and instead kept as still as possible.

'Lizzie, I promise, I will help you find a solution. There must be something we can do.'

'Like what?'

Panic flew across his eyes as he failed to come up with anything. 'I – I don't know.'

Lizzie took a deep breath, willing away the remaining moisture from her eyes. It was pointless to carry on with any other tasks after the news they'd just had, and more than anything she wanted to be alone. In an ideal world, Luc would bundle her up in his arms and kiss her until she smiled, then they'd crack open a bottle of his amazing rosé and sit and talk until they had it all worked out, but that wasn't going to happen.

'Why don't you get back to the vineyard, Luc? I need some time to figure out what I'm going to do, and I won't be very good company.'

'I am happy to stay. I can make you tea.'

The kindness in his eyes made her heart leap. Margot was a lucky woman.

'Thanks, Luc, but I'd prefer to just get my head around this on my own.'

Hurt flashed across his features as he stood, but he didn't

argue and gave her a gentle kiss on the cheek before he left. This time, her body did react. Her senses swam with the soft brush of his beard.

Just when things were going well, life, in all its aspects, had decided to throw her under the bus. It wasn't fair, and she was right back where she started – with a chateau that couldn't be saved and a heart that was as broken as before.

Chapter Eighteen

Lizzie wandered around the chateau, peering in and out of each room, taking stock of what they'd achieved and what they had left to do. Right now, it didn't feel like they'd achieved much. She knew that wasn't strictly true, but her hopes were so dashed, and her dreams laid so low, it was hard to find the positive side. Sarah would have told her to buck up. So would her mum. But there was bucking up in the face of adversity and then there was deluding yourself that everything was okay when, in fact, it was not.

Suddenly Chateau Lavande felt overwhelmingly large, and Lizzie longed to escape outside into the sunshine. She grabbed her hat and shut the door on her troubles. The sun shone, as always, and the sky was a spotless cerulean blue but it didn't make her feel better. Even the beautiful scenery of dark, deep mountains and lush lavender fields couldn't lift her spirits. The further from the chateau she got, the more she hoped to find some optimism, but as she reached the town, enjoying the shade of the beautiful stone buildings, it still hadn't materialised.

Lizzie paused at a crossroads, deciding which way to turn. There were parts of the town she hadn't explored yet and so much more to discover, but her feet carried her towards Sylvie's house. Lizzie stopped at the patisserie on her way and bought cakes, hoping that would make up for her impromptu arrival.

She pressed the bell as the sun prickled the skin on the backs of her arms and legs, and waited patiently. Just as she thought she might take a wander around town and see if Sylvie was out shopping, the door opened.

'Élisabeth! How wonderful to see you. Are you all right? Come in, come in.'

The narrow hallway was dark and cool, and Lizzie stepped inside gratefully. Following Sylvie down the short corridor, they then turned left into a bright and sunny living room. The shutters and windows were open, and a gentle breeze fluttered the gauzy curtains.

'Have you recovered from the party the other night?' Sylvie asked. 'It was a wonderful evening, was it not?'

'It was.' Dancing with Luc had definitely been wonderful. Lizzie's heart sank at the thought of him.

'Luc is a kind man, don't you think?'

A slight twinkle had come into Sylvie's eyes. She couldn't know about Margot either, which confirmed Lizzie's suspicions they were keeping it quiet because of Amélie.

'Yes, he's very kind,' Lizzie replied, her face impassive, giving nothing away.

'What has brought you to visit me?'

'I just fancied some air and found myself in town, so I thought, why don't I come and have that chat with Sylvie. As long as it's okay with you, that is? I don't want to keep you from whatever you need to do this afternoon.'

She pursed her lips. 'I am an old lady. I do nothing most afternoons. Maybe some cooking if I feel like it, or some gardening. Henri has gone for a walk. He always goes in the afternoons. It keeps him fit, but it is too hot for me today. I prefer to stay inside and I'm glad I did.'

'I brought us some pastries. There's one for Henri too.'

'He'll have earned it by the time he gets back. Sit down and I will make a drink. Then we can talk.' Sylvie held out her hand and Lizzie gave her the small box.

After a few moments of activity in the kitchen, Sylvie returned with a tray with a bottle of pastis and a carafe of water. She placed it on the small coffee table between them and handed her a glass along with a small plate with one of the pastries on it.

'So, why did you need to escape the chateau?'

'That's not quite what I said.'

'Your face tells me it is true. What is it? What has happened?' Sylvie sipped her drink and waited.

Lizzie scratched her forehead. There didn't seem any point in pretending. Everyone would know soon enough. 'I've got a quote to fix the roof. Well, not fix it, replace it, because apparently it all needs to come off, and I can't afford it. I can't even make half of it. I've no idea what I'm going to do, and I don't mean to be dramatic, but it feels like it's the end of my time at the chateau. If I can't replace it, it's only going to get worse and it'll need to be knocked down.'

Sylvie gasped. 'That cannot happen. The chateau is beautiful and has been there for generations. It is so sad to hear.' She picked up one of the tiny plates and took a bite of her fruit tart. The pastry was heavy with fresh summer strawberries that glistened under a sweet glaze. Lizzie took a bite of hers too, but the delicious flavour couldn't lift her spirits. 'There must be something we can do,' Sylvie said.

'I don't know what. There's either money or there's not. I can't just magic up more and it's only going to get more expensive the longer I wait to have it done. When it starts raining there'll be more damage. It does rain here, doesn't it? I've never actually been here in winter.'

Sylvie chuckled. 'It rains sometimes, yes. Now I know why you were so sad.'

You know half of it, thought Lizzie. She wasn't going to tell her about Luc and Margot or her feelings for the Gallic god.

'Anyway,' Lizzie said. 'Let's talk about Sarah. Tell me more about her adventures. I could do with some cheering up. You told me about the Orient Express and your friend mentioned an archaeological dig in Greece. Where else did she go?'

'I remember she also took a trip to a rainforest somewhere. I wish I could remember the exact location. She talked about seeing monkeys, snakes, and spiders as big as your head. She really wasn't afraid of anything. I could never do that; I'm terrified of them all.'

A natural storyteller, Sylvie captured Lizzie's imagination. Sarah had been extraordinarily brave, taking herself off to wherever she felt like going. A true free spirit.

'But always she came home to France,' Sylvie said. 'She loved the chateau and the town, and we all loved her.' She cast a glance at Lizzie from the corner of her eye, but Lizzie couldn't face asking more about Guillaume.

Sylvie continued talking and with their drinks all but drunk, she sat back in her chair, only a few crumbs left from her fruit tart on the tiny plate. She tapped her finger against her lips. 'I cannot believe the chateau roof cannot be fixed somehow. We all loved Sarah and she was so generous to the town. She was always throwing parties and inviting everyone, or when we got together in town, she would buy bottles and bottles of wine for the tables. She was part of the community. We cannot let the chateau fall apart.'

'So that was where her money went instead of fixing the dodgy wiring.' A smile crept onto Lizzie's lips. It wasn't what she would have done but it certainly seemed a lot more fun. She was sure that if Sarah was there now, sitting with her and Sylvie, she would be laughing and saying she regretted nothing. Lizzie could almost hear her.

Sylvie suddenly shot forwards, sitting upright in her chair. 'I have an idea.'

'Oh?'

'Yes. We should hold a fundraiser for the chateau roof.'

'What?' Lizzie felt her mouth fall open. 'No, we can't. I can't ask other people for money to fix the roof. That's not . . . right.' Sylvie scowled. 'It's a lovely idea, Sylvie, but I'm sorry, I just can't do it. I can't rely on handouts.'

'Why not? People crowdfund things all the time. Books they wish to publish, games they wish to make. People ask for money for their education, all sorts of things.' She crossed her arms over her chest like a petulant child and Lizzie burst out laughing.

'How do you know about crowdfunding?'

'I am old and French, Élisabeth. I am not senile or stupid.'

'No, you're definitely not. But don't you think it's a bit . . . I don't know . . . cheeky?'

'Not at all! Why should you not ask for help if you need it? We could have music and dancing. A concert in the grounds would be a wonderful idea, don't you think? We can sell tickets or if you don't like that idea, you can ask for donations. Then you don't have to feel so bad, do you?'

'But Sylvie—'

'No buts. It is a great idea. Even if I do say so myself.'

Could it work? Was it right to even try? Lizzie still felt like she should be doing it all herself and asking people to donate to the chateau's restoration felt wrong. As much as she wanted Sylvie's solution to be perfect, a niggling at the back of her mind wouldn't accept it.

A thick silence enveloped them, and Lizzie was about to make her excuses and leave when Sylvie said, 'Are you worried people won't donate because of Sarah and Guillaume?' The question hit her like a physical blow and her mind froze, leaving her unable to answer. 'Because whatever you may remember, Élisabeth, they were in love and it was a very long time ago.'

'But he was married, Sylvie.' The words were out of her mouth before she could stop them, the argument she'd had with Sarah replaying in her mind. 'She was having an affair with a married man.' Lizzie almost mentioned the letter Sarah had written and asked her to deliver but managed to stop herself. She had no idea if Sarah had told Sylvie about it and she didn't want to have to explain it now. 'The town must have hated her.'

'Oh, pfffft!' Indignation lit Sylvie's eyes with a fire that belied the gentle grandmother exterior. She and Sarah must have been quite a force to be reckoned with back in the day. 'Love is not so simple, *chérie*, surely you must know that by now.'

Lizzie's thoughts should have run to Will, to waiting for him to arrive on their wedding day, to the searing pain of hearing her dad tell the family and friends that had gathered for their special day that the groom wasn't coming. Those are the things she should have thought of. But the only face she saw was Luc's, followed swiftly by Margot's.

'But she broke up a marriage, Sylvie. Her free-spirited nature didn't have any boundaries then, did it? And it should have.'

'Love is complicated, *chérie*, and rarely does it run smoothly. Yes, Guillaume was married. Should they have had an affair, no they should not, but they were in love and sometimes, love is the only thing that matters. It was not their fault that they fell in love when he happened to be married to someone else.'

She said it so nonchalantly. 'But his poor wife,' Lizzie countered.

'She had affairs of her own, Élisabeth. She was not such a poor woman as you imagine. It was not a happy marriage from the start and Sarah too suffered after he passed away. Her grief was stronger than many of us imagined. She was not her usual self for a very long time.'

Was that partly why Sarah had never tried to get in touch with Lizzie? Lizzie knew she'd allowed her life to get in the way, squashing down the urge to try and reconnect with the excuse that she was too busy, or that Sarah hadn't tried either. Had there been a time when she'd been upset too? It was still no excuse for cheating and Sarah should never have dragged Lizzie as a teenager into it. Speaking as someone who was ninety-nine per cent sure Will had cheated before the wedding, Lizzie wanted to argue but it felt disrespectful somehow. With all her years behind her, Sylvie knew a lot more about life, and love too.

Lizzie had always thought Sarah wild and impulsive. Her fun-loving nature had frightened her as a shy and awkward teenager. Though she couldn't forgive Sarah, Sylvie was right that love was complicated. She had continued to love Will even after their relationship had ended. It wasn't something she could just stop doing, even though he'd seemed to. And now, her feelings for Luc were complicated. She wasn't ready to love again but she felt something for him, and he was with Margot. Complicated was an understatement.

'I know it was hard for you that Sarah was the type to

do what she wanted. Her impulsiveness scared me sometimes. But she was kind too and she loved you in her way.'

A sudden memory of Sarah chasing her through the fields unfurled in her mind. Maybe she had when Lizzie had been little, but Lizzie growing up had complicated things. They were just too different.

'Sarah could not help following her heart. It was not always for the best, but perhaps we could all learn a lesson from her, hmm?'

'I suppose,' Lizzie conceded, eager for the conversation to end. She searched for something to say. Some way to end the discussion that drove away the horrid atmosphere settling on them.

'I'm sorry I brought it up,' Sylvie said gently. 'I didn't realise it was still so difficult for you.'

'I think—' Lizzie cut herself off before gathering strength to continue. 'I think it's being back at the chateau and hearing all your stories.' There was a lot more to Sarah than the one thing she remembered. 'I feel like I wasted so much time being angry at her. I would've liked to have known her better.'

'She would have liked to have known you, *chérie*. She missed you coming back but I don't think she knew how to ask you to visit.'

With a sad goodbye, Lizzie left, her head ringing with the revelations Sylvie had made – only to bump into Margot in the street outside.

'Lizzie! It is so good to see you. I was just going to come and visit.'

A coldness washed over Lizzie's skin, but she smiled and greeted Margot as she always had. 'Hello, Margot. How was Paris?'

'Paris? Ah, *j'adore*! But we came back early.'

'You did?' Lizzie asked, picturing the vineyard, Margot and Luc so close together.

'*Oui*. I had something to do.'

Luc? Lizzie asked herself then chastised her brain for being unkind. 'Where's Amélie today?'

'Oh, she is around somewhere. She likes to go off on her own now she is so grown up. Shall we go and have a coffee? Surely you have time?' Her hopeful gaze made Lizzie feel extraordinarily guilty. She was being so nice, as usual, but Lizzie just couldn't. Not today.

'Sorry, I'm absolutely snowed under right now. I've got the article to write and – and things to do. Loads on my plate at the moment.'

'Of course. I understand. Perhaps I can call by tomorrow?'

'It might be better if I call you. Or we can meet in town or something?' Margot's eyebrows rose. 'The place is such a mess I'm worried someone will have an accident if they come in. I nearly fell down the stairs yesterday there's so much crap around.' She laughed, but Margot didn't. It was clear she didn't believe a single word Lizzie was saying. Why should she? Lizzie was without doubt the worst liar in the history of the world.

'Of course,' Margot said, warily. 'Just let me know when you're free.'

Lizzie nodded and moved around her to carry on her

way. When she glanced back, Margot was glued to the spot, watching her. Lizzie waved, but obviously Margot knew she'd been avoiding her. All Lizzie could do was hope she didn't know why.

Chapter Nineteen

For the next few days Lizzie pottered around the chateau. Luc had asked several times about the next job or suggested they sit together and come up with a solution to the roof, but each time Lizzie had rebuffed him. She didn't want to offend him or fall out, but it was important she distanced herself. Today though, Luc had come back to help. There were some things she just didn't know how to do and needed his skills for, but the solution she'd come up with was to work as far away from him as possible. Busying herself in the bedroom, a safe distance from him, Sylvie's suggestion continued to ricochet around her head.

Organising a concert sounded like a wonderful idea, but it was more work than Lizzie could handle on top of trying to sort through Sarah's things, and she still couldn't quite believe that anyone would want to help her. The town couldn't have approved of Sarah and Guillaume's affair. She'd broken up a marriage after all. Sylvie had said it hadn't been a particularly happy one but that didn't excuse Sarah's actions. In a small town like this, and her being the English outsider, they must have hated her for it. Yet they spoke kindly of her, and it forced Lizzie to question if she had just assumed they wouldn't forgive her when in fact, she was the only one who hadn't.

Lizzie came down the stairs with a black sack full of wallpaper she'd stripped from the walls. Tinny music sounded from a small radio Luc had plugged in, the French singer pounding out lyrics in a melodic accent. He was busy in the hall, fixing a floor tile that had broken in half and was beginning to stick up. It really was a beautiful floor now it was cleaned up. Well, it was cleaner. It wouldn't be sparkling until they stopped trampling all over it in dirty, dusty boots but its potential was now showing.

'You've been busy,' he said, happily. 'Are you making progress?'

He smiled up at her and her mind willed for things to be different. She hadn't thought when she'd arrived that her feelings could change in such a short amount of time. Though it had in fact been nearly five months since she'd been jilted. At one point she'd thought she'd never recover, but here she was, living a new life. For a while at least, perhaps returning to England would be best for everyone.

'Yep,' Lizzie replied brightly, trying to keep her voice light. 'A few more bedrooms to go but we can only take it one room at a time.' As he watched her, she felt the need to distance herself again and made an ostentatious show of reading her watch. 'Listen, you've been here since eight o'clock, why don't you head off?'

'Really? But I'm not finished.'

'Yeah, go. It'll wait until tomorrow. It's not going anywhere, is it? And you can't go neglecting the vineyard. That is your actual job after all.'

He stood, wiping his hands on his baggy jeans. Somehow Luc managed to look good in everything. If Will had worn those he'd have looked like he was dressing in someone else's clothes. Maybe it was because Luc didn't care about his appearance, comfortable in his own skin, whereas Will had always been just a little bit vain.

'Élisabeth, why do I get the feeling you're trying to get rid of me?'

Her cheeks flushed at being caught out. She'd thought she was being so cool about it all. 'I'm not.'

'Every time I have been here recently you have sent me home early.'

'Don't be silly,' she replied, moving around him and entering the kitchen. She threw the sack out the back door where a pile of others were growing. 'I just know you're busy with the vineyard and I don't want to take up all your time.'

That much was true.

Luc followed her and placed his hands on his hips. 'Then why don't you ever want to work with me?'

'I do.' She grabbed the kettle and filled it, eager to avoid his gaze in case her true feelings were written all over her face. 'Honestly.'

'Every time I come, you suggest we work away from each other. Do I smell?' Lizzie turned to see him jokingly sniff his armpits. 'No, I do not smell.' It was so comically out of character that she laughed. He smelled lovely, always, and that was part of the problem. Luc jerked his head up. 'Wait . . . that is it, isn't it? You do not like my work.'

'No!' Her hand shot out. 'No, Luc, I do—'

'That is it! You do not think my work is good enough, but you are too polite to say so.' He scoffed and she abandoned the kettle and moved towards him.

'Luc, no. I promise. I'm not unhappy with your work.'

'Then why are you acting so strangely? I am doing the best I can, Lizzie. I am not an expert. I did tell you that.' He became more agitated, throwing a hand through his hair. He pressed his lips together.

'Luc.' She stepped towards him and placed a hand on his arm, squeezing as tightly as she dared. 'I promise it's nothing to do with you. It's just . . .' She pressed a hand to her forehead and a scrap of damp wallpaper stuck to her skin. Luc stepped closer, his fingers reaching out and gently removing it. She was going to pass out. No doubt about it. Lizzie stepped back and took a deep breath. When she looked up, his face had lost all trace of annoyance and his eyes were narrowed with concern.

'What is it, Lizzie?'

She walked back to the kitchen table and sat down. 'Sylvie suggested something to help me, but I don't know what to do.'

'About what?'

'The roof.'

He joined her at the table and clasped his hands together.

'She had this idea for a sort of fundraiser. I don't know exactly what it would be. She said about music and dancing – some kind of concert – but I just don't know.'

He unclasped his hands, casting them wide. 'But that is a wonderful idea. Do you not think so?'

'I'm just not sure.'

'Why not?'

For various reasons, but the first one that came to mind she couldn't say out loud. She'd sound like a teenager.

'There must be a reason, Lizzie.'

To hell with it. She might as well say it. 'What if no one comes? I know it sounds stupid, but I don't want to end up a laughing stock where I put on a massive show and no one turns up.'

'Why wouldn't people come? We all loved Sarah and we love our country, our history, of course we want the chateau to survive. It's a beautiful building that we do not want to lose.'

'But why would anyone want to help me? People are going to give *me* money to fix *my* roof. Why would they do that when they have their own bills to pay and maybe their own roofs to fix.'

'Because people are kind. At least around here they are. Busy cities not so much. People there are cold and isolated, but here, we are all together. The chateau has always been important to the town. And it's not as if you are asking people to donate hundreds of euros. You are asking them to buy tickets to a concert and have a nice evening here rather than at home.'

'Sylvie suggested asking for donations, but I still can't see that raising enough money.'

'Maybe there is something else we can do?'

'Like what?'

He shrugged. 'I don't know yet.'

She sighed and tapped her fingers on the tabletop.

'Is this to do with Guillaume?' he asked gently. She stopped drumming. 'When his name was mentioned at the party, I knew something must have happened.'

Such a direct question was difficult to dodge, and Lizzie wasn't even sure she wanted to. Part of her longed to tell him. She valued his opinion and wanted him to understand why she hadn't seen Sarah in such a long time, but she couldn't go into every detail now. She'd have to stick to the bare facts.

'Sarah and Guillaume had an affair, years ago.'

'Ah,' he said calmly. 'She never told me that but then people here often assume you know things just because they are common knowledge.' Lizzie looked at him quizzically. 'I used to come around a couple of times a week to see her. Just to talk and have breakfast or lunch. I liked to check on her.'

So when she'd thought his arriving and sitting down had spoken of routine, she'd been right.

'It all came out when I was fifteen and staying here for the summer,' Lizzie continued. 'That's why we fell out. Why I never came back. She . . .' She struggled to give any more detail. Luc took her hand, urging her to go on. 'She asked me to . . .' But no matter how hard she tried, she couldn't speak about what had happened next. Sarah's reaction, the letter, her refusal. 'I just can't imagine the town will want to help me, knowing that my relative split up a marriage.' She reigned in her emotions, feeling a coldness wash over her. The same detachment she'd used for years whenever thoughts of Sarah sprang up. 'Sylvie said it wasn't a happy marriage but that's no excuse, is it? Everyone must have hated her, and cheating is cheating.'

'I agree cheating is never the answer and can never be condoned, but as you say, it was fifteen years ago. Sadly, Guillaume has gone, but from what I heard, he and Sarah were perfectly friendly before he died. They certainly were whenever I saw them. Yes, his wife did leave him, but she is perfectly happy now too, I think.'

'Sylvie said she'd had affairs as well, but that doesn't make it right, does it? God—' She lifted her eyes to the ceiling and seeing the state of it, quickly dropped them again. 'I don't want to sound judgemental. I just think you should end a relationship before you start a new one, you know?'

'I agree and I am glad to hear it.'

What had he meant by that? If he hadn't been with Margot, she would have sworn there was something more. Some deeper meaning to his words. But there couldn't be.

'Life is complicated, Lizzie, and we cannot always know why other people do the things they do, even when they hurt us.' His eyes told her he was speaking about something specific, but she couldn't tell what. 'I do not think the town will refuse to come to a fundraiser because Sarah once had an affair with a man from the village many, many years ago. The town never hated Sarah. None of us did. We all liked her, loved her *bon vivant* way of being, and we love the chateau too. It has been here for longer than any of us and we do not want to see it fall to ruin.'

'You think people will come if I organise something?'

'I do.' The firmness of his voice and the force of his nod were so powerful she felt her own confidence rise.

'I'm not sure asking for donations will raise enough money.'

'Then what else can we do?'

Lizzie glanced around the kitchen. Seeing the boxes piled at the end of the room, some of them containing Sarah's souvenirs, she had an idea. 'What about an auction?'

'An auction?'

'Yes! I can auction off some of Sarah's souvenirs. Surely someone would want some of them. They're not all stuffed camels. There are some amazing pieces here.'

'We could ask others to donate too,' Luc said, leaning forward. 'I'd be happy to donate something.'

'A case of wine perhaps?'

He shook his head. 'I was thinking more like a day's work on someone's house or something like that.'

'That would definitely raise some money. But are you sure? Wouldn't it be easier to offer a case of wine?'

'Easier yes, but not half as much fun.'

'You really prefer working on houses than running the vineyard, don't you?'

'I do. A home is a sanctuary. It is a gift to help someone make that for themselves.'

Lizzie smiled at Luc, and he didn't look away. No one knew the town better than Sylvie and Luc did, and if they said it was a good idea, then she should probably take their advice.

'Okay,' she replied. 'Let's go for it.'

'And if I may offer one more piece of advice?'

'Shoot. I'm up for all the help I can get right now.'

'You should talk to Margot. You said you had become friends. She has been an event planner for many years.' Lizzie's mood plummeted. Perhaps she didn't need *that* much help after all. 'Her organisational skills are second to none; she will help you plan everything, and I'm sure she'll be more than happy to do it.'

'I'm sure.'

Lizzie pressed her hand to the back of her neck, squeezing the tense muscles. He was right. Who could be better than Margot? But it didn't mean it wasn't going to be painful working in such close proximity to the two of them. What other choice did she have? The roof needed fixing, and this was the only viable solution she could come up with. Even if the fundraiser didn't cover the entire cost of the roof, it would make it more affordable for her to get a loan to cover the rest. She was just going to have to put her big girl pants on and talk to Margot. The summer wouldn't last forever and when the rains came the chateau would be beyond repair. She had to act now no matter how hard it was.

Chapter Twenty

'So . . .' Margot sipped her espresso, the sun shining off her enormous sunglasses, her glossy hair pinned up in a messy bun with artful strands falling around her shoulders. 'There is a lot to do to organise this event of yours, Lizzie. We will need to get started right away. You will need to decide what of Sarah's you wish to auction, and you will need to get the grounds sorted out for the bands. The grass will need cutting, we need to decide where the bands will play and where the dancefloor will be and—'

'Wow, slow down,' Lizzie said, typing furiously on her phone. 'I can't keep up.'

No wonder Margot was working for a prestigious events firm in Paris – she was clearly at the top of her game. After Lizzie had called Margot and told her about the fundraiser idea, she'd been more than a little keen to help, and though she'd been tense when they'd first met, Lizzie was relaxing again in Margot's company.

When they'd sat down, she'd wanted to ask about Luc. To just blurt out a question about how long they'd been seeing each other and to reassure Margot she hadn't been after her man at the party. Not knowingly anyway. But she couldn't. She didn't want to risk losing Margot as a friend and there was still every possibility she'd been the one to misread Luc's signals. If there hadn't been a romance there to start with, she'd look even more of a fool than she did already. As they'd talked about the fundraiser, and Margot had been her normal self, Lizzie began to relax. A trace of stiffness lingered in her muscles, but she ignored it, knowing she couldn't change anything. After all, she did want Margot to be happy, Luc too.

'Here,' Margot said, taking a plastic wallet from her bag and handing it to Lizzie. 'I have already listed everything and there is a provisional timetable at the back. I thought it would be helpful. I think having the fundraiser in four weeks will give us enough time to organise everything.'

'You're amazing.'

Margot smiled warmly. 'I know you have a lot going on with the chateau and writing your articles.'

'Don't remind me,' Lizzie groaned. The next one was due any day now, but she hadn't even started a rough outline. Until a day or two ago, she hadn't known what to write about, but now the fundraiser idea was settled that had to be the main topic.

They were sat at the tiny café Margot had taken Lizzie to when they'd had lunch. Birds hopped in and out of the nearby trees, sneaking crumbs from the ground before flying off to the safety of their nests. The world was encased in their song and the hustle and bustle of tourists out shopping. She felt so at home here and contentedly took a bite of her *pan bagnat*. It was outstanding and Lizzie could see why it was Amélie's favourite. The fresh, tasty tuna, the salty olives and the creamy egg yolk all melded together in an explosion of flavour.

'I'm sorry, but this is incredible,' Lizzie said, pointing to her sandwich.

'Almost as good as the *fleurs de courgettes farcies*?' The tip of Margot's right eyebrow was visible just above her enormous sunglasses.

'Definitely on a par. Everything I've eaten here has been amazing.'

'The freshest ingredients make all the difference. The food is what I miss when I'm away and what I enjoy when I am home. I love the elegance of Paris, but I also love the simplicity of the food here. I have never tasted a *pan bagnat* as good in Paris.'

'That's praise indeed.'

'Now, back to the list. You said a concert to me on the phone. What type of music?'

'I don't really know.' Lizzie wiped her mouth with the napkin. The deeply filled roll was so full of juicy ingredients, she didn't want to embarrass herself with drips down her chin. 'When I thought about the types of things we could do, I stupidly thought the simplest thing would be a concert with maybe one or two bands. People could bring a picnic, so we won't need chairs—'

'We will need some for those with limited mobility.'

'Yes, of course. I hadn't thought of that.'

'You would have,' Margot replied, kindly. 'I'm just used to thinking of these things, that's all.'

'What sort of music do people around here like?'

Margot took a sip of her coffee. Her burgundy nails stood out against the white of the tiny ceramic cup. Lizzie eyed her own chipped and broken nails. 'As there are a lot of older people, something traditional, maybe even classical?'

'Wouldn't that require a huge orchestra?'

'Not necessarily. We can see what is nearby. I've seen concerts with only four instruments.'

'Okay. What about something jazzy as well?'

'Ah, we do love jazz. That would go down well, and maybe something a bit more pop-ish for the younger ones? We could have a mixture.'

'That sounds great,' Lizzie replied. She was beginning to like the sound of the fundraiser, regardless of whether it raised any money for the roof or not.

'So, tell me about your article.' Margot picked up her knife and fork and tucked into her salade niçoise. She'd opted for something different to the courgette flowers too, and Lizzie had mentally added it to the list of dishes she still wanted to try before she went home. The idea of returning to ready meals or her standard beans on toast left a heaviness in her stomach and she pushed the thought away so it wouldn't spoil her lunch.

'I haven't written a single word yet so I'm seriously behind. I should probably write it this evening so I can let it sit before I submit it.'

'Is that what you do? You write it and leave it. You don't send it off straight away?'

'No. God, no,' Lizzie shook her head, her eyes so wide Margot laughed. 'My editor would be appalled if she saw my first draft. I always end up moving things around, changing words; sometimes I even totally re-write it.'

'That is very interesting.'

She'd missed Margot and even though Lizzie was a tad jealous of her relationship with Luc, she didn't want to lose her friendship. Margot was so genuinely interested in other people, kind and helpful, Lizzie considered herself lucky to know her. She couldn't believe she'd risked ruining their friendship by pushing her away for something that wasn't her fault. We can't always help who we fall for and, as everyone kept reminding her, life is complicated. She'd just have to forget about Luc as she had done Will. Even if it was easier said than done.

'What are you writing about this time?'

'I'm writing about the roof and the fundraiser. The planning of it anyway. I think my editor will like the cliff-hanger for the readers as to whether it's successful or not. I'm not so keen, but . . .'

'Of course it will be successful! I am helping you. It cannot be anything else.' Lizzie laughed. 'I know, I know, I sound full of myself, but I know how good I am at my job, and I know this town. It will definitely be a success.'

'You don't sound full of yourself. It's nice to hear a woman being proud of her achievements. So often we feel like we have to play things down. Silly really.'

'It is silly, and I do not see why we should do it. I tell Amélie all the time she should be happy to stand up and say this is who I am, and this is what I am good at.'

'You're a very good role model.'

'I do not know about that.' She dipped her head and her shoulders slumped. 'The end of my marriage was hard on Amélie and she is very angry with me sometimes, I think.'

This again explained why Margot wasn't being open about her relationship with Luc. 'She's nearly a teenager. I'm sure her hormones are going wild and sometimes we're angry with the ones we love because we know they'll still love us afterwards. She can show you how she feels, knowing you won't ever leave her. You'll always love her no matter what.'

A tightness strangled Lizzie's throat and her thoughts ran to Sarah. Sarah had loved her once and that day Lizzie had come upon her in a moment of high emotion. She understood it more now. She'd had plenty of those in the aftermath of her breakup with Will. Back then, she'd only been a teenager and her initial reaction, she still felt, had been justified. But after? When she'd hit twenty, twenty-five? There was no doubt about it, she should have tried before now to come back.

'I hadn't thought of it like that,' Margot replied, her cheeks lifting. 'That is a wonderful way to think about it. But I'm not sure it will help me keep my temper when she is being rude.'

'Maybe not, but she loves you very much.'

They continued eating and Lizzie's attention ran to the list Margot had given her. She flipped the pages over. 'This list is very long, Margot. Unnervingly long.'

'Do not worry, not all the tasks are for you. I will do all

the things in red, and Sylvie wishes to do all the things in green. It will be easier for us to do those as we speak French. That way we can ensure there are no misunderstandings.'

'Good idea.' Lizzie's French was getting better but there was no way she could organise an event with her limited vocabulary. When she'd spoken to Luc the other day, she'd encountered unexpected difficulties with the word squirrel. He hadn't understood her English and her attempt at French had been even more confusing. 'But will Sylvie be okay helping with this? I mean, she's quite old and I know this was her idea, but I don't want her feeling she has to take things on when she should be relaxing.'

'I did try to stop her, but she would not be deterred. She is tiny, like a little bird, but she can be very forceful. I was too scared to argue. But I have only assigned her jobs that involve talking to people and convincing them to come. She will let everyone know what is happening and when. And Henri has agreed to host the auction. He wants to be involved too. Or Sylvie has told him he is going to be involved and he was too afraid to argue too.'

Lizzie laughed heartily. She felt like she hadn't laughed in a long time. Not with a friend anyway.

'We will need to decide on the bands you want as a priority. Violette, who owns the gift shop, her son is in a band, and I hear they are very good. They could work well for the pop songs we want. She said they would love to play, and they do not mind about not being paid.'

'Really? That's so generous. I'll make sure I stop in and say thank you. There was an impromptu party the other night and a couple of people started playing. Do you think that might happen at the fundraiser?'

'Yes, I heard about the party.'

Oh god. Lizzie froze, wishing she'd kept her mouth shut. Had Margot heard about her dancing with Luc? Should she say something? Admit to seeing them in the vineyard together and reassure her nothing had happened, even though she'd wanted it to. Obviously, she'd leave that last part out.

Margot was looking at the list, her knife and fork resting on her plate. Lizzie couldn't tell if she was deliberately not making eye contact or simply reading. There were no obvious signs of annoyance. Was she just being paranoid? Her body tensed but before she could decide what to do, Margot continued.

'I'm sure people will start playing once the concert is over. And then you won't be able to stop them. You and Luc will be responsible for preparing the chateau. As I say, he will need to cut the grass, maybe prune some of the trees so people do not hit their heads all the time and tidy the whole place up.'

As Margot was carrying on as normal, Lizzie tried to do the same. 'It is very overgrown in places. I'm not sure if Sarah even had a lawnmower.'

Margot dismissed Lizzie's comment with a wave of her hand. 'Luc has one of those ride-on petrol lawnmowers. He will be fine. Oh, and could you maybe pick some flowers and have them in pots outside? It will look so pretty.'

'Yes, definitely. Sarah had lots of pots around the front and back of the chateau, but they've become pretty weed-infested. It'll be great to use them.'

'Perfect.' Margot ticked something on her giant list. She reached out and grabbed Lizzie's hand. 'Trust me, Lizzie, this is going to be wonderful. A night to remember.'

'Thank you, and I'm so grateful for everything you're doing. I know how busy you are with work and Amélie. I really can't thank you enough.'

'Ah, you are so sweet, *mon chérie*, but it is my passion. *J'adore* organising things . . . and people.' Lizzie laughed and ate some more of her *pan bagnat*, attempting to make it last, savouring every mouthful. 'Have you heard any more from Will?' Margot asked gently.

'Nothing since my mum told me about his Instagram post with his new girlfriend.'

'Have you been looking?'

'Stalking him, you mean?' Margot nodded and Lizzie took a sip of water. 'After we first broke up, I was doing it all the time, but I have to say, I haven't looked in a while.' She sat back in her chair. 'That's got to be progress, right?'

'It definitely is, and I am so pleased to hear it. You deserve to be happy, Lizzie.'

She did, didn't she? And even with the problems she was facing here, this was the closest she'd come to happy in a long, long time.

Chapter Twenty-One

Lizzie drew her eyes away from Luc (a.k.a. the sexiest man she had ever seen) as he wiped sweat from his brow after lopping another branch from a tree. It was like something from a nineties Diet Coke advert, and it made every nerve in her body sit up and pay attention.

They'd been clearing the grounds as much as possible in preparation for the fundraising concert and as neither of them were great with heights, they were using a pair of loppers she'd found in a shed-like building at the back of the house. While Luc reached what he could (still keeping his feet on the ground), Lizzie collected up the debris and chucked the branches in a pile a little further away.

Thanks to Margot and her contacts, a small four-piece classical band had agreed to play at the concert along with Violette's son. He'd agreed to sing some well-known pop songs though his real love was death metal (a bullet dodged, in Lizzie's opinion), and a jazz quartet were going to perform for the majority of the evening with two one-hour sets. People were certainly getting their money's worth, and with picnics and, undoubtedly, good French wine, it was going to be a wonderful evening.

Over the last two weeks, since her meeting with Margot, Lizzie had continued to stay away from Luc as much as possible, working in different parts of the garden. There had been a few times when she'd had no choice but to work with him, and on those occasions, the heat of the sun mixed with sheer exhaustion had rendered them both pretty much speechless.

After two weeks of seeing him in a tight, sweaty T-shirt and even once with it off, while he doused himself with water revealing a toned torso, she was nearing her limit. The attraction she felt towards him seemed to be part of her DNA, programmed into her. But it wasn't just a physical attraction. Luc was kind and caring and when he chose to be, he was funny. The grumpiness she'd seen at first had faded over time as they'd got to know each other, and she was seeing the real him. A kind man, eager to help others, respected by the town. But whenever her feelings surged, she reminded herself of what she had seen in the vineyard: he was off limits and that was that.

'We should have a break, yes?'

'Hmm?' Lizzie mumbled, suddenly aware that she had been absently staring at Luc.

'I said, we should have a break. We have been working for hours and it's a hot day. You should put on sunscreen.' He pointed to her shoulders. They were turning pink in the sun.

Lizzie placed her hand on her skin, feeling the heat. It might be too late for sunscreen. 'So should you,' she teased.

'I have worked in the sun all my life; my skin is used to it by now. It is not as fair as yours.'

She felt herself blush. 'Okay,' Lizzie replied. 'It'll be nice to head into the shade for a while. What are we going to do with all this wood though?'

'We could have a bonfire the night of the concert if you like. If it starts to get chilly in the evening, it will warm everyone up.'

'Sounds like a good idea. Come on then.'

She led them back through the garden towards the kitchen. With the grass now cut it was much easier to walk, but Lizzie missed the feel of the long blades tickling her legs and the wildflowers that had dotted the green landscape with colour. So far, they had cleared a large field that would house the small, makeshift stage and the picnic area. Chairs, sourced by Margot, were to be placed around the edges for the older people to sit on.

A ruffling in the long grass of an uncleared field alerted Lizzie to something moving her way. She stood on tiptoes to see Gary the goat gambolling around.

Luc stopped at her side. 'The goat is back, I see.'

'I've missed him the last few days. He's a terrible pet really. Like a really surly cat just coming and going as he pleases.'

'Ah, like my cat, Albert.'

'Speaking of which, I haven't seen him for ages. Is he okay?'

'He is fine. He has taken to staying at the farmhouse. He normally does when it is so hot. He likes the cool stones on the floor. Or perhaps Gary scared him off.'

'Gary couldn't scare anyone,' Lizzie replied, remembering how he'd charged and frightened her. 'He's a sweetheart. Come on, Gary. Come on, boy. I've got some croissants left over from breakfast you can have.'

'You know you will only encourage him, don't you?'

She grinned and seeing Luc's bright eyes meet hers, she said, 'Let's have some water.'

In the cool of the kitchen, Luc went to the sink and washed his hands and face while Lizzie fed Gary. He was lingering in the garden, and she threw the croissant out on the grass in front of him. 'Are goats actually allowed to eat bread and things like that?' she asked out loud.

'I don't know. I should think so. Especially as he is a French goat.'

Lizzie laughed and filled two glasses with water as Luc moved away to sit at the table. 'Perhaps I should do an article on goat-keeping. I've got to write my next piece for the magazine. Maybe Gary should feature more prominently. The latest article had such a great response, Hilary – that's my editor – has asked me to write something else for the website. Just a short piece but I need to think about it. She wants something about creating a Provençal garden which, considering all we've done is prune some trees and cut the grass, is going to take me quite a bit of research. I've had loads of other ideas though. This place seems to be great for my creativity.'

'I have been thinking,' Luc said. 'Once the concert is

out of the way and work has started on the roof, we can get Victor back to do the electrics. There is no point in doing too much more on the walls until that is done. He will need to drill holes to feed the wiring through. So, I thought I would begin work on the turrets.'

'The turrets?'

'*Oui*. I have been thinking about them and they are wasted space. You should use them for something. There is entry to them on each floor of the chateau, yes?'

'*Oui*,' she replied without thinking.

'Ah, very good accent.'

'Thank you.' His compliments meant so much to her it was torturous. 'Anyway, you were saying?'

'You should do something with each of the turret spaces. We can replace the floors and use them as storage or something? How about turning one into a library? That would look amazing. We could measure them and share some ideas.'

'That's a good idea. I hate seeing wasted space in a house, even one as large as this, and a library sounds gorgeous. You're really quite good at this, you know.'

'*Merci*.' He drank his water in three large gulps and moved to the sink to fill his glass again.

Lizzie took a drink of her own and enjoyed the sensation of the cold water sliding down her throat. 'And you seem to enjoy it. More than you do being a winemaker. You hardly ever talk about that, but you love to talk about the house.'

'You should give Gary some water as it is so hot. Would you like me to put a bowl out for him?'

Lizzie turned to face him. 'Why do I get the feeling you're changing the subject?'

He shrugged. 'I'm not. I just think Gary might be thirsty.' He searched in the cupboards for a bowl and once he'd located one, showed it to Lizzie. 'Is this okay?'

'Sure.' She watched him fill it and take it out to Gary who eyed him warily and, only as Luc backed away, gratefully began to drink. 'You're definitely not answering my question.'

'What was it again?'

She'd humour him. 'I said, you seem to like working on the chateau more than working at the vineyard. Why is that? I'd have thought it would be a perfect job.'

'Perfect for who?'

'I don't know. Someone who likes being here in Provence. Someone who likes being outside and being active. Someone like you.'

He sat at the table again, toying with his fingers. 'I do enjoy working at the vineyard. It is quiet and peaceful and my boss – the owner – he leaves me alone to do my own thing.'

'But?'

'But sometimes I would like to do something else. I like working on buildings. Fixing them. Bringing them back to life.'

'You'd like to do more of that?'

He pushed his damp hair back from his face and ran a hand down his trimmed beard. 'I don't know. Perhaps one day. But it is too risky. I cannot do it now.'

'Why not?'

Luc raised one shoulder. 'It is just not possible.'

'Why isn't it possible?'

He bristled and she knew she was pushing him, but she wanted to know more. They'd been working together for a while now and it didn't seem too much to ask. 'It just isn't right now.'

'But I don't see why not, I mean, you could always do it alongside running the vineyard. What do you mean it's too risky? Do you mean financially? Or is there something else?' Had he been referring to his relationship with Margot? Would working on a development business jeopardise their relationship somehow. She couldn't see why that would be the case.

'Lizzie,' he said coldly. 'I would prefer not to talk about it.'

Whether it was the heat of the day, her constant longing for him, or simply tiredness, Lizzie felt suddenly frustrated. Why couldn't he tell her? She'd opened up to him about Sarah and Guillaume and they'd shared ideas for the chateau. Why couldn't he open up to her just a little bit? It hadn't been exactly easy for her to do, but she'd managed it.

A silence began to settle, which Lizzie broke. 'I'm not sure I want to waste the turrets with just storage space. A library's a nice idea but I think we should do something more with them.'

'Okay. Like what?'

'I don't know yet.' She hadn't really had any idea but his refusal to share had made her tetchy. 'I'd just like to do something more . . . spectacular with them.' He chuckled and though she normally loved the sound, this time it annoyed her. 'What's so funny?'

'You. You are funny. I don't think spectacular is a very helpful word. What does that mean?'

'I don't know. I just think they could be . . .' She was struggling to come up with anything now. 'They could be a beautiful bathroom. Imagine that? A gorgeous roll-top bath with a view out of one of the turrets.'

'That would require plumbing and a lot of expense and time.'

Why was she even thinking like this? She was only fixing up the chateau enough to get it on the market. Her feelings were so mixed it was difficult to think with any clarity.

'Do you have any pictures?' Luc asked. 'So I can see the type of thing you want.'

She shook her head. 'It doesn't matter.'

'Of course it does. If it is what you want to do, then we should look into it.'

'No, really.' An image of herself closing the door of the chateau for the final time, descending the steps and getting into her car suddenly flew through her brain, sending a cold wave over her skin. 'Let's just leave it.'

'This is your house now, Lizzie.'

No! It was all too much.

'We could look at—'

'Please, Luc. Just leave it. Like you said earlier, I just don't want to talk about it right now. Can you please respect that?'

'Huh, like you did earlier?'

Her head shot back at that remark. She hadn't pushed that hard, had she? 'I was only curious. I've told you lots about me, but you've told me barely anything about you.'

'I am a private person.'

'Yes, I know. Like cheese.' She recounted the mechanic's words and Luc's brow pulled together in confusion. Great. Now she sounded crazy again.

'You think I'm like a cheese? How am I like a cheese?'

This should have been funny, but it wasn't. He was glaring at her, and she pushed her hands against her forehead. 'Oh, it doesn't matter. You're just – just – hard.'

'Hard? Like cold? Unfriendly?'

'Yes.' Seeing the way the words hit made her recoil. 'No, that's not what I meant. I just meant – only at first, but then—'

He stood abruptly. 'I think I know what you meant, Lizzie.'

Luc stormed out of the back door and Lizzie was tempted to run after him, but she needed some space and guessed he did too. Her head bubbled with confusion. Returning home seemed like a pretty good option right at this second. Luc was just too grumpy. At moments like these she wondered why she was so attracted to him. Deep down she knew the answer. It was because underneath it all he was kind, caring, considerate, funny . . . she could go on and on. But he couldn't be hers anyway. He was Margot's. Lizzie's heart gave a heavy thud.

And she shouldn't be thinking about doing spectacular things with the chateau. Why had she let her imagination run away with her? It wouldn't even be hers to do these things with. She had to stick to the plan of selling it and returning to England. If she didn't do that, what other option was there? She couldn't stay. She just couldn't. Her life in London was waiting for her.

Chapter Twenty-Two

With less than a week to go until the concert, the time had come for Lizzie to prepare for the auction. Lizzie gathered all the items of Sarah's she could find and took them to the living room: her base of operations. In the middle of a sea of cardboard boxes, she studied each one, deciding if she wanted to part with it or not. Had she known Sarah better, she might have made her decisions more speedily, but it was difficult when she didn't really know anything about her or where her treasures had come from. All she could do was remember the stories she'd heard the night of the party and on her trips into town and if an item related to one of those, she'd keep it. If there was a story attached, she couldn't bring herself to deposit the item in a cardboard box and give it away. But that didn't mean there wasn't a stack full of things ready to go. While searching the house and finally going into Sarah's bedroom, Lizzie had found some beautiful objects that were clearly not from her travels but that someone might be interested in bidding for. After gathering those up, she was faced with just one more room to enter.

Procrastination had never been Lizzie's favourite pastime. Normally, she was focussed and concentrated on a task until it was done, but today, she stared at the door to Sarah's study. Located at the back of the hallway, in a dark corner behind the staircase, the shadows that normally cooled the house and provided welcome shade from the heat left her with eerie thoughts of ghosts. Sarah's ghost. Her hands hung loosely by her sides and no matter how hard she tried, she couldn't quite summon the energy to lift them and reach for the doorknob. It wasn't the inevitable mess inside that was holding her back. It was that she hadn't been in there since that last day, fifteen years earlier. Lizzie had come back from a walk and found Sarah and Guillaume arguing in the living room.

The raised voices had caught her attention as she'd approached the front door, then the figures had appeared at the windows, arms flailing and gesticulating madly. Sarah had always been passionate and Guillaume, it seemed, was too. Lizzie hadn't had any idea about him or his relationship to Sarah and it had come as more than just a shock. They stood opposite each other, shouting in French, Sarah fluent as if she had never lived in England. Lizzie hadn't made out the words fired at such a rapid speed and nothing in the agitated body language had helped her either. Then all of a sudden, Sarah had said something in a short, staccato sentence and Guillaume had frozen. The moment had stretched on forever until he began to plead, and Sarah turned her back on him, stomping away. Lizzie had run in through the front door to find her in the hallway, but Sarah hadn't given her more than a cursory glance before retreating to her study. Guillaume snuck past her, shamefaced, eyes dropped. Lizzie and Sarah hadn't spoken until sometime later when Sarah had asked her to come into the study. It was then she'd asked her to deliver the letter: a letter to Guillaume's wife. A letter that in Sarah's angry and venomous mood told her of the affair.

That was the thing about Sarah. She could be free-spirited, adventurous and fun but when passionate, she could also be impetuous, even reckless.

Lizzie closed her eyes, the anger that had washed over her then flooding back now in a giant wave. How could Sarah have tried to drag her – a teenage girl – into her grown-up drama? It was so unfair, and Lizzie's refusal to be involved had caused another argument. Sarah had blamed her then and called her ungrateful, listing years of free board and lodging as a reason she should help her. But Lizzie wouldn't. She wouldn't take the letter to the poor woman and rip her world apart. Angry words reverberated off the walls of the small, quiet study as she stood up for herself. It was cruel and she'd have no part in it.

A cold chill ran down Lizzie's arms, lifting the hairs and sending goosebumps over her skin, but her hands remained at her sides. She just couldn't go in there today. After her recent argument with Luc, life was tough enough without reliving painful memories. She backed away slowly and made her way to the kitchen. A cup of tea would make her feel better. It always did.

Just as she entered, a figure appeared in the open doorway, making her jump.

'Amélie! Goodness, you gave me a fright.'

'*Excusez-moi.*' The girl peered around then dropped her eyes.

'Are you looking for someone? Me? Or Luc maybe?' It pained her to ask. Amélie nodded and Lizzie pushed down the sadness. 'I'm sorry, he's not here.' They'd been avoiding each other again: him working in the garden, her in the kitchen planting up the pots Margot had asked for. 'Is he not at the vineyard?'

'No, I just came from there.'

'Maybe he's gone into town? Have you tried calling him?'

'I think his phone is dead. He always forgets to charge it.'

Lizzie knew she couldn't send her away without offering her a drink. It was, as usual, a hot, sunny day and Amélie's cheeks were pink from her walk.

'Would you like something to eat or drink? That sun's so strong you won't want to go chasing him around town. You can wait here if you like and then wander back to the vineyard in a bit.' Warily, Amélie cast her eyes over the kitchen. 'I've got some lemonade in the fridge, and I was just about to break out some chocolate. It feels like a chocolatey kind of day, don't you think?'

Amélie hesitated, then took a step inside. 'Okay. Can I have a lemonade, please?'

'Sure. Come in. Take a seat.'

Amélie did as asked, and Lizzie poured her drink while making herself a cup of tea. When they were sat at the table, with a large slab of chocolate broken into shards, Lizzie said, 'Are you enjoying your summer holiday here?'

'Not really.'

'Why not?' Amélie clammed up and pulled her arms in closer to her sides. 'It must be very different from Paris,' Lizzie continued. 'Funny, isn't it, how we get used to everything being so busy. I always did with London and when I came here for my summer holidays it was like the whole world had just stopped.'

'You live in London?'

Lizzie nodded as she cupped her tea. Though the day was hot, her fingers still felt the chill of being near Sarah's study and difficult memories lingered icy in her system. 'All my life. But I used to hate coming here when I got to about your age. It was fine when I was younger but as soon as I hit maybe eleven, twelve, I started hating it. I never even tried learning French and I wish I had now.'

'There's nothing to do here,' Amélie replied unexpectedly, and Lizzie's heart went out to her. She knew exactly how she felt. The sun shone through the window, sending a beam of light onto the tabletop. Lizzie twisted her fingers, letting the light dance over them.

'I used to say exactly the same thing when my parents dropped me off and I'd be here for weeks with Sarah.'

'Did you like Sarah?'

Why did children always ask such direct questions? Lizzie shifted and took a piece of chocolate. Amélie did the same. 'I don't think I really appreciated what an interesting person she was when I was younger.' She thought of Sylvie's comments about love and life being complicated.

The anger of earlier memories remained, but it was like viewing them through a telescope. 'I think that, sometimes, as kids particularly, we see things as very black and white, and life isn't black and white. There's always a grey area. I would've liked to have known more about her.'

'Did you know she'd been to Timbuctoo?'

'Had she?' Lizzie laughed. 'No, I didn't know that. She'd been to a lot of places that I didn't know about. But she always came back here and I'm beginning to see why.' She looked around the kitchen at the boxes of Sarah's souvenirs still piled at the back, and out the open back door at the pastures of grass with the lavender fields beyond. So peaceful. So calm. 'You must have known Sarah quite well, Amélie.'

'She was nice. We talked a lot sometimes. Especially when *Maman* and *Papa* split up.'

'That must have been hard for you. Is your dad from the town as well? I don't think I've met him yet.' Margot had certainly never said his name or told Lizzie much about him at all.

Amélie frowned. 'Yes you have. That's why I came here.'

'I'm sorry, I don't understand.' Suddenly the penny dropped. 'Luc? Luc is your dad?' She must have raised her voice as Amélie looked slightly scared. The crazy English lady strikes again, Lizzie thought, but to be fair, it had been a bit of a shock. 'Sorry, didn't mean to shout.'

'You didn't know?'

'No, I didn't.'

'That's a bit silly. Everyone knows that.'

Luc was Amélie's dad? He'd never mentioned Amélie

being his daughter and Margot had never said Luc was her ex-husband. Maybe they'd both assumed she knew. The town clearly had.

'*Maman* and *Papa* got divorced when I was six,' Amélie said sadly.

So what had Lizzie seen in the vineyard the other day? Were they getting back together? She wanted to be relieved but couldn't quite match what Amélie had just said with what she herself had seen.

'Sarah used to let me come and play here in the turrets,' Amélie continued dreamily, looking around.

It must have been so hard for the poor little thing, her parents splitting up when she was so young. How heart-breaking for her, and though she acted like a teenager at times, now she sat before Lizzie, she really was nothing more than a little girl trying to understand the world around her.

'Did you pretend to be a princess?' Lizzie asked, remembering her days playing in the turrets.

'Sometimes. Sometimes I was running away from zombies.'

'Ah, the good old zombie game. I used to play that too. There was a great hiding place in that one,' she pointed to the turret on the other side of the kitchen. 'Right near the top. A little nook I'd slide into until they went past then I'd run all the way back down the stairs.'

'The one next to the attic doorway?'

'That's the one.'

The grin that lit Amélie's face told Lizzie she'd done the same thing, but then the smile faded. '*Maman* and *Papa* still don't get on sometimes. Sometimes they fight.'

Lizzie swallowed. She hadn't expected this, hadn't foreseen Amélie confiding anything in her. 'Do you know what about?'

'*Papa* hates that I live in Paris and don't get to see him as much. He hates Paris. He doesn't like the traffic and noise. Mama tries to tell him how boring it is here for me, but he doesn't like the city, he cannot understand what I miss.'

That explained so much, including his city girl comments. He'd been burned before, but it hadn't been a girlfriend, it had involved his wife and daughter. He and Margot were now trying to co-parent their child, and with two such different points of view and personalities, it must be difficult.

How had she not picked up on this before? Amélie was the image of Luc, with blue eyes and dark hair. Unsmiling, as she was now, she was even more like him, and Lizzie wanted to wrap her arms around her. 'It must be hard when they fight. What do you do?'

'I go for a walk.'

'You know you can always come here just like you used to when Sarah was alive. I'd love to know what Sarah told you about her travels and you still need to show me some of your photos. I do understand how you feel, though. I'm afraid when I was younger, I hated being here as much as you do. Time seemed to stand still, and all my friends were at home in London going out together, leaving me behind.'

'Exactly!' Amélie exclaimed. 'Whenever I go back, they have done so much together, and I'm always excluded. They share jokes I don't understand and leave me out.'

'It's hard, isn't it? Children can be cruel like that. But you must have some friends who don't do that sort of thing?'

She shrugged. 'One or two.'

'Then they're your true friends, sweetheart. Real friends wouldn't cut you out. They'd try to make you feel included, even if you had missed out on something.'

'That's what *Maman* says. She said I could invite someone to come down with me, but then I wouldn't be seeing *Papa* as much and he would be upset.'

'Have you asked him though?' Amélie shook her head. 'I'm sure he loves you very much and just wants you to be happy. Maybe he wouldn't mind as much as you think he would.'

Lizzie grabbed another shard of chocolate and moved the packet towards Amélie. She took a piece and popped it into her mouth.

'I wish *Maman* and *Papa* had stayed together in Paris even though they fought all the time.'

'Can I tell you something, Amélie?' Amélie nodded. 'About five months ago I was left standing at the altar in my wedding dress, waiting for my soon-to-be husband to arrive and do you know what? He didn't. He left me there and split up with me the next day.' Amélie gasped. 'For the last few months, I've been feeling just like you. Thinking about how unfair it was, how painful and hurtful and how I wanted everything to go back to the way it was. But really, now I think about it, it was probably for the best. I'm not sure I was as in love with him as I thought I was. And now, if we had got married, I'm not sure how long it would have lasted. It's taken me a while, but I think it's better to be apart and happy than together and unhappy. I'm sure it's the same for your parents. I hadn't realised how unhappy I was until I got here,' Lizzie added, more to herself than anyone else.

Her eyes made their way to the door again, to the view beyond and the heat of the day seeping in. A few wispy clouds drifted lazily in the sky, the freshly cut grass made the fields seem even larger than before and beyond that were the outlines of mountains. It was breathtaking. The chocolate was nearly finished now and never had Lizzie enjoyed a bar as much.

'I suppose they don't fight as much anymore,' Amélie said. 'Only about me not being happy here.'

'I'm sure they understand it's hard for you, Amélie. Have you told them how you feel?'

'Yes, but *Maman* says that *Papa* likes having me here over the holidays otherwise he doesn't get to see me. It makes me feel . . .'

'Guilty?' Amélie nodded slowly and sadly. With all Lizzie was hearing about Sarah, with how long she'd let their estrangement continue, she was used to that feeling. 'Can you help at the vineyard?'

'*Papa* tried to show me about the grapes but who cares about grapes?'

Lizzie burst out laughing at her honesty. 'I see what you mean. It's not the most interesting of subjects, is it? But we all have different interests and passions. I know your dad likes to work on the chateau. We were talking about doing something to the turrets the other day.'

‘He’s not going to get rid of them, is he?’ Her startled gaze almost made Lizzie laugh again.

‘No, definitely not. I’m not sure we could, even if we wanted to. But that gives me an idea – why don’t you come and help here?’

‘At the chateau?’

‘Why not? I’ve got lots of Sarah’s things to get ready for the auction, and there’ll be walls to paint soon. If I can get the roof fixed, that is.’

Lizzie prayed for the concert to be a success. Even if it only covered some of the cost, it would be so helpful. She still didn’t feel quite right about it, but according to Margot, Luc and Sylvie, everyone had been excited at the idea and everyone in town had talked to her about it when she shopped at the *marché*.

‘Maybe,’ Amélie said, still wary, but Lizzie wasn’t going to push. She’d made the offer and hopefully Amélie would take her up on it in her own time. She didn’t think Luc would mind, perhaps she’d mention it if they began to speak again. At least it would mean he and his daughter could work on some things together. Having finished her lemonade, Amélie stood up. ‘I will go and look for *Papa* now. Thank you for the lemonade and the chocolate.’

‘Thank you for your company. I really enjoyed our chat.’

Amélie flashed a smile and left. It wasn’t quite the ‘Me too’ Lizzie had been hoping for, but from a teenage girl it was the best she was going to get.

Lizzie watched Amélie walk towards the vineyard until she was out of sight. All the information from the last half-hour had made her lightheaded. She made another cup of tea and sat back down at the kitchen table. Not only had Luc and Margot been married, but Amélie was their daughter, and from what she'd said a reconciliation wasn't on the cards, so what did that mean for her feelings for Luc?

At one point, Lizzie had thought those feelings might be reciprocated, but then she'd seen him with Margot and pushed him away. If she'd been wrong, what did he think of her now? Lizzie groaned and rested her head on her hands. Had she done the right thing by withdrawing from Luc, or had she blown whatever chance they'd had?

Chapter Twenty-Three

A fierce banging on the door woke Lizzie on the day of the concert. It was barely 7 a.m. and though she'd been excited and more than a little nervous about the day, she'd managed to sleep well. She jumped out of bed, shoving on her shorts and a loose hoodie to answer the door.

'Lizzie! Why are you not dressed?' Margot looked spectacular in a pale pink jumpsuit and bright white trainers. She'd tied her hair up in a tall, bouncy ponytail and it accentuated her prominent cheekbones. Amélie stood by her side, rubbing her eyes.

Panic twisted Lizzie's stomach. 'I didn't know we were starting at seven. I thought your timetable had us meeting at nine. Did I read it wrong? God, I'm so sorry I—'

'You did not read it wrong, I am early.'

Early? Early was ten, maybe twenty minutes. Half an hour at the most. This was madness.

'I just can't help it,' Margot said, bouncing on her toes like an excited child. 'I am always like this when it is *the day*! Do you know what I mean? I am so excited I cannot wait to get everything ready. Can we come in?'

'Yes, sorry, of course,' Lizzie replied. She stepped aside. 'Go through to the kitchen and we can have breakfast together.'

'I'm not sure I can eat, but Amélie must eat something.'

Poor Amélie. She looked as dumbstruck as Lizzie at being woken so early.

'What do you fancy, Amélie? I've got cereal, toast, croissants, pains au raisin.'

'Whatever you've got is fine.'

Lizzie placed a hand on Amélie's shoulder as they followed Margot to the kitchen. 'Yeah, my brain's not quite working yet either.' To her surprise, Amélie laughed. 'I'm going to need a very big coffee today.'

For the first time since waking, excitement bubbled in Lizzie's stomach. Today was the day and with Margot by her side, she was sure everything would go to plan. She grabbed anything that constituted a breakfast food and placed it on the table with some cutlery and dishes. After making her and Margot coffee and pouring orange juice for Amélie, Lizzie sat down and ate.

She had just taken a bite of her pain au raisin when Luc appeared at the back door.

'Ah, Lizzie. Good, you're up.'

'*Bonjour*, Luc,' Margot said.

Startled, Luc edged into the kitchen, moving sideways like a crab. Tension filled the air around them though Lizzie wasn't sure if it was emanating from her, Luc or Margot.

'I didn't expect to see you so early.' He moved to Amélie and placed a gentle kiss on her head. '*Bonjour, mon trésor*.'

My treasure. Seeing him with Amélie was adorable. Lizzie could only think he'd assumed she knew Amélie was his daughter. He was a closed book and didn't share personal details readily. Their last argument had been testament to that, but he certainly hadn't seemed secretive about her. This town would be the worst place in the world to try and keep a secret. Luc must just have assumed that everyone knew, so Lizzie would too. A kindness softened his features and his eyes lit up as he smiled at his daughter. It pained Lizzie to know how bored Amélie was and how much that must hurt Luc. He stroked her head and only embarrassment at being caught staring forced Lizzie's eyes away.

Amélie moaned something at her father and Luc laughed. 'You will wake up soon enough, my little ray of sunshine.'

'But why do I even need to be here? There's nothing I can do. You could have left me in bed, and I could've come later.'

Margot glanced at Luc, her features pinched as if she'd heard this argument a hundred times before. Again, the air thickened.

'We will find something for you to do,' he replied calmly.

'Actually,' Lizzie interrupted. 'I have an idea. Amélie, you said you liked taking photographs. Would you fancy being the official photographer for today? I'll need lots of photos for my article and they might want some additional stuff for the website again. I'm a bit worried I'll get so caught up in ensuring the day runs smoothly that I'll forget to document everything: all the set-up and before and after type stuff. Would you be in charge of taking photos through the day?'

While she'd been speaking, Amélie had raised her head and though her expression was at first bored and quite firmly no, it had now changed to a hint of a smile.

'That is a wonderful idea, Lizzie.' Margot clapped her hands together. 'Amélie, you would like to do that, wouldn't you?'

'I suppose so.'

For Amélie that was tantamount to jumping up and down in her seat shouting, 'Yes, please! Yes, please!'

'Good idea, Lizzie,' Luc added. 'Amélie takes amazing pictures.'

'So I've been told. I can't wait to see them.' The air seemed to swim between them with unspoken words. Was this an apology from each to the other? 'But no photos of me till I'm properly dressed and look less like . . .' She held out her arms, her oversized hoodie covering her hands. 'This.'

'You look beautiful, Lizzie,' Margot said, taking a step towards her and touching her arm. Margot was nice, but clearly delusional. Then she pulled out the floppy sleeve of the hoodie, scowling. 'But you will get far too hot in this. It is going to be another beautiful day.'

'True. Why don't you guys have another coffee and I'll just nip and get dressed. Then we can crack on with the first job. Which is?'

'The stage arrived yesterday, *oui*?' Margot asked.

'*Oui*.'

'Then we will begin by assembling that and then set out the chairs.'

'How are you going to do that and not get dirty in that amazing jumpsuit?'

Margot laughed. 'When I say we, I mean you and Luc are going to assemble the stage while I watch.'

With everything she'd done in organising the event, Lizzie didn't begrudge her taking supervisor duties now, but how awkward would it be with the three of them working together? Lizzie crossed her arms over her chest, forming a shield at the thought. Awkward might be the understatement of the century. And with Amélie watching on, taking pictures too? This could all be an absolute disaster.

'Can you just hold this for me, Lizzie?' Luc asked, handing her the electric screwdriver.

The low stage fitted together with nuts and bolts and the different pieces were stacked to one side of the field. Lizzie and Luc were attempting to piece together the giant jigsaw puzzle. They were setting up near the house so everyone could see the chateau and remember why they were here. With the stage to the left of the large, flat pasture, the trees behind would absorb some of the noise and provide a pretty backdrop, and if the audience needed to see the poor state of the chateau before donating, they could turn and see the devastation for themselves.

Amélie had wandered off and Margot had returned to the house, leaving Lizzie and Luc alone. It was the first time all morning Lizzie had been able to relax just a little, as long as she didn't look at him or think about their argument. He was on his back underneath the stage, fastening another section together. His hair had fallen from his face and his eyes focussed intently on the job he was doing. Just being near him sent her pulse racing. So often since Amélie's visit Lizzie had thought about calling or visiting him, but what could she say that didn't give away how she herself felt about him? Still, the time had come for an apology.

'Luc?'

'Hmm?'

'I just wanted to say sorry for the other day. I was tetchy.'

He glanced at her as best he could from under the stage. 'I do not know what that means.'

She smiled. 'It means irritable. Grumpy.'

'Ah, then I am sorry too. I should not have been so tetchy. I was hot and tired and . . .'

And she'd pressed him on things he didn't want to talk about. She saved him by finishing his sentence for him. 'And we'd both been working hard.'

He smiled at her and they began to speak of other things, as they always did. The conversation was pleasant but mundane and the weight of all she knew about him, Margot and Amélie pressed down on her. In the quiet, as the day came to life, words danced on the tip of her tongue. She couldn't just ask if he and Margot were getting back together, but she had so many unanswered questions. She had to start untangling this mess of emotions somehow. One fact could not be disputed and as everyone had known it except for her, it seemed a safe route into the conversation.

'Do you know, I didn't actually know Amélie was your daughter.' She tried to make it a casual statement and downplay what a weird thing it was to say out loud.

Luc jolted, bashing his head on the frame. 'Aargh!'

Lizzie winced. 'Sorry.'

He shuffled further down before attempting to sit up again, rubbing his forehead. 'You didn't know?'

'No.'

'Didn't Sarah tell you?'

'Like I said, we hadn't spoken for quite a long time.'

'I'm sorry. I had not kept it a secret from you. Everyone knows but it must have come as a surprise.' His tone had the defensive edge she'd come to recognise, and he drew his knees up, resting his forearms on top. 'You know that Margot and I used to be married?'

'Amélie told me.'

'Oh?' Luc's eyebrows shot up.

'She came by the chateau the other day asking where you were. It kind of came out then.'

'Why didn't you say anything? We have seen each other since then, yes?'

They had, but they'd barely spoken, sticking to plans for the day and meaningless niceties. 'I – I don't really know why. It's not something you can casually drop into conversation.'

He smiled. 'No, it isn't. I hope you don't think I kept it from you.'

'No, of course not. There's no reason why you should have told me. It's none of my business.'

This seemed to be the wrong thing to say, and Luc cast his eyes down towards his hands. 'I suppose it is not.'

'She's a lovely girl,' Lizzie offered, hoping to ease the tension.

'She is. When she wants to be.' He pushed his hair back from his face. 'You must be wondering why I don't talk about her all the time. I – I am not a bad father.'

'I never thought you were.'

'It's just that I—' He took a breath so deep she saw his chest rise and fall. 'I do not always talk about her because she is away so much. It can be painful to me. I did not want to leave her in Paris, but she was at school, and it was not fair to move her. Her life was there – all her friends, her hobbies – and I could not take her away from her mama. It would have destroyed her . . . and Margot.'

'I understand,' Lizzie replied gently. 'Everyone keeps telling me life is complicated and I'm beginning to see how right they are. No one's life is simple, especially when it comes to love.'

Luc's piercing blue eyes met hers and once again, she was certain something lingered in the air between them: hidden meanings, a depth of feeling.

'I would not want you to think badly of me.'

She was just about to answer how emphatically she couldn't when Margot's voice ricocheted around the trees, indicating her arrival.

'Bravo! You are making good progress, both of you, but you really must hurry up. There is so much more left to do. *Allez, allez*,' she teased. 'Or I will not let you have a coffee break even though Amélie has put the kettle on for us all.'

Luc met neither her nor Margot's gaze as he lay back down and shuffled under the stage. Lizzie handed him his screwdriver as Margot spoke absentmindedly about an email she needed to answer for work.

She didn't think badly of him. She couldn't. Luc had more integrity than any man she'd ever known. But she still didn't know if he and Margot were getting back together, if what she'd seen in the vineyard was a rekindling of their romance. With ties to bind them so strongly together, if he chose to try again with Margot there was no way she could stop them. Not with her decrepit chateau, near-empty bank account, and dire life in London waiting for her return.

Chapter Twenty-Four

Though it was evening, the light was still strong as Lizzie paced nervously on the grass at the side of the chateau. The place had been transformed into a magical land. Strings of fairy lights hung from the trees and though their light was dim against the bright sky now, they would eventually twinkle and shine when dusk came. Lizzie brushed her hands down her dress for the seventh time in two minutes, hoping to wipe the sweat from her palms.

'Lizzie, it will be fine,' Margot said, sitting on one of the chairs they'd laid out in a large semi-circle in front of the stage. The picnic area sat in the middle and behind them were the twinkling trees. 'No one ever arrives on time. Come and have a drink and try to relax.'

She waved a glass of fizz at her. Ever organised, Margot had nipped home so she and Amélie could change, and had returned with an enormous picnic complete with a couple of bottles of bubbles. Lizzie could have kissed her if she hadn't been feeling so sick. She didn't normally

After jumping a mile in the air, Lizzie gathered herself. 'Hmm? Yes, yes, I'm fine. Bit nervous, but you know . . . Everyone gets nervous before parties and things, don't they? Important events. All that, "Will people show?" nonsense. Of course they'll show. They said they would, didn't they? And if the band starts a bit later it doesn't matter. It's just a tiny gig here in the middle of nowhere – it's not the Oscars or anything, is it? It'll be fine. It'll all be absolutely fine.' She nodded to herself and moved to the sink to get a glass of water. 'I sound like I'm having a nervous breakdown, don't I?'

Amélie giggled. 'A little.'

Lizzie joined her at the kitchen table. 'You look lovely tonight, Amélie. I like your hair up. It suits you. You have lovely blue eyes; you should show them off.' Pinkness flooded Amélie's cheeks. 'And now I've embarrassed you. Urgh.' Lizzie laid her head on the table. 'I'm going to stop talking now. Sorry.'

'Sarah would have liked the concert, I think,' Amélie said a moment later. Lizzie raised her head. 'And the auction. She liked music and parties and being the centre of attention. She . . . she would have been proud of you.' She dropped her eyes to her phone again.

Tears disrupted Lizzie's vision and she lowered her head so Amélie wouldn't notice. 'That's a lovely thing to say, Amélie. Thank you.'

The idea warmed Lizzie's heart and released some of the tension from her shoulders. If she forgot about their goodbye and thought about the person everyone else had known, Sarah was someone she'd have wanted to make proud.

'You're not auctioning off the camel, are you?'

'The mangy stuffed camel?' Lizzie raised her head to stare at Amélie. 'No, I'm not. Why's that?'

'Lizzie? Lizzie?' Luc's voice blew through the open window and a hard knock rebounded off the door. Amélie didn't answer and Lizzie gave her attention to Luc but vowed to ask her more about it later.

'It's open,' she called back.

Luc flung the door wide, clearly surprised that she had closed it. She'd left it open nearly every day to let the sunshine into the house and the sound of birdsong fill the air. He was a tiny bit out of breath, his chest rising and falling. Before she could consider how sexy he looked, Amélie stood up, and being reminded she was Luc's daughter was like a bucket of ice poured over her head. 'People are arriving, Lizzie! You must come and greet them.'

'They're actually coming? Are you sure?'

'Of course I am sure, I have seen them with my own eyes. *Allez*, a*llez!*' He gestured for her to hurry. 'Come on, Amélie, you should come too.'

'Do I have to?'

Luc looked to Lizzie as if to ask her the question. 'You don't have to,' she said. 'But it would be lovely if you were part of the welcoming committee. You've done so much to help today. Plus, you can nab us a good spot for our picnic.'

Amélie glanced at her father and then back to Lizzie. 'Okay.'

'Thank you.'

'*Oui*, *merci*, *mon trésor*.'

When they got to the field, Lizzie pressed her hands to her mouth. The place was almost full, with familiar faces from the town either sat on the chairs or on picnic rugs on the grass. Chatter filled the air as friends caught up with each other, sharing food and drink.

'I'm going to take some more pictures,' Amélie said, waving to some people she knew and moving towards them.

'Luc, I can't believe it. People came! They actually came!' She grabbed his arm with both hands, and he smiled. Heat ran through her body as if his energy were flowing into her, but she'd lost control and took a step back, dropping her hands to her sides. She quickly glanced around, unsure where Margot was but hoping she hadn't seen. 'I must go and thank Margot too. I better go find her.'

'Lizzie—'

But she pretended not to hear him.

Margot was by the stage, instructing the band they could start playing. It was a little later than scheduled, but when the orchestra began, everyone settled in for the first performance. Margot and Lizzie went to join Amélie and Luc on a giant picnic rug in the shade of a tree.

'Thank you for everything, Margot. This is amazing.'

'You're welcome.' Margot gave a tight smile and Lizzie's chest constricted. Had she seen her grab hold of Luc? Oh god, what if she had? After everything Margot had done for her.

'Do you feel better now?' asked Luc as they all sat down to watch the orchestra.

'Yes, I do. I've always been bad at waiting for parties to

start.' Lizzie was just about to thank Margot again when Margot's phone vibrated in her hand.

'*Excusez-moi*. I must take this.'

Margot stepped away into the trees. Lizzie had never seen a reaction like that from her. She was always smiling and positive. A moment later, she returned, her calm exterior cracking.

'Lizzie, I must talk to you.'

'Of course. What is it?'

'The jazz quartet. They are not coming.'

'What?' She and Luc exclaimed at the same time. 'Why not?'

'They are stuck in traffic and will not make it in time.' Margot dropped her eyes to her phone. 'I am so angry. They texted me to say they were running a little late earlier. But they haven't made any headway in the traffic and now, they are not going to make it. I am so sorry, Lizzie. It is my fault.'

Lizzie's hand shot out to hold Margot's. 'This isn't your fault, Margot. It's a pain for sure but it definitely isn't your fault. You don't control what time someone else leaves and you certainly don't control traffic jams.'

'Lizzie is right,' Luc added. 'You have organised everything down to the last detail. The band have let you down. That is not your fault.'

'You are both being too nice. I should have had a contingency, but they were so sure they'd be able to make it. So excited to play. I should not have believed them. It is the number one rule of event management: always have a contingency plan, but I did not. I thought it was just a small event, what could go wrong. I was too confident and look what has happened. I have let you down.'

'No, you have not,' Lizzie replied forcefully. 'You have not let me down and if you say that again I'll – I'll . . .'

'What?' asked Amélie, highly amused at the turn the conversation had taken, enjoying her mum being chastised instead of her.

'I'm not entirely sure, but I'll do something. There must be a solution. Could the orchestra play for longer?'

'Possibly,' Margot replied.

'I'm not sure that's a good idea,' Amélie added. 'Look.'

They peered around and though people were enjoying the classical music it was clear they wouldn't enjoy it for the entire evening. If the orchestra played for too long, they were in danger of sending everyone to sleep. What else could they do? The evening would be ruined without the main act. The jazz band had been due to play for two hours. That was a lot of time to fill and at the moment she didn't have any idea how to do it.

As hard as she searched for another solution, nothing came up. What other option was there? To cancel and send everyone home? Everyone had expected a full evening's entertainment, not an hour of classical music and then her iPod on shuffle. Would they accept a bad version of a wedding disco? Not likely. Lizzie was as outraged at the thought as they would be.

Lizzie stared around her, hoping for inspiration. The mood was one of joyfulness, but the classical music was slow, good as an introduction while people still arrived and got comfortable, but there was an anticipation of more.

Something faster, brighter, something they could dance to as they had in town.

'Wait a second! I might have a solution.' Lizzie clapped her hands together. 'Violette's son is going to play some pop songs, isn't he?' Margot and Luc nodded. 'Why don't we get him on next, then have the auction, and then ask the people who played at the party in town to play? They were playing jazz at the party, and everyone was dancing and singing along. Do you think they would?'

'Are you kidding?' asked Luc, laughing. 'Tell them they have a stage, and you will struggle to get them off!'

Margot nodded, tapping her mobile phone against her lip. 'We change the order, and we ask the locals to play something?'

'I know it's not what people expected, but it's better than nothing, isn't it? And okay, we may not make any money because we can't ask people to pay for that, but at least we'll have a great party. That's what people have come here for too.'

'I think Sarah would have loved that,' Luc said quietly and even Amélie smiled.

Lizzie's eyes were drawn to the chateau as his words sunk in. Would Sarah have approved? Yes, Lizzie was fairly sure she would have. 'And at least we'll save on that band's fees. We don't have to pay them, do we?'

'Certainly not!' Colour returned to Margot's cheeks. 'They have let us down. I am not paying them for not turning up. Luc, you and I will go and ask our friends if they would be willing to play.'

Luc pointed over his shoulder at an accordion hidden

inside a picnic basket. 'I think some of them have brought their instruments with them already.'

Lizzie laughed. 'Good! But I can drive anyone into town who needs to pick something up. I haven't had anything alcoholic to drink yet.'

'Okay,' Margot said, standing up. Everyone else did the same. 'I like this idea, Lizzie. I think it'll work.'

Though it put the future of the roof in jeopardy, what else could they do? She'd think about the chateau tomorrow; right now she had to deal with the problems in front of her.

'And after,' Margot said, 'when you are back from town, we will both have a very large glass of wine.'

'Can I try some?' asked Amélie and all three of them replied with a smile:

'No!'

Chapter Twenty-Five

Violette's son and his friends had played an unexpectedly brilliant set, including some disco classics, and everyone clapped and sang along. Violette had beamed with pride at her son and Lizzie had also caught Amélie watching him closely. Perhaps she had a secret crush. It would at least make summer holidays here more interesting for her.

'Here, you look like you need this.' Luc handed Lizzie a large glass of rosé and she took a mouthful, the delicate taste refreshing her tired brain immediately. Her neck ached from the tension of the last hour, and it wasn't over yet. The auction was about to begin.

'Thank you. I can't drink too much. I need to keep my head clear.'

'Are you nervous?'

'Terrified! Why did I ever think anyone would want to buy Sarah's old stuff?'

'Hey, there are my services to buy as well.'

'Well, I know that's going to do well, but what if it's the only one that does?'

'Stop worrying, Lizzie. It will all be fine. You will see.'

With the evening sky paling, Henri took to the stage. In his right hand he held the list she'd given him, which had a description of each item and its number. Amélie was going to hold up each object to show it off while Lizzie stood at the back with her own copy of the list, noting the amount promised and the person who'd bought it.

As Henri began to speak into the microphone, all eyes turned to him. He appeared taller on the stage in his black suit and shining shoes. Amélie waved emphatically at Luc, and he waved back. Lizzie was grateful there were no more secrets, even if there weren't really any secrets in the first place.

Henri spoke in French and Luc translated for her. 'And first up we have . . .' Henri began a description of the first of Sarah's items: a large blue vase that was pretty, but as far as Lizzie knew, wasn't associated with any adventures.

The bidding began and soon they were powering through each lot. Lizzie struggled to keep up and sometimes had to ask Luc who had secured the win as she still didn't know everyone in the town. Though the individual objects weren't raising hundreds of euros, the total was adding up. As she'd grown to know Sarah through everyone else's stories of her, Lizzie had to agree with Amélie that she would have very much enjoyed being the centre of attention and would have approved of the battles over some of the more unusual items.

Luc's offer to work on someone's house had raised one of the highest amounts and he puffed with pride next to her. They were nearly at the end before she knew it, and the penultimate lot was held up.

'Oh,' said Henri. 'I don't quite know what this one is.' He flipped the pages of his list backwards and forwards.

A wave of panic flowed through Lizzie from the top of her head down through her body. Amélie was holding up a small metal statue of Lakshmi, the Hindu goddess of fortune, wealth, love and prosperity. Lizzie's hand shot to her mouth.

'What is it, Lizzie?' asked Luc.

'I must have put it in the wrong box. That wasn't supposed to go. It's not supposed to be part of the auction.'

Whispers had begun to circulate as Henri read the list, and Lizzie was just about to step forward and let everyone know it was a mistake when the whispers grew to excited chatter. Snippets reached Lizzie's ears. Phrases such as 'Sarah told me about that' and 'She got it from India. I've always wanted to go there'.

'Lizzie?' Luc asked. 'Do you want me to stop the auction?'

'A hundred euros!' someone shouted from the back.

'Hundred and twenty!' came the reply and a bidding war began.

'Lizzie?'

She turned to look at him, a mixture of emotions swirling inside her. She didn't want to let it go. She wanted to speak to Sarah and know the story behind it. That the chance had gone forever choked her. But seeing everyone so excited at the statue, at the memories behind it, Lizzie didn't feel she could take that away from those who were bidding to own it. They'd valued Sarah as a friend and neighbour. They'd valued her more than Lizzie, Sarah's own relation, had, all because of one incident, one moment in their lives. It made her ashamed.

'It's all right,' she said quietly. 'It was my mistake. Don't stop the bidding.'

'Are you sure?'

'Look, they're so happy to have something to remember her by. Something they know meant a lot to her. I can't take that away from them. It wouldn't be right. I have other things of hers,' she added, realising the importance those things had taken on.

'If you're sure.' He placed his hand in the small of her back and the sensation nearly knocked her off balance, but she had to ignore it. He only meant it as a concerned friend and she couldn't read anything more into it, however much she wanted to.

With the auction finished, and the total impressive, Lizzie breathed a sigh of relief. Luc fetched her another glass of wine and when the evening was over, they'd count the contents of the donation boxes and see how much they'd made. Now was the time to party. The locals were playing as they had that night in town and if it were possible, they seemed to be enjoying themselves even more. Everyone was up and dancing, picnic blankets thrown aside. Food and wine were shared, and laughter filled the air as the sun set behind the trees. The vibrant sky overhead, utterly cloudless and striped with colour from burnt orange to bright pink, was the most stunning sight Lizzie had ever seen. Long shadows spread over the ground, but the night stretched ahead of them. Lizzie could easily see why Sarah had fallen so in love with France and chosen to stay. With Luc stood next to her, their shoulders virtually touching and his aftershave drifting in the breeze, she felt giddy.

'I think it's a success, Lizzie. Don't you?'

'It looks like everyone's having a wonderful time.'

'Do not worry about the roof. Even if we haven't made enough money, we will find a solution.'

The *we* set her heart on fire, but what *we* could there ever be except for one of friendly teamwork? His fingers brushed hers and she longed for his touch but stepped to the side, sure it must have been an accident.

Hurt marred Luc's features and he cleared his throat. 'I better go and find Amélie.'

She watched his broad shoulders and strong back, losing him in the crowd. Lizzie pinched her temples as tiredness overtook her.

'Lizzie!' Margot called, dancing as she came towards her. 'Isn't this wonderful?' She cast her hand out, gesturing to everything around them, everyone laughing, talking and singing.

'It is pretty wonderful. Thank you, for everything you've done. I couldn't have done it without you.'

'Ah, you are too kind, *mon ami*, but now we must talk.'

'Oh?' Nerves reached up from her stomach, grasping at her throat. 'What about?'

Please let it be the auction. Please let it be the auction.

'About Luc.'

Oh god.

Margot crossed her arms over her chest. 'Luc is a good man, *oui*?'

The question floored Lizzie. She'd expected a more keep-your-hands-off-my-man start. 'Sorry?'

'Oh, my friend. Come.' Margot wrapped her arm around Lizzie's shoulders and led her to two empty seats.

This was it. This was where Margot accused her in front of everyone of going after her man. Of trying to steal the father of her child. Stone-cold dread ran down her spine. Perhaps being left at the altar wasn't going to be the most publicly humiliating thing that ever happened to her. This was.

'Margot, before you say anything, I just want you to know that I had no idea about you and Luc and as soon as I did, I – I—'

'Lizzie, calm down. Have another drink.' Lizzie took a sip of her wine, but her hands were shaking. 'I saw what happened with Luc just now when he tried to hold your hand.'

'Margot, I swear.' Lizzie turned to face her. As much as she wanted to hide, she needed Margot to believe her. 'He must have just accidentally brushed my hand. He would never have tried to hold it if you two were getting back together and I wouldn't have reached for him knowing that either. It must just have been—'

Margot burst out laughing. 'What are you talking about, Lizzie? We are not getting back together.'

'You're not?' Her heart burst, rattling around her chest like a pinball. 'But at the vineyard . . . I saw you—'

'You saw us what?' Margot's expression was quizzical rather than angry.

'I came to the vineyard to see Luc, and I saw you both there, in the vines. You were so . . . together. It was when you'd said you were going to Paris for the weekend.'

'Oh, Lizzie. What did you think?'

'I just assumed you were a couple. That maybe you had a secret romance you didn't want to tell anyone about. Possibly because of Amélie. I didn't know then that Luc was Amélie's father and when I did, I thought maybe you were getting back together.'

Margot laughed heartily, pressing a hand to her chest as if this was the funniest thing she'd ever heard. When she'd calmed down, she took Lizzie's hands. '*Non. Non!* Amélie and I came back from Paris a day early because we had a massive fight. She was rude to me; I was rude to her. Teenage girls are hard to handle, sometimes. I went to see Luc to tell him about it. I felt so bad for losing my temper with Amélie and not being the "adult" one, but he was kind to me and told me I am not a bad mother. He is always kind.'

Lizzie thought back to the first weekend she'd come to see Luc at the vineyard and heard voices arguing. That must have been Margot too. 'Luc's right. You're not a bad mother. You're amazing.'

'It does not always feel like that. Sometimes it feels like war and that weekend, it certainly did. But I love my daughter and I want her to be happy. She does not want to be here all summer but if she is not, it is hard for her to see her father. He comes to Paris sometimes, but he hates the city. He misses her, but it causes arguments. Arguments between me and Amélie and between me and Luc.' She paused for a moment and tilted her head to catch Lizzie's eye. 'So, you were hoping to see Luc that day you came to the vineyard?'

'I – I was.' There – she'd admitted some of her feelings for him. She wasn't prepared to share how she spent most days yearning to see him or thought about him first thing in the morning and last thing at night. She couldn't confess that her heart ached whenever the prospect of returning to England and leaving him behind flew into her brain.

'I heard about the party and you dancing with Luc. You have feelings for him, I think? Real feelings?' Margot pinned Lizzie with her large, pretty eyes.

'I don't know. My heart still hurts when I think about love and trusting someone else again, but I – I do like him.'

'Is that why you pushed me away?'

It felt so strange talking to Margot about her ex. Lizzie was about to protest but the words died on her tongue. Margot had the measure of her. What was the point in denying anything? 'I didn't want to get in the way of anything and, after Will, my heart couldn't cope with any more upheaval. I'm sorry if it seems petty. Believe me, I didn't want to lose your friendship, but after Will, and Sarah's death and all the problems with the chateau, I just needed some space.'

'I understand.'

It was Lizzie's turn to laugh now. 'You're far too understanding and far too nice. I don't deserve it.'

‘Of course you do. Now, back to Luc. You must understand, that I will always love Luc. He was my husband, we had a life together for many years, and we share our beautiful daughter. But I am not in love with him anymore. We have both moved on and I am happy with someone else.’

Relief mixed with embarrassment and Lizzie watched the pale rose liquid in her wine glass.

‘What I am trying to say is that you have my blessing. I can tell Luc likes you and I could tell from the moment you mentioned him that you like him too.’

He liked her? Lizzie’s body tingled with happiness. She’d hoped, sometimes suspected, but had never been certain.

‘Luc does not easily give his heart away. I did not say anything about our past before because I didn’t want to make things awkward between us. When I met you, I knew we could become great friends and I didn’t want to jeopardise that, but I think it is better now that we get everything out in the open. *Oui*?’

Lizzie nodded. ‘*Oui*.’

‘What are you going to do? I think you upset him before when you would not take his hand. That was a big gesture from Luc. He is not overly romantic, but he is kind and caring and small gestures like that mean a lot to him. Perhaps you should go and find him?’

Lizzie’s head spun from the adrenalin running through her system, her conversation with Margot and the party atmosphere surrounding her. ‘Are you sure it won’t be awkward for you, Margot? What about Amélie? I don’t want her to hate me.’

'Amélie hates every adult. She is twelve. But she will understand in time. Do not let life pass you by, Lizzie. If Sarah could teach any of us anything, it was that life should be enjoyed and chances taken. Now, I will help to clear up a bit, but then Amélie and I are going to go home. She will be horrible tomorrow if she is very tired.'

Margot leaned forward and kissed Lizzie's cheeks before winding her way into the crowd for a final dance.

The sky had turned a deep, dusky blue with stars shining overhead as everyone left. The fairy lights now glittered against the dark in golden glory as Lizzie searched for Luc. She'd tried to find him through the rest of the evening but hadn't discovered his whereabouts. She had the horrible feeling he was avoiding her. She studied the groups that were leaving with cheery waves, and the stage and dance-floor to see if he was still there, but his handsome face never once appeared in the crowd.

As the last visitors said goodbye, and the chateau fell once more into silence, Lizzie gave up hope, her heart heavy. She wasn't quite sure what she'd have said to him even if she had found him, but knowing she'd hurt him by refusing his hand, she was desperate to make things right. To say or do something that would show him how she felt. The evening had been a success and though she tried to focus on that, it was difficult to rid him from her mind. She picked up one of the donation boxes and circled around to the back of the house, to begin counting.

The light from the kitchen spilled out onto the grass, the house forming long shadows as she headed inside. The unexpected figure hunched over the table made her jump.

'Luc! I thought you'd gone.'

'I could not leave without knowing how much we made.' He gave her a small, guarded smile.

'I'm glad you're here,' she replied, placing the donation box on the table and sliding into the next seat. He relaxed a little.

To Lizzie it felt like the air between them hung heavy with emotion and she had no idea how to disperse it. There were so many things she wanted to say but had no idea how to start. She wished she could gather her courage and grasp the moment and as she began counting, she tried several times to let the words out, but each time fear held her back. What if he'd changed his mind? What if she wasn't really ready for this after all?

Eventually, after losing count several times as her mind wandered, she focussed on counting the notes and coins in front of her.

Time passed, but Lizzie had no idea how much when she sat back, astonished. 'I can't believe it. We did it. We did it, Luc! With the auction as well there's enough here to fix the roof. The main roof anyway. The turrets might have to wait, but this combined with the money from Hilary I was saving for the electrics, and I think the amount Sarah left me will be enough to fix the roof. I just can't believe it. It's – it's unbelievable.'

Tears formed in her eyes, and she buried her head in her hands. The town had been so generous. She'd been wrong to think that they wouldn't, or hadn't forgiven Sarah. It truly seemed they'd never hated her in the first place. Only she herself had, but she was making things right now.

'Hey,' said Luc, wrapping his arms around her shoulders, their weight and strength comforting, acting like a balm to the emotions swirling inside. 'Don't cry, Lizzie. This is good news, is it not?'

She lifted her head and turned to face him. 'I'm just so grateful. So happy. I don't really know what to do. How do I thank everyone?'

He didn't answer and the silence trapped them together in a world where only they existed. It was just the two of them in the darkness of the night. Luc's sweet, warm breath fluttered over her skin and his hand cupped her cheek. With his thumb, he brushed away a tear as his eyes darted over her face, settling on her mouth.

Without a second to think, she lifted her head so their lips met in a tender kiss. Luc's mouth came to hers with a willingness that thrilled her. As they fell into each other, their kisses became more ardent and more eager. Luc pulled her up to standing, his arms wrapping around her waist, pulling her into him. A hand ran up her back, holding her firmly, its warmth seeping through her clothes onto her skin.

They parted for a second as though speaking silently to each other, checking that this was what the other wanted after the confusion of earlier. Her eyes were wide, urging him to continue. His were fiery with passion, and he kissed her again even more fervently than before.

She had no idea what happened next: how they made it to the bedroom, who took off which piece of clothing, but soon they were in her bed. It was as if they were one person, so in tune that every action was synchronised, every need and desire predicted then fulfilled. Lost in his kisses, in the strong arms wrapped around her, she gave herself completely to him, and to the love and desire she'd kept locked away for so long.

Chapter Twenty-Six

In the bright morning light, Lizzie awoke to find the bed empty, and she looked around for Luc, a slight sense of panic forming inside. The sound of the shower drifted to her, and she relaxed, smiling at the memory of everything that had happened the previous night.

It had been like nothing she'd ever experienced before. In her experience, albeit limited, a first time with someone could be cringeworthy, awkward and sometimes even embarrassing. Hers and Will's first foray into sexual antics had been far less passionate, she realised now. Last night with Luc had been on a whole new level. Their bodies had entwined tenderly, and there was a deep passion that had been missing from her relationship with Will. Luc, she knew, didn't give himself to just anyone and goosebumps flew over her skin at the memory of his touch, and the intense way he looked into her eyes as they made love. Butterflies fluttered in her stomach at the memory.

'Good morning, *ma chérie*,' Luc said, walking back into the bedroom. She looked up to find him half dressed in his jeans, but without the shirt he'd worn yesterday. Her eyes roved over the toned torso she'd run her fingers down last night and the strong arms that had held her firmly, as if he never wanted to let go. Luc sat on the edge of the bed and brushed a lock of hair behind her ear.

'Good morning.' She didn't say she thought he might have done a runner like Will had the first time they'd slept together. He'd regretted it, worried it was a mistake. Perhaps it shouldn't have come as such a surprise when he'd done the same thing on their wedding day. Luc, it seemed, had no regrets. She certainly didn't. There were many experiences in life she regretted: wearing skyscraper heels to her first job in London rather than commuting in trainers like everyone else; that first date with the guy who thought his recent STD diagnosis was a suitable topic for discussion at the dinner table; the time she'd had a dodgy one-night stand with someone who, she found out the next morning, still lived with his parents; last night, however, was not one of them. The only thing she regretted was that she hadn't done it sooner and considering her recent romantic history, that was saying something.

He kissed her again, slowly and tenderly. 'You look very beautiful this morning.' She didn't believe it, but she'd take the compliment anyway. 'But you cannot sit around in bed all day, *chérie*. Now we have the money for the roof, we should get started organising everything. I will call Sébastien and tell him we are ready to proceed – he will need time to organise scaffolding and supplies.'

Lizzie groaned. 'But it's Sunday. Can't we just stay in bed and eat croissants and drink some of your fabulous rosé?'

'You cannot get around me by complimenting my wine. Come, it is already half past ten.'

She lay back and pulled the pillow over her face, listening to Luc's chuckling as he finished dressing and went downstairs. When she released the pillow, the sun spilled through the gap in the curtains and she bathed in the light. Her whole being was filled with happiness. Her past was finally slipping behind her. She wasn't holding it in her mind anymore. Life was moving on. She was moving on, and it was all thanks to France.

Hearing Luc potter in the kitchen, she dressed, hurrying downstairs when a knock at the kitchen door and additional voices caught her attention. Had someone come to pay their auction fee already? She ran into the kitchen and her heart paused mid-beat. It was Margot and Amélie. Despite all she'd said yesterday, was Margot really okay with her and Luc? Would she think badly of her that something had happened between them so quickly?

'*Bonjour*, Luc, you are here already?' Margot flashed Lizzie a cheeky grin as she bounded into the room.

'Yes, I . . .' Luc scratched the back of his head, his eyes darting between Margot and Amélie. While Margot smirked, clearly finding the whole situation endlessly entertaining, Amélie was scowling, her eyes narrowed on Lizzie. The withering look made Lizzie shrink.

Eager to fill the silence, Lizzie said, 'Luc was saying he wanted to call Sébastien and tell him we have enough money for the roof.'

'Really?' Margot beamed, clapping her hands. 'Why, that is excellent news. I thought we would have after the auction, but I was not sure. That's why Amélie and I stopped by – we had to know for certain, didn't we, darling?' Amélie shifted her gaze momentarily towards her mum and gave a curt nod. 'So what are you two up to today?'

'Nothing!' Lizzie shouted, then lowered her voice. 'Nothing together. I mean—' She glanced at Luc, who seemed as confused as she was. What was she blathering about? 'Probably sorting out the roof and then I'll be tidying again. You know, back to work on the chateau and Sarah's stuff. My mum's still after the bits Sarah wanted her to have. I should have sent them by now, really, but I haven't got around to finding them.'

'Would you like to come for lunch with us?' Margot asked. 'Both of you?'

Amélie gave Lizzie a look that could only be described as murderous. Lizzie shook her head. 'No, thanks. I'm wiped out after yesterday and I need to write up my article while everything is fresh in my mind.'

Work had been her shield for months and here she was using it again, but this time it felt dishonest. The truth was, she'd have loved to have lunch with her friend and with Luc, but Amélie clearly wasn't ready for something like that. The girl wasn't stupid. None of them had said anything had happened but it was clear from the tension in the room and Lizzie's own nattering like a lunatic, that something had changed.

'What about you, Luc?'

'Lunch sounds nice, Margot. Thank you. Lizzie, are you sure you won't join us?'

'No, honestly. But if you could call Sébastien to let him know we're good to go, that would be great.'

'Come with us now, *Papa*,' Amélie said, moving towards him. Luc opened his arms to hug her, and Amélie snuggled into his chest. 'Please?'

Lizzie had the sneaking suspicion Amélie was doing everything she could to get him away from her. 'You should definitely go, Luc,' Lizzie said, cheerfully. 'Yesterday was crazy. You deserve a break, and like I said, I'd really like to write up my article while last night – the party! – is fresh in my mind.'

Margot stepped forward. 'Are you absolutely sure you won't join us, Lizzie? You too worked hard yesterday and deserve a break.'

From the way she met Lizzie's gaze, it seemed Margot also thought Amélie was up to something and didn't want Lizzie to be put off. It was sweet of her to make sure, but there was no point in making life difficult for them all. Amélie needed time, that was all.

Time.

Did they have time? She'd be leaving when the chateau was fixed up and the thought made her stomach turn over.

'Lizzie?' Margot asked gently.

Everyone had turned to look at her and panic deadened her limbs. 'Sorry,' she replied, feigning chirpiness. 'I just thought of something I need to do for my mum. You guys go on, I really need to get started on some bits.'

Margot and Amélie exited; Amélie much more cheerful

now her papa was leaving with them. Luc lingered for a second.

'Are you sure you're all right, Lizzie? You have gone very white.'

'Yes, honestly. I just remembered something Mum wanted me to find for her. It was really important, so I better get on. Honestly. Go.' She laughed and gestured towards the door.

Luc gave her a kiss on the cheek and when his lips met her skin, the panic rose again, so strong it overpowered every other emotion. With a wave, he left, promising to call her later.

What was she going to do? Lizzie went to the living room and sat down. She couldn't stay in the kitchen where they'd all just met. The awkwardness still lingered in the air. Her ringtone echoed around the empty space, and she answered it. 'Hi, Hilary. What are you doing calling me on a Sunday?'

'I just had to know how the fundraiser went. Did it work? Did you get enough money?'

Lizzie allowed herself to relax a little as her brain focussed on a different subject. 'Yes, we did. We can't do the turrets, but we can do the main roof, so it's brilliant news.'

Hilary squealed. 'Fantastic! Oh, Lizzie, I'm so happy for you – and I've got some more fabulous news too.'

'Oh?'

'The "Living the French Dream" articles are going down an absolute storm. Everyone, and I mean everyone, is in love with them so I can give you an additional five hundred words for your next article. We want to make a big feature out of the fundraiser, but I held off saying anything in case it didn't go as well as you'd hoped. Readers are going to be so happy, and I think we should do regular in-between updates on the website too. This is it, Lizzie!' she said, happily chatting away. 'This is the next step for you. The promotion is guaranteed for as soon as you get back. We were thinking maybe another couple of features until you sell would be great. We don't want to push our luck with the readers and bore them. Lizzie?'

'Wow,' she replied, her heart dropping to the pit of her stomach. She should have been elated. This was what she'd dreamed of for months. This was what she'd come out here for, but a horrible taste had settled in her mouth. 'That's amazing, Hilary. Thank you.'

'Are you sure? You don't sound too pleased.'

'I think I'm just in shock,' she replied, honestly. She really was in shock, her brain unable to form any kind of logical thought.

'Well, with the roof fixed you'll be able to sell, won't you? So, when do you think you'll be back? Is a couple of months okay?'

'I – I don't know.' She marshalled her thoughts. 'We're contacting the roofer today, so I'll let you know once I've spoken to him.' She cleared her throat, hoping she'd hidden the waver in her voice.

'Are you sure you're all right, Lizzie?'

'Yes, yes. Just a bit worn out. Possibly a little hungover.' She was actually stone cold sober, but she couldn't let Hilary think she was ungrateful.

'I understand. Let the news sink in and we'll chat later. Oh, I'm so happy for you, Lizzie. Once you get that roof fixed, sell up and come back, we'll need to talk about other regular articles, who you want to interview, what your plans are. Great things are coming for you. I can feel it, and after everything you've been through, I can't think of anyone who deserves it more.'

'Thanks, Hilary. Speak soon.'

Lizzie hung up and buried her head in her hands. She couldn't give up her life in London, but she was excited about where this thing with Luc could go. It was early days, but it was the most passionate, most powerful start to a relationship she'd ever experienced. She wasn't quite ready to admit it to herself, but the word love floated on the periphery of her mind whenever she thought of him. What would happen to them when it was time to leave? What would happen to her friendship with Margot? She didn't want to hurt Amélie either.

Pulling a cushion onto her lap, she held it tightly.

The phrase *life is complicated*, which everyone seemed so fond of here, sat front and centre in her brain. How had her life become so tangled?

Chapter Twenty-Seven

Within a week, scaffolding had been erected around the chateau and a team of men were working on the roof. France clearly had more than its fair share of handsome men as most of the guys were attractive and toned. In the heat they'd stripped down to just their shorts, ridding themselves of T-shirts and vests, their golden skin glistening in the strong summer sun. Lizzie had to admit, it made a nice change from the flabby builders' bums she'd grown used to in England. Even some of the ladies from town had cheekily mentioned what a wonderful sight it was when they came to pay their fees from the auction.

'Are you still watching them?' Lizzie teased Luc as she brought a tray of coffees for the workmen. 'I thought you were heading back to the vineyard.'

'I am. I am just learning what they do.' He pointed to a group of the men working together in harmony. 'You see how they pass the tiles to each other. It is like a well-oiled machine.'

She placed the tray down and slid her hand into his, resting her head on his shoulder. He turned to face her, pulling her in for a kiss. The feel of his mouth sent fireworks through her body.

Lizzie and Luc had spent their days together working on the chateau and their nights rolling between the sheets, the desire for one another growing daily. The trouble was her love for him was growing daily too. Part of her still refused to use that word exactly. She added qualifiers like it was a 'summer love' or 'French love'. Any word would do as long as it set it apart from the rest of her life. She couldn't contemplate going back to London or think about how fast time was passing. She'd also thought about staying away from him but couldn't bring herself to do it.

Begrudgingly, he pulled away. 'Ah, I really must go, *chérie*. I cannot put off the vineyard any longer.'

'Shame.' She reached her arms around his neck. 'Are you sure you haven't got five more minutes?'

They kissed again, only separating when the workmen spotted them and began to cheer. Though embarrassed, Lizzie laughed as Luc left, promising to come round again later. He had barely turned the corner when her phone rang.

'*Bonjour Maman*,' she trilled happily.

'Oh, Lizzie.' Her mum's voice was fluttery with worry.

'What is it, Mum? Are you okay?'

'I'm fine, it's just . . . well . . . Will's been in touch, darling.'

'Will?' Her stomach dropped to the floor. 'What did he want?'

'He wanted to know where you were. He said he'd called that friend you were staying with, but they wouldn't tell him anything. I said you were out of the country, and he could crawl back into the hole he came out of.'

Despite her shock, Lizzie chuckled. 'Well done, Mum. Did he say anything else?'

'He wanted to apologise to you. He gave me some guff about knowing he was wrong to act as he did, and he wanted to apologise to your face. Your father said his conscience is obviously eating him. Should I have told him where you were? He knows you've blocked him.'

'No. Don't.' The two small words were a huge statement for her. She'd have given anything for her old life back not long ago. Now, though, she didn't want it, or at least him, in it.

Amélie began walking towards her from the opposite direction her father had just gone in. Lizzie said, 'Listen, Mum, I'm sorry, I have to go. But don't worry, I'm fine and you've done the right thing. I don't want to see him.'

'Good. You do sound so much better, darling. It's lovely to hear. Keep it up.'

'Will do. Bye Mum.' She smiled at Amélie, pretending everything was fine, though the mention of Will had shaken her. 'Hello, Amélie. Are you looking for your dad? He literally just left. You can probably catch him up if you run.'

Since that morning a week or so ago, Amélie had been wary of Lizzie and particularly clingy with Luc. Lizzie and Margot had chatted about it during lunch the day before, and Lizzie understood that it must be hard for her. She had apparently acted the same way when Margot met and began dating her new partner, but things had calmed down eventually. Lizzie suspected that though Amélie didn't enjoy her summers here, she had always had the benefit of her father's undivided attention and now she feared she'd be forced to share it. Lizzie promised to do everything she could to ensure that didn't happen. She'd never get in the way of Luc and Amélie spending time together.

Amélie crossed her arms over her stomach, wrapping them around her protectively. 'I was looking for you, actually.'

'Me? Oh, okay. Shall we go in the house? I was going to make myself a coffee anyway.'

Amélie followed her around to the kitchen door and inside the chateau. As usual, Lizzie offered her a drink and after making her own they sat at the kitchen table. Amélie watched the men pass the door, peering as she heard their voices.

'Is everything okay, Amélie?' Lizzie asked.

'Yes, but I – I wondered if you needed any help at the chateau.' She shuffled nervously in her seat.

'Help? What sort of help? Did you want to come and paint or help me with Sarah's stuff? I was thinking of making a list of the things in boxes, like I did for the auction.'

'I don't mind. *Maman* thought it would be a good idea if I did something, though. She said I'm always moaning about being bored so I should do something constructive. You did say before that I could come and help.'

'You certainly can. I'm hoping you'll be able to fill in some of the gaps for me. You said Sarah told you about some of her travels. Do you think you could identify what fits to what story?'

'Possibly.'

'Does that job sound okay or did you want to do something else? You can be honest, Amélie. I won't mind.'

'No, that sounds fine.'

'Do you want to get started today? I've already moved a lot of things down into the living room. I had to for the auction. It might be a bit noisy though; the workmen are right outside, going up and down the scaffolding.'

'I don't mind.'

'Come on then.' She led Amélie to the living room and found paper and pens for her. 'Are you sure you don't mind going through each box and listing what's in there?'

'Positive.'

'Well, if you get bored and need a break, feel free to go for a wander. I'll let you know when I've made lunch but do help yourself to anything from the kitchen if you get hungry. There's more chocolate in the cupboard by the sink and there's lemonade in the fridge.'

Amélie nodded and gave Lizzie a genuine smile. It lit her pretty eyes – the same shape as her mother's, but the colour of her father's – and it brought her face to life.

Progress at last.

An hour later, Lizzie called Amélie down to have some lunch. She'd set up charcuterie, fresh bread and some of the tasty local goat's cheese as well as a small salad. The workmen normally brought their own lunch, but she couldn't help taking out a similar board for them.

'Help yourself,' Lizzie said, waving towards the food.

There was far too much for the two of them, but Lizzie didn't want Amélie to go away hungry. Amélie's expression had returned to unsmiling, and it made the atmosphere tense, but as the adult, Lizzie acted as if everything was fine. 'How's it going, Amélie? Have you found anything interesting?'

Amélie took some bread and scooped some of the goat's cheese onto her plate with a knife. 'I've only been through one of the boxes so far. There were so many little things in it. I remembered Sarah telling me about one of the objects though. The little blue-stone brooch with the gold around it? That was from a man who fell in love with her in Rome. She'd gone there to work for a writer, typing up his work, and he wanted her to stay.'

'It sounds like she left behind a string of lovers everywhere she went.'

'Sarah was really interesting. She'd travelled to so many different places and done lots of different things. She'd been a nurse, a journalist, she'd volunteered on archaeological sites. She had lots of great stories.'

'I bet she did. I wish I could remember some of them.'

'I think she must have been very pretty when she was younger. Have you seen any photographs of her?'

'No, I haven't. She must have lots from her adventures. I'm guessing they're all in her study. I haven't been in there yet.'

'Why not?'

Lizzie paused, taking the bowl of salad and adding some to her plate. She didn't really fancy it, but her hands had needed to hold something, and it was the first thing they'd grabbed. 'Actually, did you want to carry on today, Amélie? You're welcome to come and go as you please, I don't expect you to come every day or anything like that.'

Amélie shrugged. 'I don't mind. I'm enjoying it actually.'

'Good.' The question dodged, Lizzie added bread and cheese to her plate.

'She told me all about you,' Amélie said, and Lizzie almost dropped her fork.

Though the words had been said softly, in Amélie's child's voice, they hit Lizzie like a punch to the gut.

How could Sarah have told anyone about her? She'd thought Lizzie was boring and unadventurous, and after that final row she'd thought her rude, ungrateful and selfish. At least that's what Lizzie had spent the last fifteen years assuming. And to have spoken about her to Amélie? Sylvie she could understand, but what possible conversation could Sarah and Amélie have had about her?

'What do you mean?' Lizzie asked, trying to keep her voice level. She took a sip of water to quench her dry throat.

'She was very proud of you being a journalist. She kept all your magazines. She made Antoine the newsagent order them in especially. She'd always show me some of the articles when I came back for holidays.'

Lizzie hadn't come across them yet. If Sarah had done that, and she had no reason to doubt Amélie's word, they must be in the study. The one room she hadn't touched.

'I didn't know that,' Lizzie admitted, unable to find any other words.

'And she talked about when you used to stay here. She said you used to have lots of fun.'

'We did.' Pushing the words past the lump in her throat, Lizzie remembered campfires and games of hide-and-seek. All things she'd forgotten or not allowed herself to remember.

'Why don't you know much about her?'

Amélie was innocent and childlike in many ways, but she was also a perceptive young woman on the verge of those first steps into adulthood. Lizzie placed her knife on her plate and scratched the back of her head. She'd only told her parents about the row with Sarah, making them promise never to say anything and they'd kept their word. Will had never known. He'd never really seemed that interested. He'd always had an ability to place things in the past and list them as finished, not worth thinking about anymore. Was that where he was now? Clearly not if he was trying to get in touch to apologise, but the idea of being Will's past didn't hurt anywhere near as much as it once had.

Looking at Amélie now, her expression open and the question honest, Lizzie revealed a little more.

'We had an argument. At the time I didn't think it would be the last time I'd see her, but that's how it turned out. I refused to come back, and my mum never made me, though she wanted me to. She thought Sarah and I could talk things through but as a teenager I didn't want to, and I was much more focussed on other things. Then when I got into my twenties, time just slipped away . . . I wish . . .' She took a deep breath. 'I wish I'd made different choices now.'

'I think Sarah did as well. When I asked about you, she

used to say something about life being complicated but she'd made it more complicated than it had to be.'

Had she been talking about their row or her relationship with Guillaume? Lizzie had always felt justified for refusing to be dragged into the middle of Sarah and Guillaume's affair and Sarah had never contacted her to apologise. Had she regretted not doing that?

'Did you know she got that camel from Egypt?' Amélie continued, clearly unaware of the emotional turmoil that one simple question had started. 'She went on a holiday there and on a day trip to the pyramids she ran away from the group and went exploring on her own.'

Lizzie laughed and it was like pressure being released from a valve. 'I can imagine her doing something like that.'

'She had to hitch a ride on a camel's back to her hotel and the tour guide gave her such a telling-off she felt about five years old. She said she bought that camel at the hotel gift shop and was going to give it to him when she left to annoy him, but she ended up keeping it.'

Seeing how much Amélie knew about it and knowing she'd asked about it the night of the auction, Lizzie said, 'Would you like it, Amélie? I need to put it through the washing machine first, but you're welcome to have it.'

'Can I? Really?'

'Of course. It sounds like you were close to Sarah. You should definitely have something to remember her by.'

A tear came to Lizzie's eyes as she said the words, and she noticed Amélie's too were glassy. Her lip quivered and instinctively, Lizzie went to her and put her arms around her. 'Don't be sad. I'm sorry I made you cry.'

'I really miss her sometimes.'

'Me too.' She meant it far more than she ever thought she could. When Amélie shuffled to wipe her eyes, Lizzie pulled away. She didn't want to crowd the girl or overstep any boundaries. 'The Sarah I'm getting to know wouldn't want us to be sad. She'd want us to be happy that we we're here and remembering her. Let me grab you that camel and we'll put it on to wash now, shall we? That way you can take it home with you.'

As she placed the plates in the sink, Lizzie knew she'd no longer be able to escape the study. At some point she'd have to go in there and with everything Amélie had just said, she was more worried than ever at what she might find.

Chapter Twenty-Eight

With Luc by her side and a team of men on the roof, the chateau was soon on the mend. Thanks to all the work she and Luc had done on the garden in preparation for the concert, the place was looking better every day. At least, the outside was. Inside was still a little hodgepodge, with rooms waiting to be stripped and re-plastered, but Luc was spilling over with decorating ideas and the gloomy atmosphere was shifting. Light penetrated even the darkest corners and the chateau no longer felt neglected. It was coming back to life. Slowly but surely, progress was made, and the magic Lizzie had felt as a child was returning.

On another glorious morning, with the sun high in the sky, Lizzie and Luc were taking a moment together outside. They lay on a picnic blanket, her head resting on his chest, both staring at the clouds above them. Butterflies flew around settling here and there as Lizzie focussed on the rise and fall of her breath, feeling the deep inhales and long, slow exhales in her body. Totally relaxed in Luc's company and in the middle of peaceful Provence, the moment was tranquil and heavenly. It was a far cry from how she'd felt when she'd been here as a teenager and how she'd felt when she'd first arrived, frazzled by love and life, obsessed with work to the point that her mind had no space for anything else. Today her mind was free, her thoughts open to the smallest of sensations: the grass on the back of her arm, the breeze drifting over her face, the heat of the sun on her cheeks.

'*Ma chérie*, have you fallen asleep?'

'Hmm?' Lizzie opened her sleepy eyes and turned to look at him. She stretched, feeling the length of every muscle.

'I thought you were, how you say, out for the count.'

'No, I was just relaxing.'

'I didn't think you knew how to do that. Not when you first arrived anyway.'

'Hey, I know how to chill out. I was maybe a bit of a coiled spring, but I'll have you know I can kick back and relax with the best of them.' She rolled onto her belly and kissed him. 'Just like I'm doing now.'

Luc kissed her back, cupping the back of her head, his fingers entwining with her hair. His kisses had the power to dissolve her, and her heart pulsed whenever he held her. As long as she didn't think about England and the end of her Provençal adventure. When her mind wandered to those thoughts, gloom settled, weighing her down. She knew she'd have to think about it sooner or later. Just not today. She pushed back at those thoughts once again as they tried to dampen her happiness, focussing on the feel of Luc's lips pressed against hers.

'Oh, *excusez-moi*! *Pardon*,' came a voice she didn't recognise.

She pulled away from Luc, blushing, and he flashed his eyes at her, a mischievous grin on his face. Lizzie stood and turned around, assuming it was one of the workmen, surprised to then see a suited man averting his gaze.

'Can I help you?' Something about him was familiar but she couldn't place him. Perhaps she had seen him in town more casually dressed, or had he been at the concert?

'I was passing and saw the roof being fixed. I see you took my advice to fix it up a little before putting it on the market.'

The market? Oh god, it was the estate agent she'd spoken to when she first arrived.

Lizzie glanced at Luc to see deep lines furrowing his brow. He came towards her as the estate agent continued talking.

'So, I thought I would stop in and see if she's now ready to sell. Or at least will be soon. There seems to be a lot of progress. The roof will be fixed very soon, *oui*? And I may have a buyer interested in this sort of property. Mid-summer always sees a rise in interest. After people holiday here, they are full of the idea of buying a property. Some do, some don't, but this would be just the type of thing they like. Even if it needs some work . . . But not too much!' He chortled, but neither she nor Luc responded. 'It's not too big or too small. It is just right. Like Goldilocks and the three bears.' His laugh resounded around the quiet garden.

Luc's expression had turned thunderous and the hurt in his eyes made Lizzie queasy. 'Lizzie?' he asked tentatively. 'What's going on?'

'I – umm—' Her brain had frozen with panic, but the estate agent carried on talking.

'*Bonjour!*' He moved forwards, his hand outstretched. 'I am Charles-Claude Baudin. Are you Miss Summers' umm . . . partner?' Mr Baudin didn't wait for a response but galloped ahead, determined to shove both his feet in his mouth along with his legs and anything else he could fit in. 'I valued the chateau not long after Miss Summers arrived. Unfortunately then it wasn't really worth trying to sell, but I can see that repairs have been made and it is now ready. Did you still want to proceed, Miss Summers?'

Both Mr Baudin and Luc turned to her. Why had she let him carry on talking? She should have said something or shoved something in his mouth so he couldn't speak.

'Lizzie,' Luc croaked. 'I cannot believe that you would do this. Please tell me it is not true. You were staying. I know you wanted to sell at first but that changed. You gave the impression you were staying . . . for good. The fundraiser, taking donations for the roof . . .'

Mr Baudin's face finally registered the strained atmosphere and he realised his words hadn't helped at all. 'I should perhaps go,' he said, backing away. 'You still have my card, I believe? Yes? Good.' He didn't actually wait for an answer, and virtually ran back around the house to his car.

'Lizzie?'

'Luc, it's not quite what you th—'

'Don't tell me it's not what I think. I have heard that

before and it was exactly what I thought. Be honest with me. You are planning to sell the chateau?'

'Not planning exactly,' she replied, her voice small, the words pathetic even to her own ears.

'But I thought – we all thought—' The fierce hurt radiating off him winded her.

He began walking away, striding purposefully back into the house. She followed him, her skin reacting to the sudden change in temperature as they entered the cool kitchen and on through to the living room where his tools and phone were.

'Luc, hang on a minute. It's not—'

'I cannot believe you would do this, Lizzie. I thought you were staying. We all thought you were.'

The vivid memory of Sarah and Guillaume arguing in this room flashed into her mind. As the memory replayed, anger, guilt, and confusion materialised in her veins, creeping through her. Why was she always made out to be the bad guy? Sarah had done it, Will had done it, and now Luc was doing it. But she wasn't always to blame. Though it hurt her to see Luc so aggrieved, he'd made an assumption, not her. She'd never promised anything. She straightened. 'I never said I was staying here, Luc.'

'But you have been here for months.' He cast a hand out, thrashing at the air. 'The fundraiser – we all thought you could make the chateau a home again—'

'Yes, a home for someone, but I never said that person would be me.'

'No, you just let us all believe it. You deceived us.'

His words wounded her. 'That's unfair, Luc. I've never

deceived anyone.' If people had assumed things, that wasn't her fault. She'd always been clear about her intentions.

'You have deceived us all.'

The anger in his voice echoed around the room but she wouldn't be dictated to. 'Luc, I'm sorry if that's how you feel, but I never said I was moving here. From the start I've made it clear my life is in London.'

'But your editor said you could work from here. You were staying to live the French dream. These are things you said, Lizzie.'

She had, but she hadn't meant for them to be taken as permanent. 'I was staying until the chateau was fixed enough for me to sell it. I told you that, didn't I?'

'No. You have never said that.'

Of course she had. She was sure of it. 'I can't stay here, Luc. There's a promotion waiting for me in London when I get back.'

'And what about us, Lizzie?'

An icy blast hit her skin. He had no idea how much she'd agonised over the prospect of leaving, hoping they could work something out. The idea had torn away at her heart. Before she had time to answer, to form her incoherent thoughts into something understandable, Luc scoffed.

'I see.'

'No, Luc, I—'

'When?' he demanded.

'When what?'

'When will you put it on the market? How soon, Lizzie? How soon till you bring that man back? When the roof is finished? That will be any day now. You have deceived all of us. Me, Margot, Amélie, Sylvie . . . everyone who has helped you. You have betrayed us.'

'Betrayed? How can you say that to me, Luc?' She crossed her arms over her chest, a defensive shield but her anger grew. 'If this is about the money for the roof, I didn't like the idea of taking money from people. That's why we asked for donations and did the auction. Ask Sylvie, she'll tell you.'

'Sylvie thought you were doing what Sarah had done. Moving here, making a life. And this is not just about the money, Lizzie. It is about how we feel about you. People donated because they thought you wanted to make a home here. Because you were happy here and wanted to stay, like Sarah did. But that is not true at all, is it?'

Luc grabbed his mobile phone and stalked past her.

'Luc, wait, please. Let's both just calm down and talk about this like adults.'

'There is nothing more to say. You are exactly what I thought you were: a city girl, playing for a while at a quiet life. You have no appreciation for this—' Once again he threw his arm out in an arc, encompassing more than just the chateau. 'It is all about money and ambition to you. Not about people. Not about the quality of life. Not about love.' He paused after this last remark, his voice cracking. The word pounded at her skull. 'Call your estate agent, Lizzie. Perhaps the sooner you leave the better.'

At that comment, something inside Lizzie exploded. All the pain she'd kept bottled up from her parting with Sarah and all she'd discovered since, shot to the fore. Here she was again having a huge argument with someone who had meant something to her. First Sarah and now Luc. The bottled-up emotions fizzed over, and she snapped.

'Why are you speaking to me like this? I may have ambitions, Luc, but at least they're mine.' She slammed a hand onto her chest. 'They don't belong to anyone else. They can't be taken away from me like my wedding day was. And at least I'm making something of myself. If you love this quiet life then I'm happy for you, but some of us want to be more and at least I'm not too afraid to try.'

'What is that supposed to mean?'

'At least I'm trying to make my dreams come true, which is more than can be said for you. You want to run your own business refurbing houses but you're too afraid to take a chance. Why is that?'

He didn't answer immediately, and she let the question hang in the air. After a second, Luc responded, his voice having lost the anger only to be replaced by a low, hurt-ridden growl. 'It is complicated.'

'I am so sick of hearing that!' Lizzie balled her fists. '"Life is complicated", "Love is complicated". Why is it so complicated, Luc?'

'Because I have a child to support,' he shouted back. 'Amélie is, and always will be, my priority. My dreams come second to her, and Margot cannot support them both. It is my duty. She is my daughter.'

His answer nearly knocked her off her feet and she realised then what a callous, hurtful remark she had just made, just as Sarah's had been towards her all those years ago. Of course he would always support Amélie and it probably meant he had little capital to start his own business. She'd been quick to judge, just like Sarah.

The need to run away from the chateau almost overwhelmed her, but she stayed put. His angry eyes didn't flinch from her face, but she couldn't bear to see the pain she'd caused.

'Luc, I'm sorry.'

He moved to the door, careful not to touch her. 'Call your estate agent, Lizzie. This is not the place for you.'

Chapter Twenty-Nine

Two days later, her eyes still red with tears, Lizzie contemplated the walk into town. She'd much rather have stayed at the chateau, away from everyone else, but she was running out of food. It was Sunday and the house was silent. Lizzie wanted to hide from the world, just as she had when Will had jilted her. Her heart ached from Luc's angry words and from the pain she'd caused him. Did he really believe she'd deceived everyone? As far as she was concerned, she'd always made it clear she'd be returning to London. Surely Luc was exaggerating.

As she sat on the sofa, her arms wrapped around her curled-up legs, and a piece of stale baguette on the plate in front of her, there was no other option but to visit the *marché*. She needed fresh food and wine. Lots and lots of wine. At the moment, she had no idea if she'd ever see Luc again. She couldn't face phoning or texting him and the fact that he'd made no effort to contact her made her even more resolute not to apologise first. Luc was wrong, she hadn't kept it a secret. Her plan had always been to return to London and though she'd had an amazing time here, growing to love the place, he'd simply misunderstood her intentions. He'd taken it for granted she would be staying. Sylvie and Margot would know different. It was just Luc's grumpiness taking over again, the harsh exterior she'd first met coming back.

Scraping her hair back into a ponytail and wrapping it in the band she had on her wrist, she cleared her plate and took it to the kitchen. A glimpse in the mirror told her it was no time to bother with make-up. Not only could she never in a million years hide the dark circles under her eyes or the puffiness of her eyelids, she simply couldn't be bothered. The chances were, she'd cry it all off again anyway. As much as she didn't want to accept it, she'd been falling hard for Luc and his grumpy ways. She hadn't intended to and if anyone had told her before she left for France that was what was going to happen, she'd have laughed in their face. Her heart had been too torn, too broken, but being in Chateau Lavande, in Provence, discovering a new life had healed her. Now it was all falling apart again.

Lizzie's sight misted with unshed tears as she grabbed the wicker basket she normally used for her shopping and closed the kitchen door behind her.

The walk had become so familiar to her over the weeks she'd been here that she'd almost stopped noticing how wondrous it was, but today, with a heavy heart and eyes seeing things more clearly, she noticed everything anew.

The purple lavender fields opened before her as she

came to the end of the chateau's grounds. Though surrounded in scaffolding, the chateau remained beautiful. Some of the shutters were still off kilter with broken hinges and the outside needed repainting, but as the new tiles replaced the old, the building was being reborn.

Mr Baudin had been so excited at the prospect of putting the house on the market, but since he'd mentioned it, Lizzie hadn't been able to share that enthusiasm and not just because of Luc's reaction. All those months ago she'd longed for the day she could get shot of the place, buy somewhere in London, and get on with the rest of her life. Yet being here had calmed the tempestuous seas of her life, or at least, her outlook on it. She'd relaxed and breathed in a way she never had in London. Was she ready to give all that up?

Fields of amethyst rolled away, and to her right, in the distance, was the small wall she'd climbed over into Luc's vineyard. Her chest tightened remembering the nights they'd shared together. She'd never felt such passion and desire. There'd been a connection between them, something strong but intangible like a rope binding them together. But he wanted nothing more to do with her now. She didn't belong there. He'd said the words himself and they'd hurt more than anything Will had ever done.

Eventually, the scrubby dust track came into view, and she breathed in the scent from the chunky lavender bushes. London seemed so far away. Not just geographically but mentally too. It would be so strange to throw herself into the hectic morning commutes, the cold glass offices and the time limits on everything: lunchbreaks, evenings, bedtimes. She hadn't realised before how freeing Provence had been. She'd kept her own schedule, managed her own workload, been her own boss. It would be a big adjustment to go back to her old life.

The familiar buildings of the town were upon her within minutes. The pale pinks and creams of the walls masked by the fragrant bougainvillea bursting into life. The painted shutters in blues, greens and creams open to allow in the sun. The cobbles felt even more uneven under her feet, and the sights and smells of the *marché* already coming towards her were more vibrant than on any other day, her senses sharpened by the idea that soon she'd be leaving this all behind and returning to London. A place that seemed so grey and dull by comparison. Lizzie moved her basket from one arm to another, ready for the final few steps to the *marché*. Luc was wrong, she reminded herself. Luc was wrong. Not only had she not deceived anyone, he'd simply misunderstood their conversations. Sylvie and Margot and everyone else would know the truth.

Turning the corner into the market square, the *marché* bustled before her. She took a moment to enjoy the colourful awnings of each stall and vivid displays underneath. She'd miss this when she left. Not just the food, bright and glorious and in the sunshine, but the process of buying it, of seeing and smelling it and being surrounded by such fresh produce. Going to the local supermarket wasn't the same and the idea of pre-packaged sandwiches and the ready meals she'd been living off before almost turned her stomach. She'd be giving up so much by returning.

Entering the throng of people all queuing for the various stalls, she smiled at the stallholders she'd come to know. First was the cheesemonger, but he didn't smile back. Perhaps he was simply busy dealing with the queue. There were lots of people waiting.

Next was Pierre the charcuterie seller. She chose the items she wanted and handed them to him with a warm smile.

'*Bonjour*, Pierre,' she trilled.

'*Bonjour*,' he replied, taking the items from her. She waited for their usual small talk to begin but he didn't say anything.

'It's a beautiful day, isn't it?'

'It is. You will be sorry not to see them when you return to England.'

'Yes, I will.'

'It is a shame. A great shame.' He handed over her change.

'*Merci*, Pierre.'

'*Au revoir*, Lizzie.' Something about the way he said it tugged at her heart. He sounded so disappointed in her.

The possibility that Luc hadn't been exaggerating turned the knot in her stomach to a stone that sank to the bottom of her belly. Then Violette gave her a similar look. A look that said, 'You've let us all down', before hurrying back inside her shop and Lizzie chewed the inside of her cheek as she carried on. What else could she do? She had to buy some food. She passed where Luc's wine stall normally stood, but he wasn't there. Had he deliberately not come in case he ran into her?

'Margot!' Lizzie cried, waving at her friend as she

stepped out from behind the crowd. At least she could explain it all to her. Make sure the record was straight.

Margot's pace continued, her eyes focussed ahead on her next destination. Surely Margot wasn't ignoring her too.

'Margot!' Lizzie called again, waving.

The shoppers nearby stared at her before tutting and turning their backs. Embarrassment inched up Lizzie's spine. She wasn't being treated like a local anymore. She was no longer one of them. It hurt, but not as much as the thought of losing Margot too. Lizzie carried on after her, compelled to make sure she didn't feel the same as Luc.

'Margot, is everything okay?'

Margot slowed and finally came to a stop, her back to Lizzie. She turned and her normally smiling face was dark, her mouth a thin, angry line. 'Lizzie, I do not think—'

'I take it you've spoken to Luc.'

'Yes.' She raised her chin. 'He told me you are selling the chateau. That you always intended to sell it.'

'But you knew that,' Lizzie replied meekly.

'No, Lizzie, I did not know that.' Her tone was sad rather than angry. 'In all our conversations you never once said you were selling the chateau and returning to England. Like Luc I thought at first it was what you wanted but then, after you stayed for so long, after all the effort you put into the chateau, I thought you were staying here. I cannot believe that all the things we talked about, all the things I confided in you, and you did not tell me the truth.'

Lizzie thought hard, replaying their conversations in her

head. Surely she'd said something about her intention to sell, or hinted as much. But as she thought back, she could see that she hadn't. She'd talked about problems she was facing with the chateau as someone who was fixing the place up to stay and even more than that, she'd talked about her life in London as if it was done and dusted and left behind.

'Margot, I didn't mean to. I never deliberately—'

'It does not matter if you did it deliberately or not, Lizzie. You have hurt us all.' She wrapped a hand around Amélie's shoulders, pulling her closer. Regret and sorrow passed through her expression, but her mind seemed made up. Amélie wouldn't even look at her. Any closeness that had grown between them was gone.

'I understand,' Lizzie replied. She held back the tears swimming in her eyes. 'I'm sorry.'

'So am I.'

Margot shuffled away, and Lizzie felt another piece of her world fall apart. She'd lost friendships after she and Will split up but this one cut deeper because she knew now Luc had been right. She hadn't meant to, she hadn't deliberately deceived anyone, but she *had* deceived them and now she had to deal with the consequences.

Lizzie turned to make her way back through the *marché*, praying she wouldn't run into anyone else. She couldn't face any more heartache. She pulled out her sunglasses and put them on, hoping to hide the tears, but luck wasn't on her side. Luck had most definitely made a hasty exit from her life as Sylvie marched towards her.

The tiny birdlike woman grew with every step as she stomped along. Had she been looking out for her? She wasn't even carrying a shopping bag.

'Élisabeth, tell me that all these gossips, all this rumour, is not true. You are not selling the chateau.'

'I – Not yet,' she conceded.

Sylvie reacted with a sharp intake of breath. Her hand flying to her chest. 'Oh, Élisabeth, no. Why would you do such a thing? We all thought—'

Though her heart was racing, Lizzie tried to stay calm. She didn't want to fall out with Sylvie, she was too fond of her. 'I know what you all thought, Sylvie, and I'm sorry.' Her voice cracked, but she carried on. 'I didn't mean for you all to think that. I honestly thought I'd made it clear that I'd be returning to England. You couldn't all think I'd just leave my old life behind and move here.'

'Like Sarah did, you mean? What was wrong with her decision? She was happy here.'

'I know she was, Sylvie. But I have a career back home and—'

'You have a career here, do you not?'

'I do, but—'

'But nothing.' Her accent had become heavier as her anger grew. 'If you do not want to stay, fine, we will not try and convince you. I just hope whoever moves into Chateau Lavande will appreciate it the way Sarah did. She did not always get things right, but she loved every minute of her life there until the day she died. She would never have had it any other way.'

'Sylvie, I'm sorry.'

'I am disappointed in you, Élisabeth. I thought you were cleverer than this.'

What did she mean by that? Lizzie was going back to a budding career. She'd been hurdling the career ladder rather than climbing it. Before she could implore Sylvie to understand, she marched past her and carried on her way. Lizzie couldn't face calling her back. She'd had enough humiliation for one day and Sylvie's words had sliced through the remnants of her composure. Dropping her eyes to her basket, she pushed on. She had to get out of here and away from everyone. From all the people she'd hurt, however much she hadn't meant to.

Chapter Thirty

Brushing tears from her cheeks, Lizzie made her way back through the fields to the chateau. How she wished Luc would be there to greet her, giving her a chance to explain. She'd been so closed off from everyone that she'd never been clear about her intentions. Luc had been right; she had deceived people. Not willingly. She wasn't a scammer or a con artist. She just hadn't been honest enough. It was no wonder given everything she'd been through, but she'd embraced so many new things since she'd been here, felt so many new sensations, she could, and should have taken that final step and trusted again. Would the town have supported the idea? Who knows, but it would have been better than how they felt now.

Lizzie turned the corner of the chateau to see a figure standing at the kitchen window, peering in through the glass.

'Will?' A static shock sparked in her chest.

He spun, his eyes wide, taking her in. 'Lizzie. Wow, I mean . . . Wow, you look great.'

'What are you doing here?'

Where was his girlfriend? For some reason, she checked her watch, as if knowing the time would give her the answer.

Will took a step towards her. He looked good. The familiarity of his square jaw and clean-shaven face offered something to her bruised heart. 'I came to see you. I thought we should talk.'

'Talk?' Anger rose up, her brain replaying the scene of her at the church waiting for him. The humiliation flooded back. 'Talk about what?'

He reached out but she pulled away. 'I've made a mistake, Lizzie. A horrible mistake.'

All she could hear was the thudding of blood in her ears. So many times she'd prayed to hear those words. When she'd called him late at night, sometimes a little drunk but always truthful about the pain inside, he'd never once wanted to talk. Soon he ignored her. He hadn't gone so far as to block her, but he certainly never answered. It was like a brick wall had been built between them and now he wanted to tear that wall down.

Emotionally exhausted from her argument with Luc and her trip into town, Lizzie couldn't bear another scene. Her instinct was to send him away. She still had hopes Luc might come by and they could talk things through, but the chances were slim. What would Luc think if he saw Will? She didn't want him to think even less of her than he did now. If that was actually possible.

Will's eyes were dull with what she hoped was regret. 'Please, Lizzie?'

'I suppose you better come in.' She made her way to the kitchen door.

'This is quite a place, isn't it? You never told me your aunt lived in France.'

'I did, actually.' Though she hadn't confided everything about Sarah, she had told him her aunt lived here.

'Did you? I should have remembered that.'

Walking to the sink, Lizzie filled the kettle. 'How did you know I was here?'

Will sat down at the table, moving things out of his way and clasping his hands in front of him. 'I saw your latest article – some of your Instagram photos were in there and figured it out. I'm sorry to turn up unexpectedly, but I had to see you, Lizzie.'

She turned to face him, resting her back against the worktop. 'Well, you've found me now. What do you want?'

He scratched the back of his head. His hair had been cut much shorter. She didn't like it. He was still handsome, but it made his features sharper, colder somehow. 'I understand why you're angry with me, Lizzie. I do. I've behaved horribly. I should never have done what I did. I panicked. Suddenly getting married seemed like such a big deal—'

'But it didn't seem like a big deal when we were planning the wedding for over a year. When we were checking out venues, tasting cakes or booking DJs?' He had no answer. The whistling of the kettle gave her a chance to calm down. With shaking hands, she made the tea, keeping her eyes away from Will's as she grabbed the milk from the fridge.

She knew he'd be watching her, trying to figure out what to say or do next. She took the two cups to the table and sat down opposite him.

'Lizzie, I wish I could tell you exactly what's happening, but I don't know. All I know is that I wanted to marry you for so long. That's why I proposed, and I loved all our wedding preparations. But then, the night before the wedding, I panicked. I was scared. Scared that, for some unknown reason, we weren't right for each other and that if we married it would be harder to do anything about it. I know it doesn't make sense. I didn't want to hurt you, Lizzie. I'd never hurt you on purpose.'

Except for the day you left me at the church, waiting for you to arrive.

'But it was all a mistake, Lizzie. It was all my mind playing tricks on me.'

A part of her wanted to laugh at the ridiculousness of it all. Was he really sitting here telling her this after the months of torment she'd been through?

'And what about your new girlfriend?' She met his gaze, eager to see his reaction. Will dropped his eyes to his cup and removed his hands from hers.

'It's over.'

'Another mistake?' She didn't want to sound cruel but what was she supposed to do? Let him walk back into her life and fall at his feet. No way.

Will's cheeks coloured. 'I know this sounds bad, Lizzie, but it was a rebound thing. I didn't realise it at the time, but I threw myself into it, ignoring that deep down I knew I'd made a mistake.'

'So even when you posted that picture on Instagram, you knew it was a mistake?' She was starting to feel sorry for the pretty woman in the picture. It seemed Will had treated her badly too.

'No. No. It's all so complicated.' He rubbed his temple. 'What can I say, Lizzie? I wish I could explain everything in a way that makes sense, but I can't. My feelings didn't make sense – they don't make sense. I've messed everything up. Everything.' He gripped her hands but all she could think was that they weren't Luc's. His were gentle and caressing. Will's were unwelcome. 'I panicked about getting married and made the biggest mistake of my life. Then I met her, and I was hurting so much I thought starting something new would help me get over you, but it didn't. It just made me realise everything I'd lost. All because I was too stupid to tell you I was scared and ask to put the wedding off a bit. Please believe me, Lizzie, when I say I've realised now what an absolute idiot I've been. If we could do it all again, I'd run down that aisle and say I do before you changed *your* mind.' He laughed but it was an awkward, self-conscious laugh that brought a blush to his cheeks.

'There's something I need to know.'

'Anything.'

'Did you ever cheat on me?' She kept her gaze locked on his, ensuring she'd catch any lies on his face.

He didn't flinch. 'No.'

'No?'

'No. I swear to you.'

She wanted to believe him. He hadn't given anything away and it seemed she had no choice but to believe him.

At least she could put that fear to bed. Looking at him, there was a vulnerability in his expression that tugged at her heart and something inside reminded her of all the years they'd spent together.

She'd run away to France to escape everything back home and now she wanted to run away from France back to England. Back to the career that had comforted her so much. Was Will now a part of that future too? The familiarity was tempting. She could remember the comfort she'd once taken from his arms around her after a bad day. The way they'd watched movies together, laughing and joking. But was the memory of it enough? She could only imagine what her mother would say. She'd loved Will and was as devastated as Lizzie by the breakup, but it would take a long time for her to forgive him. Could Lizzie just fall back into their relationship? Could she trust him? She wanted to so desperately, but a niggle at the back of her mind held her back.

'Will, what exactly are you asking me to do?'

'I want us to get back together, Lizzie. I'm not saying dive back into wedding planning. I know how much I hurt you and when we do get to the wedding stage again, you might want something different this time, but I want us to be together. I've missed you so much.' He raised his hand as if to reach out, but held back. 'I've missed waking up with you every day, falling asleep with you at night. I've missed watching TV with you snuggled on the sofa, talking through half the things we want to watch.'

She'd missed those things too. The good times, the safety and security of it all.

'I thought,' Will continued, 'we could sell this place and buy somewhere in London. Together. Think of the type of place we could have, Lizzie. It would be the perfect home we always dreamed of.'

Lizzie's head spun. As the heat of the day seeped in through the open back door, she suddenly felt very hot and tired. It was all too much. All she wanted to do was cry for the friends she'd lost in town and for Luc, and the love that could have been between them. She stood, bringing their conversation to an end.

'I need some time to think, Will. What you've said – what you're asking – it's a lot to take in. Are you staying at the *gîte* in town?'

'No, a hotel about an hour away.'

Of course. Will liked the nice things in life and a small, cosy *gîte* wouldn't be for him. He'd probably chosen a hotel with five stars, a swimming pool, a decent restaurant. That's just how he was, and she'd loved that about him once. Loved the places he'd taken her for romantic weekends away.

'I'll call you, okay?' Lizzie said. 'How long are you staying for?'

'A couple of days.'

'You understand I need some time?' She rubbed her forehead, weary and drained. 'It's a lot to think about.'

'I get it.' He got up and made his way towards her. Again, his hand reached out, but he withdrew it. 'But you have to know, Lizzie, that I love you. I've made some horrendous mistakes, but I do love you more than ever. You're the only person for me. The one I want to grow old with. The one I want to—'

'I get it, Will, but please, I just need to be alone for a while.' She desperately wanted to believe him but couldn't shake the feeling he was laying it on a bit thick.

With a dip of his head and a sad smile he made his way out of the kitchen door. His gaze wandered over the impressive lines of the chateau as he left and something about it rankled.

The prospect of escaping back to Britain and picking up her life from before it had all fallen apart was incredibly tempting. Her career had gone from strength to strength, a promotion was guaranteed, great things were ahead. If they sold the chateau, they would be able to buy somewhere decent in London, living the life they'd always dreamed about together. Will had made a mistake and now knew for sure that she was who he wanted. Everything about his words and actions seemed genuine, but a piece of her heart had closed to him, and she wasn't sure she'd ever be able to unlock it. Not after what he'd done.

Lizzie went to the fridge and pulled out a bottle of wine. Luc's wine. Just holding it made her feelings stir. He never really left her thoughts anymore. She'd have to bury her feelings for him deep down inside if she went back to England, but then, he never wanted to see her again anyway. No one did. The town had made it clear how betrayed they felt. She'd even hurt Margot and Amélie.

The joy had been stripped from her life here in France and she didn't know if she'd ever be able to get it back. Running to England and the familiarity of Will and her growing career seemed like the safest option all round.

Chapter Thirty-One

The door stood before her and already Lizzie's breathing had grown faster. Before she could go anywhere, she needed to find the items Sarah had given her mother and after an extensive search of the house, the only place they could be was the one room that remained untouched: Sarah's study. With her thoughts on returning home, the time had come to finish this last job.

There'd been no word from Luc or Margot, nothing from Sylvie either, and Lizzie had been too scared to attempt another visit into town. Will, however, had been in touch frequently. He'd texted a couple of times each day to wish her good morning and ask what she was up to, then in the evening he'd bid her goodnight, adding that he wanted to hold her like he used to. Unsure of what she was supposed to say, Lizzie held back, giving answers that she'd have given to her mum. She wished him goodnight too and hoped he was enjoying his hotel, maybe adding a polite enquiry as to what he'd had for dinner. It felt like he wanted to say more, but she couldn't risk hearing it. However much she had once wanted him to say that he loved her and wipe away the months of pain, she wasn't sure she could ever trust him again. Perhaps it would simply take time to rebuild what they'd once had and when she sold the chateau and returned to England, she'd be in a better place to decide.

Armed with a cup of tea and a roll of black bin bags, Lizzie took a breath and finally opened the study door. The room was stacked with papers. The desk that ran along one wall was covered with an array of magazines, journals, random sheets of paper and letters. Behind it, shelves were packed full of books and dusty glass boxes that contained some of Sarah's most exotic souvenirs. Given that the pieces Sarah had given her mum were jewellery, Lizzie was expecting there to be a small safe in the office, or a locked drawer. There were keys on the enormous set she hadn't yet found a matching lock for. On first glance there was nothing. She'd have to clean it all to make sure.

Edging in, Lizzie ignored the age-old anger at Sarah and the bitter exchange between them adding to her already fraught emotions. She'd get in and get out again. That was it. She took another deep breath in, holding it for a second to pause her racing heart, and then let it out slowly.

As she had with the kitchen table, she began to sort through a stack of papers, throwing out the rubbish and piling up anything that could be important.

Clearing the desk was a long and arduous task and as lunchtime approached, Lizzie took a break, sitting back in the creaky wooden office chair. Her neck ached from hunching over and though she'd made good progress, there were still the four drawers of the old wooden desk to go.

Four small feet clacked across the hallway floor and Lizzie knew instantly who they belonged to.

'In here, Gary,' she called.

His little head appeared around the door frame, those funny ears flopping over at the tips. He bleated and trotted in, gazing around him.

'Nothing to fear, Gary. Here, you can chew this.' She handed him a flyer and he held it in his mouth before finding a space on the floor and sitting down. She'd miss him too when she left. 'I hope you came in through the back door. I still need to find where you've been sneaking in from.'

Outside the window, the men were hard at work on the roof, but their enthusiasm had dimmed. Songs were sung much more quietly, and they smiled at her less. They too clearly felt the same disappointment the town did, but were finishing the job anyway. She missed their jokes and the cheerful atmosphere they'd brought with them.

As Lizzie sat, it occurred to her that another cycle of the chateau's life was coming to an end, just like it had when she'd first arrived. Even if she pictured a young family moving in, it still felt like something would be lost. Gone forever, never to be found again. She'd always thought that once it had left her family, a new chapter would begin in its history, but now it seemed more like a whole new book would open and it wasn't one she was keen on reading. She wasn't ready for it to have a new life with other people who didn't know Sarah or her family. She bit down on her lip to stem the emotions rising inside.

A tinny ping echoed around the room and Lizzie grabbed her mobile phone from her pocket, checking the screen. It was Will. She tapped to read, her temper rising. He was asking if she needed any help clearing the chateau. If there was anything he could do to help her make her decision. Lizzie considered replying but chose not to. Was it purely bad timing that he'd come when he had, or had he heard about the chateau and then decided they should get back together? As uncharitable as the thought was, a warning lurked in her brain. She wanted to trust him so badly, but memories of his betrayal held her back.

Ignoring Will's message, Lizzie pulled open the top drawer and began work again, throwing papers into the black sack. A few handfuls in, she grabbed an envelope noticing it had the sealed side down. She turned it over to see her name and address written on it in block capital print. Lizzie's forehead pinched in confusion. She ran her thumb over the writing and shivered. When had this been written?

Lizzie's heart gave a hard thud. She suddenly remembered Sarah telling her to always write addresses in block capitals to make them easier to read. It had apparently saved her from getting lost several times on her adventures when her pronunciation failed her. There'd been a story about Morocco – about bazaars and backstreets – another memory Lizzie had buried.

Puzzled, Lizzie let the bin bag sink down between her

knees as she turned the envelope over and opened it. There was no card inside, and her fingers began to tremble. She pulled out a letter, written in Sarah's neat handwriting. Some of the words had faded over time, but as she began to read it was clear and concise, as Sarah herself had been.

Dear Lizzie,

I won't bother with formalities. All of that *how are you* nonsense. You will, I know, be wondering why I left Chateau Lavande to you since we haven't spoken in fifteen years. The answer is simple: because I want you to have it.

I remember fondly the summers you spent with me even when you were a sulky teenager. Even though the last one was eventful for all the wrong reasons, I was always happy you came.

I should have contacted you sooner, I know that. But for a long time, I was angry at you, and when Guillaume died, I was consumed by a crippling grief I had never felt before. It wasn't until recently that I came to realise the misunderstanding that happened between us. So silly really, and such a waste of precious, precious time. You may not think it now, in the bloom of youth, but time is precious, and I've wasted too much of it being stubborn and refusing to make the first move to mend our broken relationship. I always thought of you not only as a niece, Lizzie, but as the daughter I never had. I was happy not to have children of my own, but if I had had a daughter, I *would have wanted her to be just like you. Most importantly, I think that, as you grew older, we would have become friends, closer than friends, if we had only given each other the chance.*

Before you read any more of this letter, please read the other one I have enclosed herewith. I hope it will help correct the misunderstanding between us, a misunderstanding that was caused by my temper and hurt all those years ago.

Lizzie reached back inside the white envelope that had sat steadily on her lap. Another letter, smaller and written on aged writing paper without an envelope nestled inside. Lizzie gasped as she opened it, seeing immediately the name at the top. It was the letter that had started everything. The letter that had ended Lizzie's contact with Sarah. The letter addressed to Guillaume's wife.

The argument right here in the study flashed back into her mind. Sarah had asked her to deliver it. She hadn't wanted to go into town, probably for the same reasons Lizzie herself hadn't wanted to today: worried that everyone would hate her and shame that those she'd befriended thought badly of her.

At the time, Lizzie had refused. She'd assumed it was a confession that Sarah had been having an affair with Guillaume, unceremoniously unveiling the truth of their relationship to his poor unsuspecting wife. Telephoning, sending a text message or email, they weren't Sarah's style at all. A letter had been far more dramatic. Lizzie had assumed Sarah's motives in her anger and hurt were vengeful and when she'd asked Lizzie to take it into the village and post it through their door, she'd refused to have any part in it.

Was it different now she knew they had loved each other deeply? That his wife had been having affairs too? That Guillaume's marriage was unhappy from the start? Lizzie's throat tightened as she read and slowly, she realised how wrong she'd been about everything.

The letter was an apology. Heartfelt and endearing. A confession of falling in love at the wrong time, of knowing that they should have owned up and knowing that hurt lurked around the corner for all of them. Lizzie couldn't condone Sarah's actions, she still felt there was no excuse for cheating, but she did at least now understand. Sarah had gone against her conscience and wanted to apologise to the woman she'd hurt.

The phrase 'life is complicated' resounded through Lizzie's mind as she went back to Sarah's letter to her.

I've come to realise that you believed the letter was me informing Guillaume's wife about the affair. That I had set out to hurt both him and his wife by telling her everything, but it was not. I know I could be reckless at times and our relationship had been passionate and stormy. To be honest, it was the type of affair I've always loved most. The most adventurous and, at times, the most fulfilling, but not always sustainable. As it was, news of the affair travelled fast enough after you left that there was no need of a letter at all. Guillaume's wife found out that very day from Guillaume himself. The town was shocked, but they forgave us and came to understand our love for each other was true, if untimely. Though Guillaume and I tried, after a few years our relationship became a rewarding companionship, and we remained friends until his death.

Now it will be my turn to take that final journey and I have to admit, despite the many adventures I have been on, this is one I am nervous to take. The doctors have confirmed I have only weeks left to get my affairs in order and that is the reason for this letter. I have changed my will, but I wanted something to go with it so that you would better understand the gift I have given you, and Chateau Lavande is a gift.

I have always loved you, Lizzie, and it is for this reason I wanted you to inherit the chateau. I have had many adventures in life and in love, but Chateau Lavande has always been the love of my life. My sanctuary. I would not change a moment of my life. It has been lived on my terms and I've squeezed every last moment of excitement from it.

I know you may wish to sell the chateau and if you do, that is your decision, but I hope you will consider keeping it and taking a chance on life and love. Your mother has kept me informed of everything that has been happening to you and I want you to know that *you only ever need to be true to yourself. A man can be a wonderful lover and companion, a career can be rewarding and fulfilling, but true happiness can only come from within. I want you to be truly happy, Lizzie. To live your life on your terms and squeeze every last drop of pleasure from it.*

Chateau Lavande is yours and I hope it will give you as much happiness as it has me.

With all my love, and my deepest apologies,

Sarah

Lizzie finished reading the letter with tears falling down her cheeks. Sarah must have intended to send it but had become too sick. Lizzie choked back sobs. She'd been so wrong about Sarah – and about everything, it seemed. Chateau Lavande hadn't been a final chore for her to complete, a final message from Sarah; at least, not in the way she'd assumed, and her summers here hadn't always been terrible. Lizzie knew she'd been a sulky teenager, driven by a fear of missing out on what her friends were doing, of them leaving her behind, but there were so many good moments she'd forgotten. Some had already surfaced over her time here, but there were many more in her memory, if she allowed herself to unlock them.

And Sarah was right that she had always lived her life solely on her terms. She regretted nothing and had taken every opportunity given to her, whether in life or love. Sarah had been brave. Far braver than Lizzie had ever been. Until recently. She'd taken the chance to move out here and had finally been truly happy. Her love for Luc, because that's what it was, no proviso needed, was the strongest she'd ever felt for anyone, and though she loved her job and her career, it hadn't filled the dark holes in her life caused by a broken heart and a broken life. As she looked back on her months here in France, she realised how full her life had felt. How complete.

Could she really run away from all this? Give it all up to move back in with Will? The town had forgiven Sarah for her affair with Guillaume, if indeed they'd ever been angry with her at all. Could they do the same for her own plan to sell? In time, if she stayed, it would, she was sure, all be forgotten.

The pieces of Lizzie's life suddenly fell into place. Wiping her eyes, she saw the stack of magazines Sarah had kept of her articles. This room would make a wonderful office for her to continue writing, and if *Lifestyle!* didn't want her anymore, she could always free-lance. She had so many ideas for articles already listed down, and her mum would be overjoyed to know the chateau would be lived in and loved by her. She would work to mend her friendship with Margot and Sylvie and continue to restore the sense of joy Sarah had brought to Chateau Lavande. And as for Luc, she wouldn't give up. He was right to be hurt and she'd do everything she could to make sure he knew how sorry she was.

In fact, there was no time like the present. He may not want to see her, but taking a leaf out of Sarah's bold and fearless book, she was going to try.

'Don't eat anything, Gary, okay?' But he was asleep, curled up in a ball in the corner of Sarah's study.

Still holding the letter, Lizzie charged out of the front door and on towards the vineyard.

Chapter Thirty-Two

As always, the fresh air was perfumed with flowers and ripening fruit. Lizzie couldn't imagine her life without it now and as she walked on, she basked in the sun, the breeze on her face, the grass sweeping gently against her legs. Though she wanted to run to Luc, she didn't want to arrive hot and sweaty. It wouldn't exactly be the romantic moment she was going for. Though there wasn't anything to say that there would even be a romantic moment. There was nothing to say that Luc would forgive her. All she could do was hope, and ignore the fear creeping up on her.

In her excitement at finally realising where she belonged and where her future lay, Lizzie hadn't considered the possibility that Luc may not want her anymore. He may not be able to forgive the hurt she'd caused, and even if he did, it might take far longer than she expected for him to speak to her again, let alone love her.

In her mind, she hoped for a movie scene. One of the

ones where they run through an airport, swim a lake, or leap onto a boat already sailing away from the dock. Surrounded by the beautiful countryside, she'd admit her mistake to Luc, and he'd sweep her into his arms and kiss her. But what if he refused to talk to her? What if he looked her up and down and decided no thanks, not for me?

Lizzie's pace slowed at the doubt edging further into her mind, settling over it like a black cloud. Then the vineyard appeared, its low stone wall encircling it. She remembered climbing over it drenched to the bone, the first time she'd seen rain-soaked Luc looking all handsome and heroic. Grumpy and standoffish as he was, she knew now it had all been an act. That underneath was a kind, caring man. A man who'd mended her heart.

Sarah's letter said she didn't need a man to make her happy and that was absolutely true. Regardless of Luc's reaction she was staying and following the path here. She didn't need Luc, but she wanted him. She wanted to share this journey with him. Discerning courage from the letter still clenched in her hand, Lizzie marched on, climbing over the wall and into the lines of vines. She ducked underneath the heavy bunches of grapes, eager to make it to the farmhouse.

Lizzie's phone rang and she considered refusing the call, but when she saw it was Will, she had to answer. She was sure of her decision, and there was no point in putting things off. Today was all about taking control of her life, facing the future and doing everything she could to make that happen.

'Lizzie, I'm sorry to ring, but I'm heading back to London tomorrow and I – I just need to know how you feel about me. I understand you can't just forgive me, but I can't go without knowing there's some hope for us.'

'Will—'

He kept going. Had he always done this? Talked on and on without giving her space to think or respond? 'I keep seeing us in a sweet Victorian house in Greenwich, or a cool flat somewhere. Just us, together, you know? I don't want to push you. I know I've no right, but I mean—'

'Will, stop.' There was stunned silence on the other end of the line. 'I can't. I just can't.'

'You can't forgive me?'

'I can't go back.'

'What do you mean?'

'I mean that—' She pulled a leaf from a branch, running it between her thumb and forefinger. 'I can't go back to London. I'm staying here. In Provence.'

'But what about us?'

She shook her head, though he couldn't see. 'I'm sorry, Will. Things are over between us. I can't go back to being with you.' She thought of his inscrutable face when she'd asked if he'd cheated. She still wasn't sure he'd told her the truth and that, on top of all her other doubts, was enough. But though he'd hurt her badly, she didn't want to hurt him. She didn't feel the need anymore. There'd been a time when she had wanted to, when it felt like that was what he deserved, but not anymore.

'But I made a mistake, Lizzie.'

'I know, Will. But sometimes you can't just apologise

and turn the clock back. I don't think I could ever feel the same way about you as I did before and I'm wondering now, if you didn't make a mistake after all.'

'What do you mean?' His tone was hard.

'You clearly weren't happy with our relationship to do what you did, and I think you might have been right. Maybe it wasn't everything I thought it was. We were happy for such a long time, but things changed. Maybe you changed first but . . . I've changed now and I'm not going back to England. I'm staying here at the chateau.'

'Lizzie, this is mad. How will you afford it?' Will's voice had grown stronger, carrying an angry undertone. Lizzie ignored it. She'd be ending the call shortly anyway.

'That doesn't matter, Will. That's my business. Just know that I'm sorry and I hope things work out for you in London.'

'But Lizzie—'

There was nothing more to say. He was a part of her life that was done and finished. She'd never regret the time they'd had together, but her life was moving in a different direction, and she couldn't wait any longer. 'Goodbye, Will.' She hung up, hot from their discussion, her heart pounding from the confrontation.

As she exited the vineyard, Lizzie paused. Luc was outside the farmhouse, painting the shutters on the windows. His T-shirt clung to his back, showing the muscles that lay underneath. Muscles she'd traced her hands over on what had been, without doubt, the greatest night of her life. This was the man she wanted. The man who, if she was going to attempt a relationship with anyone, would be the one she chose. Like a big bass drum her heart thudded against her ribs.

'Luc?' she said tentatively.

He spun, surprised at seeing her. His face was covered in speckles of paint, and she wanted to walk over and wipe them away.

'What are you doing here?' He wasn't happy to see her, but his tone was neutral, no longer angry. Something else passed over his features, something she dared to hope was more than just confusion.

'I—' How did she begin? There was so much to say. So much damage to undo. But how to find the words. Sentences raced through her mind, but she couldn't pin a single one down. Yet she'd started to speak, and she had to say something. She had to tell him the most important thing. The thing she'd come here for, regardless of the consequences. 'I've decided to stay.'

Luc stayed where he was. No running to sweep her into his arms, no lifting and spinning her around, overjoyed at her announcement. Instead, he carefully placed the paint-brush on top of the open paint can.

'I found this letter,' Lizzie continued, holding it out so he could see the crumpled mess in her hand. 'It's from Sarah. She told me she'd left me the chateau because she wanted me to grow old there. To live my life on my terms and make the most of every moment, just like she did, and it made me realise something.'

'What's that?' He asked the question quickly, eagerly, and hope sparked inside her.

'That I've been the happiest I've ever been here, in these

past few months.' She glanced down at the ball of paper, loosening her grip so as not to destroy it. 'The chateau's a pain, and it's going to take a long, long time to get it back to its best. It may never look its best, but I can't leave it. The chateau, the town, have felt more of a home to me than anywhere I've ever lived before.' She glanced up to see him watching her. His bright blue eyes mesmerising, she couldn't look away. 'You were right. I did deceive everyone. I honestly didn't mean to. I just didn't think when I spoke and—'

In a second Luc was in front of her, his arm outstretched. 'I'm sorry, Lizzie. I should not have said that. I was hurtful. Of course you hadn't decided to just move from London to Provence forever. You had your own life. I wanted to come and apologise but I didn't know if you wanted to see me. It was wrong of me to presume. It is my greatest fault.' He ran a hand through his thick, curly brown hair, pushing it back just for it to spring forwards again. 'I always think everyone wants this life, as I do.' Lizzie had begun to increasingly see the world through his eyes. The peace, the tranquillity, and the belonging.

'I should have been more honest about my plans, Luc. Not just with you. With everyone. Especially myself. And I should never have said you were too scared to follow your dreams.' She dropped her gaze as guilt filled her. 'It was insensitive. I was angry.' She shook her head. 'I was out of order.'

'You were right,' he said gently. A soft smile lit his face. 'I have been too scared. I do want to support Amélie, but I do have money I could use towards starting a business.

I just wanted to keep life simple. What is it you English say? Not to rock the boat? But life is always complicated, one way or another, and I should not let it stop me. I should be braver. Like you.'

'I don't think I'm brave. I just know now what I really want. And I don't want to go back to London. For the first time, I've felt really alive here. Like I was finally living my life how I wanted.'

Luc shifted closer. They were millimetres apart, the heat of his body igniting hers. Her feelings for him solidifying and anchoring her to the ground.

'And then there's . . .'

'There's what?' he asked, his breath tickling her cheek. His hand brushed the hair back from her face, tucking it behind her ear. The light touch of his fingers sent shivers down her spine.

'Well, there's Gary the goat. I couldn't possibly leave—'

Luc's lips met hers, his fingers racing from behind her ear, holding her face. His other hand came to join it, caressing her cheek as she kissed him back. The world slid away as his arms enclosed her. Her fingers were in his hair and on the back of his neck. He had to know how much she wanted him in her future.

Breathless, they parted.

'You're a crazy English lady, you know that?'

'I know.'

For the first time, she loved that phrase. She was crazy, uprooting her life and staying here, just like Sarah had done all those years ago. A kind of peace settled in her mind. Sarah would have approved, she was sure, and though Lizzie couldn't tell her she was sorry, or that she forgave Sarah for her actions, it was as if the chateau, and Sarah, knew exactly how she felt. The past was finally behind them.

'I'd better tell Margot,' she whispered, unable to raise her voice to anything more.

'Later,' Luc replied, sweeping her into his arms and carrying her inside the farmhouse.

Later would be fine. After all, neither she, nor the chateau, were going anywhere.

Chapter Thirty-Three

The final piece of scaffolding came down and the village cheered. Lizzie popped a champagne cork and a stream of delicious bubbles flooded onto the grass. She laughed as Luc tried to catch some of it in tall, thin glasses.

'The roof is fixed!' Lizzie announced to the assembled crowd. 'So please help yourself to food and drink.'

Using the last of her money, Lizzie had treated her friends to an informal picnic. She'd bought as much food and wine as she could afford and, of course, everyone else had pitched in even though she'd told them not to. It was her way of apologising for the confusion she'd caused over the chateau's future and thanking them for forgiving her.

She'd told Hilary of her plans to remain in France and she'd been happy for Lizzie to continue with the regular feature, quoting reader numbers and comments at her. It was going down well, and ideas were thrown around for other articles she could write and topics they could explore. The promotion still hadn't been decided but Hilary had been supportive of her plans to go freelance, promising they'd still want a regular article about her Provençal life for as long as readers were enjoying it. The permanent post was to be based in London, but Lizzie didn't mind if they chose someone else. She'd realised that life was full of so many other things that gave her joy and writing from the chateau, in the middle of beautiful Provence, was more than enough to keep her happy.

After she'd spent the rest of the day – and night – with Luc, they'd braved the town together, hand in hand. Wide-eyed stares and surprised glances changed to smiles and congratulations as she'd told them all her news. Sylvie had hugged her as if she were one of her own grandchildren, while Margot and Amélie were overjoyed. Well, perhaps overjoyed was the wrong word for Amélie. From the way she tutted when Luc and Lizzie held hands, it was going to take a while for her to get used to her dad dating again. Still, Lizzie felt decidedly grateful. A tut and an eyeroll she could deal with.

'I am so proud of you, Élisabeth,' Sylvie said, embracing her and placing a kiss on each cheek. 'And Sarah would be too.'

'Thank you, Sylvie.'

'Even though it took you longer to realise it than her.' She waved a hand dismissively. 'I will not hold it against you. You realised it in the end and that's what matters.'

'What exactly have I realised?' She wondered if Sylvie knew the depths of everything she'd discovered about Sarah and herself, and about life and its complexities.

'That Provence is the most wonderful place in the

world!' she declared, giddy as a schoolgirl. 'Of course you would want to live here!'

Lizzie laughed as Luc took the champagne bottle from her, filling more glasses. 'It certainly is,' she replied, earning a smile from Luc that made her tingle all over.

Sylvie sauntered off, Henri holding her under the arm as Margot arrived.

'The chateau is looking so much better already. What is your next job?'

'Oh, umm, the electrics, filling the holes in the ceilings, repairing the shutters, repainting the outside before the winter hits. Take your pick.'

Margot laughed. 'You will have a lot to keep you busy. You and Luc.' She cast a glance at him, and Lizzie followed. He'd lost the champagne bottle and was dancing in front of Amélie, who giggled, pretending to cringe with embarrassment. Gary the goat was snuggled next to her, enjoying being petted and fed errant bits of food. When Margot's gaze returned to Lizzie, Lizzie forced the silly smile from her face. Though Margot had said time and time again everything was fine, Lizzie still felt strange at being such good friends with her boyfriend's ex-wife. 'He is a good man, Lizzie. I hope that you will be very happy together. And very happy here.'

She raised her eyes to the chateau and saw it as she had as a child. The fairy-tale palace came to life once more and though she wouldn't be charging up and down the stairs as Cinderella or playing zombies in the tower, she was making the chateau her own. It needed a beautiful name plate once the front door was repainted. Something in purple, as 'Lavande' did mean 'lavender', after all. Perhaps a white sign with a lavender border and the name written in swirling letters. It would take years to get everything done, but the prospect excited rather than disappointed her, just as it excited her mum. Her parents had been overjoyed that she was staying at the chateau. They'd miss her, of course, but hearing, and hopefully soon seeing, her so happy was all that mattered to them.

'There is someone I'd like you to meet,' Margot said, drawing Lizzie's attention back to the moment at hand.

'Okay. Who is it? Is it your partner? You said you might bring them. I can't wait to meet him.'

'Just wait there, okay?' Margot patted her arm and went off into the crowd.

Lizzie did as she was asked, smiling at the townsfolk who'd come out to the chateau and sipping her almost empty glass of champagne. Luc would be opening some of his wine soon, but they'd decided that a job as big as the roof had to be celebrated with something bubbly, and of course, French.

When Lizzie looked up from her glass it was to see Margot walking towards her with another attractive woman by her side. Her hair was slightly shorter, resting just on her shoulders, but the shaggy cut was just as stylish. She was wearing a pretty floral dress and trainers, which Lizzie very much approved of.

'Lizzie, this is my girlfriend, Marie.'

For a second, Lizzie assumed she meant girlfriend as in, a friend who is a girl, but seeing the adoring look that passed between them and the way Margot threaded her arm around Marie's waist, she understood fully. Though surprised, she was ecstatic to see her friend so happy. Lizzie thrust her hand out. 'It's so lovely to meet you! Do you mind if I hug you? Is that okay?'

Marie's arms widened and a smile spread over her face. 'That would be wonderful. I am so happy to be here. Margot has spoken so often about the chateau and about you. I feel I know you already.'

Though she couldn't say exactly the same, Lizzie replied that it was lovely to meet her too. Perhaps Margot had kept Marie's gender a secret for the same reason she'd held back about selling the place.

'I admire that you are refurbishing such a beautiful house. It must be a lot of work.'

'My to-do list is quite long,' Lizzie joked.

'But what an adventure.'

She could almost hear Sarah laughing at Marie's words. 'It certainly is that.'

'Lizzie, who is this pretty lady?' Sylvie bustled over to join them. 'Some friend from London, perhaps?'

'Umm, actually . . .'

'Hello, Sylvie,' Margot said. To everyone else her voice probably sounded as confident as usual, but Lizzie could hear the nerves underlining the words. 'I've been meaning to introduce you. This is my partner, Marie. We live together in Paris.' As if fearing Sylvie's response, Margot defiantly shared a kiss with a slightly stunned Marie.

There was a moment's silence and it felt like everyone had turned to watch.

'Well,' said Sylvie. 'You are most welcome! You must come and meet my husband, Henri. He will probably try and dance with you later when he has had too much to drink, but I will tell you when to run away, so you must not be scared.'

Sylvie chuckled at her joke as Marie was led away. She glanced over her shoulder and Margot shrugged, advising her to go with the flow.

'See,' said Lizzie. 'It was all right in the end. No one cares that you're in love with a woman.'

'How did you know?' asked Margot.

'I think, deep down, though I didn't realise I was doing it, it was the same reason I never made it clear I was selling the chateau. I was worried what people would think. Perhaps you were worried too?'

'Possibly,' Margot conceded with a smile.

'Actually, I'm glad I've got you on your own. I was wondering what you thought of something.'

'Oh?'

'Do you think Amélie would like to help me write a book about Sarah, her life and her travels? She did so many amazing things and I don't want her life to be forgotten.'

Margot's mouth widened and Lizzie began to worry. 'But that is a wonderful idea. Why did we not think of it ages ago? Amélie?' she called, looking around for her daughter. When she spotted her, she waved her over. 'Amélie, come here.'

'Yes, *Maman*? Am I in trouble?'

'No, this time you're not. Lizzie has something she wants to ask you.'

Lizzie repeated the question, stupidly nervous. This would be such a good opportunity to bond with Amélie, and something she really wanted to do.

The typical teenage sullenness fell from her face and her cheeks lifted. She nodded furiously. 'I would love to do that.'

'Really?' Lizzie's chest felt lighter. 'We could include some of your photographs of the area to show where she lived, and we can interview everyone and gather together their memories of her and her stories—'

'And we can photograph her souvenirs.'

'Exactly. I thought it would make holidays here a bit less boring. Oh, and I'm going to speak to Monsieur Mercier about letting me keep Gary.'

'You are?'

'Well, he seems to like it here and I kind of like having him around, don't you?' Amélie nodded, her thick curly hair falling backwards and forwards as she did so. 'And goats are way better than puppies.'

'We could get a puppy later.' The hopeful note in Amélie's voice rang loudly. 'Then Gary won't get lonely.'

'I suppose we could. I still need to find out where he's getting in, though. He can't turn a doorknob and walk in himself.'

Amélie cocked her head. 'He uses the back door.'

'Does he?'

'The one on the conservatory. The left panel is broken, and it tilts up. Did you not know that?'

'No, I had no idea. So he's got his own cat flap.'

'His what?' asked Margot.

'Cat flap. You know, like a big letter box in the door for cats to get through.'

'Oh, I see.'

'A goat flap,' giggled Amélie, and Margot and Lizzie joined her. 'I'm going to tell *Papa*.'

Amélie ran to her father and Lizzie watched as she recounted their conversation. Luc hugged his daughter close and after Amélie returned to feed Gary, he came to Lizzie, placing his hand in hers and a kiss on her lips.

'Are you ready to get back to work on the chateau, Lizzie? Tomorrow we can—'

She silenced him with another kiss. 'Let's just enjoy today before we plan tomorrow.'

Lizzie turned to her new home. She had no idea how long it would take to fix it all up; she imagined that one day it might be filled with Luc and Amélie, possibly other children. Would there be more nights like the concert, with dancing and laughter? From here would she follow in Sarah's footsteps and explore parts of the world she'd always wanted to visit? An infinite number of possibilities lay ahead of her, and she was looking forward to the adventure of finding out.

Acknowledgements

I always find writing acknowledgements hard and normally take ages to get started, but for the first time I know exactly where I want to begin! I want to start by thanking all the readers and authors who have shown support for my new alter ego Annabel French. You've all been amazing and I mean that from the very bottom of my heart. A special shout out to author friends Sarah Bennett, Samantha Tonge, Jaimie Admans, Belinda Missen, Leonie Mack and Anita Faulkner. Your friendship means the world.

And to my fellow bookworms, I really can't thank you enough for your company on this weird and wonderful writing journey. If you've been with me a while, thank you for sticking around and if we're meeting for the first time, thank you for picking up my book! I really hope you've enjoyed it.

I'd also like to thank my lovely agent Kate Nash at the Kate Nash Literary Agency. There are so many things I love about Kate, but one of the main things is how tirelessly she works to support her authors. She really is one of the best agents in the business and I am beyond grateful to have her in my corner.

The team at Avon have been an absolute dream to work with and the energy and care they show towards their authors is really heart-warming. Particular thanks go to Thorne Ryan, and my wonderful and incredibly talented editor Elisha Lundin. Both of these ladies know their stuff and are just plain lovely people too! But my thanks also go to all the Avon team for the beautiful cover and for doing everything you can to market my book.

Finally, thanks as always go to my family for their unwavering support, even when my head is so full of a story I'm sending the kids to school in uniform on non-uniform days, I haven't got the faintest idea what's for dinner and I've forgotten a million and one other things because deadlines are looming! To all my family, I love you.

Will the magic of Christmas mend her broken heart?

Christmas at the Chateau

The next festive romance from Annabel French.
Available to pre-order now!